BEYOND
❧ THE ❧
BUST

Much love,
Enjoy
Julien
Bradley

Kevin
Dawn

Miranda
Lynn

JULIEN BRADLEY

WISE
INK

ISBN 13: 978-1-63489-632-0

Library of Congress Catalog Number has been applied for.
Printed in the United States of America
First Printing: 2023

27 26 25 24 23   6 5 4 3 2

Cover design by Jay Monroe
Interior design by Vivian Steckline

www.wiseink.com

*To the future and the activists, organizers, supporters,
and cultural workers dedicated to the
defense of the world's water systems.*

PROLOGUE

The stealthy, youthful figure slipped silently through the bedroom window, her toes dangling a foot from the ground. She cursed, then let go of the sill. Landing with agile grace, Lil Sis blended into the dark of the night. If discovered, she'd be beaten within an inch of her life, but there was little chance of that. Grandmother Moonbeam had taken a sleeping pill before bed, which typically knocked her out until two in the morning when she got up to pee. Even that effort had been too much for Grandmother as of late; she'd taken to wearing adult diapers. After the white lawman had come with the news of Sissy's disappearance, the old woman had stopped caring about pretty much everything. Wetting herself was the least of her concerns.

Things had gone from bad to worse after a cast-iron skillet slipped from Grandmother's hand, smashing her little toe. What started out as a bad bruise had quickly developed into a festering wound, spreading like wildfire to the rest of her toes within a matter of days. A brittle diabetic, Grandmother had sought help from the community healer, who'd made a poultice for her wound and tasked Lil Sis with changing it daily. It was an awful job. The foot reeked a putrid odor, and the gangrenous flesh wept through her moccasins by day's end. Even a kid could see it was only a matter of time before the foot would have to be amputated. When that happened, Grandmother would be put into a nursing home and Lil Sis shipped off to foster care. She planned to be long gone before then.

The young girl crouched down in the open space between the house and the street, duckwalking toward the kennel. As she approached, two dogs lifted their heads simultaneously. She put the key in the lock. Since she was the only one who cared for the dogs, there was no way of knowing how long it would be before anyone would think to tend to them once she was gone. It would be cruel to leave them helpless. She wasn't worried about the German shepherd; he had a home with the white woman, Mony Strong, who would come for him as soon as she learned of Lil Sis's "disappearance." Her fear was for Rainstorm. Her mutt would have no one once Lil Sis and Grandmother were gone. Better to let the dog run free—at least she'd have a chance, maybe find a new home. The alternative was too sad to think about.

Lil Sis unlatched the kennel door. "Come on, you two—I need your noses, eyes, and ears." The dogs rose soundlessly and followed.

While Rainstorm trotted off ahead, sniffing and leaving her scent, Shep stayed at Lil Sis's side. She reached over and scratched behind his ear. He was an exceptional dog, loyal and obedient, cunning and smart. It was easy to see why his owner placed great value on him. Shep had come to her family the day the lawman brought the news about Sissy. As he'd bullied Grandmother into an explanation for why Sissy's jacket was found at a murder site, Lil Sis had told Mony in private about the man and woman who might have taken her older sister. It had only been a partial truth, but even the fib had revealed the grave danger she and Grandmother were in, prompting Mony to urge the sheriff to provide protection for her family.

The sheriff's lack of concern was nothing new—white people only showed interest in the Indian community when there was something in it for them—but Mony Strong had become livid at his response. If she'd held an ulterior motive for loaning her dog as protection, she'd kept it well hidden, even from Grandmother's keen senses. Grandmother never said it aloud, but she liked having the big dog around. Shep seemed to like Grandmother too, for he often sat near her when she was out in the front yard with her wheelchair during her "neighborhood watch." Strange things were happening on the Rez as of late. People were agitated, jumpy—even the old women at the community center lacked their usual chatty gossip and spoke in hushed whispers. Sissy wasn't the only girl missing from the Rez. Bad men had been seen lingering on the edges of reservation land like ravenous animals. There was a sense of foreboding hovering in the community. Something big was about to happen.

The two dogs followed as Lil Sis retraced her steps across

the backyard and disappeared into the shadows, making her way to the designated rendezvous. She could have walked the path blindfolded. She'd been instructed to dress in black pants and a black hoodie, but she'd chosen to wear her red basketball shorts and a gray T-shirt instead. It was too damn hot for pants.

Though it was already past ten o'clock, the temperature still hung in the low eighties. You didn't need a meteorologist to sense the pending storm. Heat lightning danced across the western sky, and a distinct fragrance of moisture lingered in the air. Thunder rumbled off in the distance. The six o'clock news had reported that a tornado had touched down in a man camp over by Watford City. No one was hurt—too bad. God should have scrubbed it from the earth entirely. Man camps were evil places where bad men did bad things, especially to women and children.

Lil Sis noted a slight breeze rustling the leaves in the trees. It did nothing to alleviate the intensity of the heat, nor did it break the humidity. Tucked between the low bluffs of the Missouri River, she'd heard white people proclaim, *If a tornado ever got in the valley, it would decimate the town.* There was little chance of that—while many forces were at work trying to destroy her Indigenous community, the weather wasn't among them.

She'd traversed several blocks undetected when she reached the community college campus on the other end of town. She liked the campus and had spent a good portion of her summer afternoons there. Designed to teach the community youth more about their culture, the programs were run by college students fulfilling educational requirements to complete their own coursework. Some of the activities were lame, like beadwork—Lil Sis hated anything to do with a needle and thread. But some of the classes were interesting, like horseback riding. The bus ride was long and boring, and the horses mostly walked along a winding trail around the hills over the Little Missouri River, but occasionally one or more of the horses would get frisky and start to gallop in the open fields. It was then that Lil Sis felt truly *Indian*.

The wind picked up now, tussling her long black hair into a giant mess of tangles. Lil Sis stood next to a tree along the boulevard and quickly braided the unruly strands into a ponytail. Her stomach gave an egregious growl—not a good sign. She'd been told to eat a big supper before leaving the house, but all Grandmother Moonbeam had made that night was bologna on fried bread—not very filling. As she reached for one of the candy bars in her backpack, words of warning suddenly echoed in her ear: *Ration your food. There is no way of knowing how long it will be until the next meal.* Blushing, she stowed it away.

When she reached the edge of campus, wind whirled into miniature dirt devils, obstructing her view of the designated rendezvous. Far away from the streetlights and student housing, the pre-chosen location had been selected due to its proximity to an open field. At a specified time, Lil Sis would have to make a run the length of a football field to a small cluster of trees out in the middle of the prairie. If all went according to plan, a transport would be waiting.

Settling behind some shrubs, she rested her back against the foundation of the building. Shep and Rainstorm sat on either side. Lil Sis stroked each behind the ear, grateful for their company. Since Sissy's disappearance, the dogs were her only real companions, and she realized for the first time how lonely she'd been without her big sister. Sure, they'd fought and argued, but with their father dead, their mother run off, and Grandmother's health failing, they were all each other had. A queasiness roiled in her stomach. Sissy wouldn't like that she'd brought the dogs along. It wasn't part of the plan.

The sweat along her hairline started to cool, making her shiver. Maybe she was subjecting the dogs to a fate far worse than being locked safely in a kennel. Her actions could jeopardize the plan. She shook her head, pushing the thought out of her mind. *What's done is done.* It would be up to her to convince her sister of the dogs' value. Besides, had she left them behind, the great dog might have been used to track her. He was smart, but not smart enough to understand he was being used against his friend. Rainstorm, too, had come a long way in her tracking skills. Blessed with hunting dog genes, Rainstorm was good at sniffing out small game, another skill which might come in handy later when it came to foraging for food. Mony had told Lil Sis that Shep would teach Rainstorm how to protect the family, and he had.

The first fat raindrop plopped against her arm, and Lil Sis huddled closer to the building. It was uncomfortable, literally having her back up against a wall—she felt hemmed in, trapped. She tried not to think about it.

Now was not the time to panic—best to keep calm and stay focused. After all, her big sister was counting on her. Sissy always praised her craftiness in finding a way out of traps. It might be a skill she'd have to call upon tonight. Surviving in the world as a runaway was a new thing for her. She would have to rely on all of her skills.

The rain came more steadily now. In the flashes of lightning, Lil Sis could see the wall of water sweeping across the open field in her direction. A clap of thunder rolled across the sky, and wind began slamming gusts of rain against the building. Rainstorm huddled close to her side. Despite being tucked under the overhang, Lil Sis's clothes were getting soaked, and she regretted not wearing the sweatshirt and jeans as she'd been instructed. Heat and humidity still clung to the air. Despite the warmth, her teeth began to chatter; she wrapped her arms around her bare legs, pulling them against her chest in an effort to keep warm. A melancholy took hold, and the thought of returning to her bed in the comfort of Grandmother's air-conditioned house felt enticing.

It will be over soon. Just a dash across the field and you'll be in a warm truck, reunited with your sister. She was tempted to pull out the letter she'd stowed in the pocket of her shorts. Just holding it could restore her courage. Thank goodness she'd had the wherewithal to store it in a plastic bag, or it would be soaked as well. It was the last contact she had with her sister. It was far too precious to let it get wet.

Lil Sis hadn't told a soul about the letter, not even Mony. Truth be told, the two sisters had been planning to run away for months. She'd been sneaking clothing and other personal belongings out of their shared bedroom for a while now, setting them in a black garbage bag for pickup. She had no idea where Sissy kept everything, but she trusted her sister. And yet . . .

Running away had always been part of Sissy's plan. Not the dead woman floating in the lake.

Maybe she'd found out about the sisters' plan. If so, was it possible Sissy had been involved in the murder? The sheriff seemed to think so. He hadn't come out and said it, but he didn't have to. It was the way all white people thought: An Indian was always guilty.

Mony Strong seemed worried that Sissy might be dead too, but Lis Sis knew her secret. Her only regret was hiding the truth from Grandmother Moonbeam. The poor old woman had worn herself to the bone with worry. If only she hadn't dropped the frying pan on her toe, making everything so much worse.

But it was important for people to believe her sister dead, even Grandmother. Otherwise, they would always be looking over their shoulders. Someone would always be searching for them.

The lawman and Mony kept asking Lil Sis what she knew about a person named Hitch. They were barking up the wrong tree. Hitch may have prostituted her sister, but that had been part of Sissy's plan as well. *How else would two teenagers find the means to finance an escape?* Sissy had asked. *And fucking for money is better than getting fucked for no money at all.* Lil Sis didn't know anything about that.

She was still waiting for her "first moon" and had no
choice but to take her sister's word for it.

It was a strange thing, trust. Lil Sis often wished Sissy
would have placed more trust in Mony Strong when she
had the chance. She was convinced Mony would have
helped her sister, had she allowed it. The white woman
had a smart dog, money, and power, and she wasn't
afraid to talk back to the sheriff—very helpful qualities,
in the young girl's opinion. None of it mattered to Sissy. It
wasn't part of the plan. Best to stay focused on the plan.

Across the open field, Lil Sis spied three sets of headlights traversing the wet, sandy soil from opposite directions, converging on the cluster of trees in the middle.
They were gathering early. Sissy's letter said they would
come for her at midnight, but it was only a little before
eleven. Lil Sis watched the scene unfolding as best she
could through the torrential downpour. When the trucks
reached the trees, some people got out and stood in the
headlights' beams. They passed an object back and forth
between them, looking as though they might be talking.
It was hard to see if Sissy was among them.

Just then, a member of the group pointed over to the
college. Abruptly, the headlights in the field went dark.

On the street in front of her, two cars slowly made
their way in her direction. That was odd—the street was
primarily a service road used to access the loading bays
behind the building, so why were they there at this time
of night? They didn't look menacing, until a bright-beam
spotlight started scanning along the base of the building.

Campus security? Lil Sis wasn't going to wait around and find out.

She started to crab-crawl away from the light along the building and managed to round the corner before the beam caught up with her. Exposed, she frantically searched for a better place to hide. She shot a quick glance out at the people standing in the prairie. They had to have seen the spotlight. A clasp of thunder sounded, followed by a large *boom* that startled Rainstorm. The streetlights went dark. Lil Sis used the added darkness to look for better cover, but Rainstorm lay on the ground, paralyzed with fear. Sissy had rescued her as a pup during a storm such as this, and ever since the dog had never fared well during thunderstorms.

Looking up at her with pleading eyes, the dog whimpered quietly. She whispered comforting words, but it only made the dog whimper louder. Lil Sis looked around with panic. She had to resist scolding—it would only make the whining worse—but she couldn't just abandon her dog. She didn't know what to do, but Shep did. Nuzzling at Rainstorm's flank, he coaxed her into moving. To Lil Sis's relief, they were back in motion. She shouldn't have been surprised. The great German shepherd was smart. Both dogs were smart, really, just in different ways. She prayed their combined intelligence would be enough that when the time came and she gave the command, both dogs would run.

She continued to creep along the building and reached the next corner, grateful for the cover of dark. There weren't many places to hide. The cars were still moving slowly in her direction, but at least they were far enough away that she might be able to make a dash for better cover before being exposed by the spotlight. Her knees were aching from the awkward position, but she'd endure the pain. Getting caught simply wasn't an option. Farther from her rendezvous spot, she had to figure out where she could hide, then get the truck driver's attention without being seen by the cars. Sissy had never mentioned a plan B. She had to rely on her wits now.

Lil Sis glanced once more at the three vehicles out in the open field before she slipped around to the other side of the short wall. They were moving fast toward the college, coming for her. *Thank God.* But what would happen if the cars and trucks met?

First things first—*find a place to hide.*

In the dark shadows behind the building, Lil Sis navigated between bushes, shrubs, and dumpsters. There were a couple of campus vans parked in the back lot. She thought about checking if any were unlocked, then decided against it. Some of the new vehicles had theft alarms. A horn blowing out her location was the last thing she needed.

She chose to hide behind one of the dumpsters to wait things out. It was away, but hopefully not too far away that she'd miss her ticket out of this mess. The dogs huddled close to her, each of them shivering a little. She began to shiver too, soaked to the bone—or maybe it was from fear.

The two cars rounded the block and continued scanning with the big spotlight along the base of the building.

Because the dumpster sat on wheels, there was a small gap of exposure. Looking around her, Lil Sis found a loose piece of cardboard and tucked it in front of her to hide her feet. She sat stone still, moving only her hand to pet Rainstorm, who licked at her nervously. Both dogs intuitively understood the need for quiet. Thunder clamored all around, echoing off the walls of the building as lightning flashed like daylight. Lil Sis knew if the three of them stayed close together, they would be safe.

That feeling disappeared when the trucks' headlights reflected off the wall behind her as they bounced over the curb onto the service road. They were on a direct collision course with the two cars shining the spotlight. One of the trucks raced in front of the lead car, blocking it from moving forward, while another pulled up alongside. The last truck pulled in behind, effectively boxing the two cars. Several passengers from the trucks methodically got out and started shouting at the cars' occupants. Lil Sis could only make out a word or two, but they were clearly angry.

The people in the cars didn't get out, and the people from the trucks started banging on the cars' doors and windows. More shouting, before an unmistakable sound of gunshots rang out between a clasp of thunder.

"Holy shit," she gasped, then clasped her hands over her mouth. It seemed unlikely her voice had carried over all the noise from the storm, but it didn't matter. Shep made a low growl at the scene, unfolding and creeping toward the ambush. Lil Sis snagged him by the scruff of his neck, scolding in a whisper, "Are you trying to get us killed?" Shep sat back on his haunches but continued to make a low menacing growl. Again, she told him to hush, and this time the dog obeyed.

Lil Sis peeked around the dumpster and saw a body lying in the road—then all hell broke loose. More gunshots, more people on the ground. *I have to get out of here, but where?* Her first thought was home, but her foolish attempt to run away had taken her one-time sanctuary off the short list of possibilities.

She inched her way to the edge of the dumpster, then darted for the next source of cover, scuttling behind the front tire of one of the school vans as the two dogs quickly joined in line behind her. She held her breath, wondering if she'd been spotted, but the street sounded like an all-out war, augmented by the crashing of the storm. *Why are they fighting? Is it because of me?* Both parties had to know she was around somewhere, otherwise why were they there?

In that moment, she grew conscious of the fact that she'd unwillingly become a witness.

Lil Sis gathered the two dogs close to her, fighting back the tears welling in her eyes. "Shep, you have to take Rainstorm home. Can you do that for me?"

Shep canted his head to the side in a knowing response. "Good boy." A tear trickled down Lil Sis's rain-streaked cheek, and she realized how she'd grown to rely on the dog. She would miss him terribly. Brushing away her tear, she whispered, "When I go, you run with Rainstorm. I'll meet you at the house." Of course, neither of the dogs had any way of knowing that she was lying, but at least it gave them a chance. Shep readied himself to sprint into action. Rainstorm copied his stance.

Easing around the front of the van, she slid her back along the passenger side, away from the fighting. Leaning her back against the sliding door, she took a couple of deep breaths and prepared to make a run for it. Her plan: ring the security doorbell of the closest dorm and hope someone would let her in. It wasn't much of a plan, but it was all she had.

Lifting onto her toes in a sprinting stance, she looked at Shep. "Ready?"

Lil Sis never got the chance to execute her plan. As another thunderclap rattled the building, the sliding door panel on the van flew open. From behind, a large pair of hands clasped over her mouth while another pair of hands yanked her inside.

The dogs never made it home either. The second she'd been pulled into the van, both leapt in after her, the door sliding closed behind them.

CHAPTER 1

MONY

"N—ate," Mony moaned, pressing the heel of her hand against her lover's sweaty forehead. Writhing beneath him, she tried to shift her hips away from his devilish tongue. It was impossible. "S—low down. Please—slow down."

Not quite two months had passed since Nate's surgery. He still experienced intermittent shortness of breath with exertion and hadn't been cleared for rigorous activity, but that didn't stop him from testing his limits, especially in the bedroom. Mony felt the smile spreading across his lips.

"Can't help it. I love the way you taste."

Anyone who didn't know them would have had a hard time believing this mega–rockstar could have a thing for an ordinary country veterinarian. Even now, in their early fifties, they seemed an unlikely pair. But those people wouldn't know their backstory, or the years these second-chance lovers had spent apart.

Mony brushed her fingers over the exit-wound scar below Nate's right shoulder blade. It was just above the spine—that the bullet hadn't rendered his lower extremities useless was nothing short of a miracle. Nate had beaten the odds, making a full recovery despite his blood anomaly, thanks to their son. Perhaps it was this recent brush with death that fueled Nate's passion, or maybe it was the years he'd spent waiting for his lover to come back to him. Whatever the reason, he exerted his sexual prowess like a man in his twenties, the surgeon's recommendation be damned.

"Don't you think that's enough orgasms for tonight? We need to get some sleep." Nate nipped at her inner thigh, and she let out a yelp. "Stop that!"

Nate rested his cheek on her thigh. "I'm not tired."

Mony tousled his thick hair. "Did it occur to you that *I* might be tired?"

"Are you?"

Ignoring the question, Mony tugged on Nate's longer-than-normal locks. "I'm surprised Gloria hasn't taken a pair of scissors to you yet."

"Don't think she hasn't tried."

It was a peculiar fate that had reunited Nate and his brother Massey with their mother Gloria. Had it been a long-range plan, plotted by her father before he died? Buddy had run into Nate's mom several years ago while looking for a place to winter the honeybees in the southwest—at least, that was the story. But had it really been happenstance? Or had Buddy been looking for her all along? Whatever the case, he'd left ample clues for the brothers to find their mother, and for her to find her way back into their lives.

Nate slid along beside her back, spooning his naked body behind her. "Don't I satisfy you?"

Where the hell did that come from? Is he kidding? The man knew ways of pleasuring a woman that would make her beg like a puppy.

No, Nate's stamina certainly wasn't an issue. Despite his refusal of opioid and narcotic painkillers, he had progressed quickly through his physical rehab, relying only on Arnica. At first his doctors had scoffed at the homeopathic approach—Nate's meds of choice were nothing more than sugar pills, they'd said, and unmanaged pain would slow his healing. Nate had simply smiled and done as he pleased, proving them wrong. What his doctors should have been paying attention to was the aftereffects of PTSD he carried from his near-death experience. Nate's fear of addiction and his concern for a normal sex life had distracted him from emotionally dealing with the egregious event.

One would think that, having witnessed firsthand the damaging effects of addiction related to unresolved trauma, he'd have been more open to counseling. His father, a Vietnam veteran, may have been a successful politician, multi-business owner, NRA advocate, and community patron—but he was also a high-functioning alcoholic. It had taken a divorce from Nate's mother and several decades of unhealthy living for Kip Ferguson to acknowledge that problem. By then, the liver damage, clogged arteries, and addiction had been securely established. Adamant in avoiding the same fate, Nate had given up all of his vices—save one.

Will it be enough?

Mony wiggled in his arms, rolling over to face him. From the first time they'd made love to this moment, the intimacy they shared had always transported her to a time of shared loss of innocence, the fruit of that copula- tion, and the love that had never died. She looked into his glimmering eyes. "Don't be like that. You know I love your mouth all over me. But tomorrow is an early day, and we'll need to be sharp if we're going to go toe to toe with Trevor and the rest of your bandmates."

Nate squeezed her tightly, taking her breath. "Always the voice of reason."

She managed a winded laugh. "Remember that when you're discussing concert security." All at once, he released his hold, shifting away from her. When he spoke, he sounded pissy. "I'm not the only one who needs security."

"Really? Well, you're the only one who's been shot."

The level of commitment Nate retained toward a group of men who hadn't performed together in twenty years was mind-blowing. Mony tried to be supportive, but it was difficult. Maybe it wasn't about the men as much as it was about finishing a project. If it was a project he needed, though, there was a highly profitable oil business her dad had left the both of them. Kip's health wouldn't hold out forever, and it was time for the next genera- tion to step up to the plate. Problem was, Nate wasn't in- terested. Mony wasn't entirely sure she wanted it either, but she didn't like the idea of him living in the spotlight again. It was just too *dangerous.*

Nate pressed his lips to her forehead. "I can see where

this is going. As much as I love makeup sex with you, let's quit while we're ahead. You're right about an early morning. I could really use a good night's sleep."

Mony slipped quietly out the front door so as not to disturb Nate and his mother's morning coffee. Normally she'd have joined them, but her lingering foul mood and restless sleep made for poor company. She needed space to reflect and cool off.

Outdoors, she took a deep breath, savoring the cool, dry air. The sun hadn't quite crested the horizon. When it did, it wouldn't stay cool for long. There were reasons people in the Southwest took an afternoon siesta; the midday summer heat here was unbearable. It was a lifestyle very different from the one back home in Minnesota.

The decision to spend Nate's convalescence at the ranch owned by his estranged mother and Mony's deceased father had been a hasty one. After all, this was the same woman who'd abandoned him as a child. *What could possibly go wrong?* On the upside, the ranch was located within the Bill Williams River National Wildlife Refuge, providing much-needed privacy at an easy driving distance from the rehab center in Lake Havasu City. Maintaining a low profile was paramount on Mony's priorities—a point of contention between her and Nate's bandmate Trevor St. James. Trevor was bent on capitalizing on the publicity generated by Nate's shooting, whining constantly about "lost opportunities." Mony didn't give two shits about that. What she did care about was not letting that money-hungry asshole run their life, and she'd shut that shit down with a vengeance.

Despite the pros of staying at the ranch, however, she wasn't fully onboard with the decision. A forty-six-year relationship deficiency wasn't something easily rectified by her standard. Hell, she and Nate had a lot of catching up to do. It was a situation she knew all too well, given her estranged relationship with her own mother. Complicating matters was the ever-present natural tension created when two women inhabited the same household, especially while fixating attention on one man. However, despite her reservations, Nate's mother Gloria had proven a gracious host and seemed eager to fulfill her adult son's desire for a relationship no matter the terms. So Mony kept her mouth shut—for now.

Strolling through the tranquil inner courtyard of Gloria West-Hernández's hacienda, Mony understood why her dad had kept the sanctuary a secret. Very few places existed in the world where one could enjoy such peace. That didn't negate the awkwardness of the situation. Only recently and quite by accident had Mony, Nate, and Massey learned of her father and Gloria's "arrangement." Gloria had filled them in on superficial details using the honeybee story as a cover, but Mony had her doubts about that. Since her father's death, she was learning in all sorts of ways just how much planning he'd done over the years. Gloria claimed the ranch was a business proposition, but it didn't feel all business—evident in the way Gloria spoke of Buddy in tender tones, staring at Mony as if she were looking at her lover's ghost.

Mony exited the pollinator haven and made her way across the open driveway toward the stable, where two tricolored horses frolicked blissfully in the corral. A tall, broad-shouldered man, skin gone dark and leathery from too many years' exposure to the elements, was putting out fresh hay. He looked up momentarily, his long black and gray hair hanging loose around his face. Waving, the man lifted his chin in a nod—their morning greeting.

Mony had made it a point to earn the Indian's good graces. It had been his suggestion she bring her mustang to the Arizona ranch. An impulse decision, perhaps, but the ambiguity of when or if she would ever return to her farm and veterinary practice in Minnesota made bringing her horse to the ranch seem like a logical choice. Besides, she didn't want to keep boarding her late husband's last gift with strangers.

Mony called to Slow Joe, "Is the jeep gassed up?"

The Indian kept an eye on his work and tore off another chunk of hay, tossing it into the trough. "Enough to get to Parker. Nate seems set on making music for that ina'adlo' record company."

Mony climbed up onto the corral fence and perched herself on the top rail. Nothing was a secret on the ranch, but she liked that Slow Joe was on her side. *Ina'adlo'* was Navajo for *fraud*, a term which described her opinion of Trevor perfectly. It drove her nuts how fervently her lover defended the man, but she had to reconcile that fact if the two of them were to ever have a chance at a meaningful relationship. She had to start trusting Nate's decisions, despite his poor track record.

Pulling a carrot from her pocket, she snapped it in half. The horses immediately noticed and trotted in her direction. "You're going to ruin their appetite doing that," Slow Joe scolded.

"Since when aren't vegetables part of a good diet?" Mony held out a stick for each horse, waiting for Joe's rebuttal.

A female voice responded, "You're spoiling those horses just like Buddy did."

Mony turned to see Gloria West-Hernández approach, sporting a wide-brimmed cowboy hat, riding boots, and a dazzling smile. It always caught Mony off guard how strikingly beautiful Nate's mother was. Even in her senior years, Gloria retained much of her natural poise and beauty from her pageantry days as a Fiesta San Antonio queen. It was easy to see why Kip had fallen in love with her, and why she'd become a catalyst of mistrust between two friends.

Gloria stood on the gravel next to Mony. "Do you still have time for a ride this morning?"

An accomplished equestrian, Gloria too had insisted Mony bring her horse to the ranch. *Let the animal enjoy the true scope of its nature.* In her former life working a full-time veterinary practice, Mony hadn't had the time to indulge in the luxury of becoming a proficient horseback rider. Gloria had fixed that. They often rode together now, the mountain trails along the Bill Williams River pleasingly therapeutic for both of them. It was during their one-on-one time that Mony had uncovered just how much

Gloria thought of her dad and the solace she found in his daughter's presence.

Mony turned to face her. "I'm afraid I can't this morning. Nate and I are heading up to Vegas to discuss the future of his band's unfinished album."

A frown marred the wide smile on Gloria's face. "That's today."

It wasn't a question.

Both women shared the same opinion of Trevor. But unlike Mony, who was far more verbal in the matter, Gloria chose not to interfere with her son's life, even after learning there had been nothing spontaneous about the impromptu concert prior to Nate's shooting. Trevor had been laying the groundwork for months during Nate's self-imposed exile in Vegas after a falling out with Massey.

"Ojalá no te fueras," Gloria said in commiseration. *I wish you wouldn't go.*

Mony nodded in agreement.

Despite a restless night, Nate hopped into the passenger seat upbeat and cheerful. Gloria stood at the gate and waved as they drove down the long driveway toward Highway 95 in the borrowed vehicle. Mony would have taken Nate's new Ford F-150, if it weren't so infamous. In the sleepy retirement community of Lake Havasu City, it had become headline news when she and Massey had taken it on a high-speed chase, fleeing a couple of *neo-Nazi pistoleros*. Now the North Dakota license plates and the distinguishing bullet holes in the tailgate were a dead giveaway. Mony was in no mood for dealing with the rabid Mile High City fans lurking in the area, hoping to get a glimpse of the Fergmeister.

Still, she thought the current situation ridiculous. A drive in a borrowed car was one thing—a limo was entirely different.

As they pulled onto the blistering airport tarmac, they were greeted by their driver for the next leg of the trip, dressed in full chauffeur attire and ready to open the stretch limo's door. Mony tried to show some empathy for the man, but the desire to fly to Las Vegas in her own plane was too overpowering. Nate said accepting the gratuitous offer was a show of faith—*bullshit*. A limo could have picked them up at VGT just as easily. Still, she held her tongue. This was Nate's decision. She had to trust him, not Trevor.

When the driver popped open the back door, Mony hesitated in accepting the offered courtesy. She'd vowed long ago never to accept a ride in the back seat from an unfamiliar driver, after paying an irrevocable price for her naivete those many years ago. It was an irrational response, considering Nate would be sitting beside her, but sometimes past experiences had a way of clouding logic.

Nate nudged her. "Come on, babe, get a move on. It's hotter than hell out here. Ladies first. Or maybe you'd rather sit in the Jacuzzi?"

Mony looked to the rear of the limo, where water bubbled in pointless luxury. Sighing, she climbed awkwardly into the backseat. Nate gracefully slid in behind her.

Before closing the door, he said to the chauffeur, "Don't take it personally. She hates not being in the driver's seat."

As he took in their surroundings, Nate gave a low whistle. The amenities in the limo were off-the-wall ridiculous. He must have sensed that the flashing neon and strobe lights were already giving Mony a headache, because after a few moments he began fiddling around with the remote, searching for the off button. Once that was accomplished, he started checking out the video game console and wet bar. Watching him act like a kid in a candy store, Mony had to suppress a laugh. It was a bright spot in what was certain to be an exhausting day.

Nate pulled an expensive bottle of liquor from the wet bar. "Too bad I'm not drinking. But you look like you sure could use a stiff drink."

Mony met his gaze and forced a smile. "That obvious, huh?"

"You look like you're about to jump through a window." Nate placed the bottle back on the bar and took hold of her hand, giving it a tug. She slid over to his side. Draping an arm over her shoulder, Nate brushed the nape of her neck, running his fingers along her hairline. "Geez, woman, you're sweating like ole Wilbur. You need to relax and enjoy the ride."

Mony leaned her head against his chest, making a conscious effort to slow her breathing. It felt as if she were losing a grip on all her defense mechanisms. "I'm not used to being chauffeured around," she said, irritated by her transparency. "Besides, I get carsick riding in the backseat."

"Are you kidding? Do you know what the wheel base is on this beast? Maybe this queasiness has something to do with the meeting today."

Mony wasn't worried about the meeting. She could handle Trevor and Gem Richards, his flunky second. What she couldn't abide was confinement. "I told you, if you want to get back together with the band, I will support your decision."

Nate turned his body to face her. "Mony, it's not about what I want. I *need* to do this. I'm not ready to go back to North Dakota and face all of the people I let down. Plus, there are too many memories. I need to occupy myself doing something else."

"I'm not pressuring you to go back to North Dakota, and no one there begrudges your time away. Everyone knows what you're recovering from. Besides, the only person you let down was yourself."

Nate was glum. "What about Shawn?" he asked. "If I'd have stayed in Williston, Shannon would still be alive."

"Just how would your presence have made a difference? Shannon made her own risky choices long ago and paid a terrible price for those decisions."

"Are you saying she deserved it?"

Mony bolted upright and gave Nate an incredulous look. "Christ! Are you trying to pick a fight? Don't be stupid. I would never think or say that."

"What are you saying then, Mony?"

"I'm saying she got involved with dangerous people—"

"People like that asshole Finch—"

"—Cindy Van Dyke, for one. Shannon set her ridiculous

quest to uncover information about me and you into motion over thirty years ago. It blinded her to the danger she was in."

Nate let out a heavy sigh. "Mony, you're the one with blinders defending Finch. He's as responsible for Shannon's death as if he'd pulled the trigger. He's only working with Sheriff Wagner now to save his own sorry ass."

"My God, why are you talking about Finch?"

As Nate reached for the bottle of liquor, Mony snatched it from his hand. For a moment, he looked startled—then he glared. "Give me that."

"Or what?" Mony slammed her fist on a panel of buttons, and the sunroof above them began sliding open.

"What the hell are you doing?" Nate asked, and grabbed for the bottle.

The open window whipped Mony's hair around, making her look like a maniac. Before he could grab it, she flung the bottle out the window, making an unceremonious splash in the hot tub.

As he stared at her, dumbfounded, Mony reached for Nate's outstretched hands. "Why are we fighting over John Finch? Haven't we got enough shit to deal with, without being at each other's throats?"

He grabbed her hands as if they were a lifeline. "God, I'm sorry, Mony, I'm sorry. I don't know what got into me. I guess I'm more anxious about the meeting than I thought." Nate pulled her to his chest. "I don't know how to get past all this. I can't act like nothing happened. The bees, and the oil business . . . I want it to be over. You know, a fresh start from everything that's happened. But we have so much fuckin' unfinished shit to deal with."

Reeling from her own desperation, Mony returned the embrace. "No one's expecting you to pretend nothing happened. I'm on your side, remember?"

"I meant it when I told you I'll do whatever you want to do with the business. I'll support you. But I don't know the oil business; I know music."

"It's not just the oil business. I don't know how I'm going to handle all the attention you'll receive getting back on stage."

Nate loosened his grip. "What do you mean?"

"I'm scared to death that being back in the spotlight means you becoming an easier target. Everyone knows you're the popular one, and now the world knows you're a multimillionaire as well."

"We're both in the spotlight as long as we own an oil business."

"Not the same."

"It is to me. What happens when the next good-looking oil representative tries to sweep my oil baroness off her feet offering to buy out the family business? How am I supposed to compete with that?"

Mony pulled away and looked her lover in the eye. "Don't be ridiculous."

"Who's being ridiculous? Dad and Massey have the oil business under control. They don't need us except to vote on decisions."

"At least if we were to become more involved in the oil

business, I wouldn't have to share my lover with a million lustful female fans."

"Are you jealous?"

Mony stabbed at the button to close the sunroof and tried to straighten her windswept hair. It was pointless. "Maybe, but I'm also practical. If Trevor's intent on drawing a younger crowd, he isn't going to want his love-ballad front man ball-and-chained to a middle-aged widow."

Nate leaned forward and pressed his lips to Mony's forehead. "I'm over the hill too, you know. I just don't let a number define my age. Besides, I would never have had my appeal if it hadn't been for my favorite spank-bank cougar."

"*Ew!*" Mony stopped fiddling with her hair and punched him in the shoulder.

"What?" he asked, and gave an innocuous grin. "It's true. The memory of a college woman coming to my tent when I was seventeen and making love with me is forever etched in my brain. Now that I know I have a son with her, just think of the great song lyrics it will make. Better than Tommy and Gina."

"I don't think Dane would appreciate—"

"Let's not talk about that now. I don't want to spend the rest of this awesome ride talking about business. I think we should get naked and make use of that hot tub."

Mony gave a cursory glance at the privacy partition. "Are you crazy? I'm not getting naked on a major US highway."

Nate clicked the remote, dimming the lights to soft hues of blue, purple, fuchsia, and green. "Well, we'll get naked right here then. It's soundproofed—our driver won't even hear all the sounds you make while I have my way with you."

"Don't you think we should spend the drive getting ready for this meeting? I'm sure Trevor will have a team of lawyers ready to pounce the moment we arrive."

"Oh, thanks for reminding me." Nate hit the intercom button. "Eddy, be sure to make a pit stop at VGT airport before our meeting."

"Yes, Mister Ferguson."

Mony furrowed her brow. "What are you up to?"

"We don't need a team, just one—and he'll be landing about the time we arrive in Vegas."

She narrowed her eyes. "What? You couldn't have led with that?"

Nate closed the privacy partition and began taking off his shirt. "I did. Like I said, trust me."

CHAPTER 2

MASSEY

Massey walked down the airstairs of F&A Oil's private jet to meet Mony and Nate on the tarmac. Mony reached for him first. "I would have slept a whole lot better knowing you'd be here for this shindig," she said, wrapping him in a hug. "Why the secrecy?"

Massey grasped his shoulder satchel and gave Mony a one-handed return hug. "I didn't want Gloria to know I would be in the area. She'd have expected me to stop in for a visit. We don't have time for that today."

Mony pulled back from him. "Did you think I'd rat you out?"

"It's not that," Massey said, unwilling to divulge the real reason for concealment. Facing his mother took a kind of emotional energy he had no intention of expending today. Just seeing her for the first time in forty-six years a few months back had taken every ounce of strength he possessed. He needed to be in the right headspace before embarking on that endeavor again. "I wasn't even sure I

35

would make it myself until the last minute. I didn't want to build false hope."

Mony looked at him skeptically but said no more. As she released him from her hug, Nate stepped in. "If I were a gambling man, which I am, of course, I'd have put good money on you showing up."

Massey returned the embrace with genuine affection and felt the tension between his brother's shoulders relax. The two of them still had significant unresolved issues they needed to face, but that too would have to wait.

"Come on," Nate said, slinging an arm over Massey's shoulders. "We have a limo waiting."

Massey took hold of Mony's hand. "All right, then—let's see what sort of havoc the trio of trouble can stir up today."

CEO Trevor St. James stood waiting in the Shooting Star Records lobby. As they approached, he reached for Nate's hand and then pulled him in for a shoulder bump. "Hey, man, so glad you made it." Stepping back, he looked Nate up and down, then patted his belly. "And you've put on some weight since the last time I saw you." He turned to Mony. "We'll have to rectify that, won't we, Miss Muse?" he asked, moving in for a kiss.

Mony took a step back and extended her hand. "Mony Altman-Strong, and I think Nate looks healthier than ever."

His smile unwavering, Trevor took the proffered hand. "All because of you, Mony Altman-Strong." He looked to

Massey. "Big brother is here too. Good to see you, man—and under better circumstances, wouldn't you say?"

Indeed—the last time they'd spoken, after Nate's disappearance, had been a far more confrontational meeting. "I promised you then that I would bring him back to discuss finishing the demo," Massey replied. "You can see I'm a man of my word."

Trevor shook his hand. "I never doubted it, Massey Ferguson. May I call you Massey?"

As he escorted the trio through a long corridor, the CEO continued his small talk. "Tell me, is the oil business still booming up there in North Dakota? I hear rumors you're headed for a bust."

Massey suppressed a laugh—the drop in oil prices was anything but new. He indulged the chatter with information easily found in a daily middle-market newspaper. "How's the music business going for you?"

A slight frown marred Trevor's forehead. "Not as lucrative as the oil business."

Well, at least not for Trevor, Massey thought. He'd been monitoring the public outlets regarding Trevor St. James's business dealings. Lead guitarist for Mile High City and self-made entrepreneur, Trevor had done very well for himself after the band's breakup years ago. Investing heavily back in the music industry, he'd purchased the band's former record label Shooting Star Records and moved its headquarters from Los Angeles to Las Vegas. Next, he'd bought up a string of off-the-strip nightclubs throughout the city, selling them off a few years later. For his next trick, he'd invested in an urban renewal project in an abandoned warehouse district, renovating the largest warehouse into what became the Mile High Club. The venue had gained notoriety as an underground clearinghouse for major labels scouting for their next new act.

"And the renovation project, how's that coming?"

This time, full-on tension spread across Trevor's face. "I've got my best people managing the construction. We should make the deadline."

It was difficult for Massey to fathom the money it must have taken for the city and zoning commissioner to turn a blind eye to the cleverly hidden exclusive rooftop amphitheater in the first place—Las Vegas had strict rules about outdoor venues. All of that cunning had gone to shit, however, during the band's impromptu reunion. It had been the 1987 U2 liquor store rooftop video in downtown LA all over again. Traffic had been backed up for hours. The cat out of the bag, the nightclub had faced significant fines for city zoning and ordinance violations.

The upside to the debacle was that Mile High City had amassed enormous publicity, generating considerable buzz of a reunion album. Even after Nate's shooting, rabid fans were waiting with bated breath, wondering if dreams would become a reality. In the meantime, though, Trevor was up to his eyeballs in debt and under a strict timeline.

Disquiet still looming behind his eyes, their host artfully changed the subject. Ushering the three of them into the boardroom, he said, "Everyone's just grabbing lunch."

To the right of the room was a lavish spread of food across a white linen banquet table. On the left, the Mile High City band members sat gathered around the boardroom table conversing quietly—all except drummer Tim Thompson, who was chowing down on a plate full of saucy chicken wings. As he looked up from his food, a smile rose to his face. "Hey, Trevor, you didn't tell us we could bring our old ladies."

The burly, six-foot-four man went straight for Mony, wrapping her in an unapproved bear hug. "This must be the chick our old mate's been singing about all these years." Massey could see Mony grimace under the weight of his strength.

Finally, Tim stepped out of the way as a man dressed in an expensive tailored suit advanced with a more urbane approach. Lead singer Rocky Rhodes took Mony's hands in his and gave her an apropos kiss on the cheek. Nate bristled, but Rocky paid no notice; stepping back, he held on to Mony's hands, spreading her arms as if sizing up a new suit. "Well, I can see where your daughters get their stunning looks. Welcome to the club."

Nate banded his arm around Mony's waist, breaking the connection. "Best back off," he said with a warning grin. "Mony's got a keen eye for bullshit."

Rocky obliged and gave Massey a condescending side glance. "Hey, Trevor, it was my understanding this was to be an informal gathering. I didn't realize I should have lawyered up."

"It is informal," Nate cut in. "My brother is in town on a different matter."

Massey noted a slight furrow in Mony's brow but said nothing.

Trevor gave an uncomfortable laugh. "You're always

getting ahead of things, Rocky. I told you, the only lawyer that would have any say at this table is one we all decided on—that and an agent."

Bass player Cody Brandon broke the tension by shaking Nate and Massey's hands before offering his to Mony. "It's great seeing you again, Massey, and it's a pleasure to finally meet you, Mony." To the general assembly, he added, "I, for one, am glad that all three of you are here."

Trevor took Mony's elbow, moving her toward the banquet table. "Gentlemen, Mony, let's all grab a plate of food and sit down. We have a lot to discuss."

Taking his cue, Massey asked Trevor, "Can you point me in the direction of your building advisor's office?"

A surly, non-conversive young woman wearing classic Converse shoes, distressed jeans, and a Shooting Star Records T-shirt escorted Massey down the hall, stopping in front of a large office. Knocking lightly, she ushered him inside. Gem Richards was standing in front of a floor-to-ceiling window facing a new construction lot, talking on her cell phone. She failed to notice them as they entered.

"I told you, that's not good enough," she snarled into the receiver. "That deadline is nonnegotiable. I don't care what other projects you have. Your workers will be there—today. There will be severe repercussions if we lose this investment because of your inability to follow a timeline. Do I make myself clear?" She clicked a button and slung her cell phone into the office chair. "Goddamn contractors."

Massey's escort cleared her throat. "Gem, your eleven o'clock is here."

Gem whirled around, grimacing. "What's wrong with you, Connie? Can't you knock?" Her eyes met Massey's. "You're my eleven o'clock?"

The escort ducked out quickly, closing the door behind her. Massey smiled and took a seat in front of the desk, dispensing with the pleasantries. "Please sit down, Ms. Richards. We have much to discuss."

Defiant, Gem stood a beat before taking the power position behind the desk. "I hope this is about how you're going to convince Nate to fulfill his obligation to finish the album."

Massey shook his head. "I've already told Trevor: Nate makes his own decisions. This is regarding your brother."

Gem's face morphed into a look of disdain. "I have nothing to say to you, Ferguson. I already told Detective What's-her-face; I haven't spoken with my brother in a couple of years."

"Was that before or after his involvement with the prostitution ring for the oil worker camps in Wyoming?"

Her eyes grew wide. "How do you—you can't prove that."

Massey reached into the satchel, retrieved several eight-by-ten glossy photos, and handed them to Gem.

She snatched the photos and flipped through a couple before visibly cringing, then slapped them face down on the desk. "The detective already showed me these disgusting things. It proves nothing."

"Are you saying pictures lie, Ms. Richards?"

She eyed him coolly. "What do you want, Ferguson?"

"Not me; it's your brother who needs your help."

She snorted. "Since when does he not? My help usually involves bail money. I'm sure you're aware that my resources are tied up right now."

"What if I told you there may be a chance to get your brother out of the white supremacist group without making him a martyr?"

"Ha! Harland is no martyr. Is that all?"

Letting silence hang between them, Massey used the opportunity to glance around the room. His eyes fell on a framed photo on her desk. He picked it up. "Is this the Durango–Silverton train in Colorado?"

"Yeah. What of it?"

He set the frame reverently back in its place of prominence. "It must have been exciting as a kid to have a family picture taken with a couple of Hollywood celebrities. Me and Nate have a similar picture with a couple of astronauts when our family was vacationing in Florida. We were pretty young at the time, so we didn't fully appreciate the novelty of the experience. We were more interested in Disney World. The photo must be a great conversation starter for your new clients."

Gem picked up the picture, studied it, and sighed. "Harley is beyond my help."

"That's not entirely true—though he is in some pretty deep shit. What if I told you there is still a chance he could get out alive, serve his time, and start a new life? That is, if he hasn't committed murder."

She set the picture on the desk. "My brother's too much of a coward to be a killer."

Massey pressed the issue. "If he *has* killed, he's lost his only bargaining chip. Nate will see to it."

Gem bristled visibly at the mention of his brother. Massey had suspected for a while that a possible "friends with benefits" relationship had existed between Gem and Nate during his self-imposed exile in Vegas. How serious had the relationship been to Gem? He was about to find out.

"A washed-up old rock star doesn't wield that kind of power," she spat.

"If you believe that, you haven't done your homework. Maybe Nate doesn't, but our father, Senator Kip Ferguson, does. I guarantee Shannon McDonald's killer will be prosecuted to the highest degree. Being the prime suspect, your brother's fortunate North Dakota no longer has the death penalty. He will be charged as soon as I return to North Dakota. If convicted, Gunsel will face first-degree—"

"Don't call him that! And you're lying." She rose from her chair and began to pace. "Detective Gomez told me you already have a suspect, some lawyer from Chicago."

"You mean John Finch? He's not the murderer."

She stopped pacing. "Are you calling the detective a liar?"

"John Finch is not the murderer."

Gem paused at the window, staring out at the construction next door. "What's in it for me besides a drained bank account?"

Massey smiled inwardly at human predictability. "Don't you want to know the details first?" When she didn't respond, he filled her in on what he knew of the shooting that had taken place on the reservation.

Gem scoffed. "Why should I care about a squabble among a bunch of Indigenous people?"

"Indigenous and white people," Massey clarified. "Your brother was among the bodies left for dead. He's handcuffed to a hospital bed at Mercy Medical Center with a gunshot wound, similar to the wound Nate sustained—only he's been less fortunate."

"What do you mean?"

That got her attention.

"Nate received prompt medical treatment from a team of medics shortly after his incident. Your brother was left bleeding for several hours before he was found."

She turned to face him. "Will he live?"

"It's too early to say with any confidence."

Gem walked to the dry bar in the corner of the room and grabbed a jeweled decanter along with two glasses. She poured three fingers into each and offered one to Massey, who took it. Shooting her drink, Gem spoke in a tone of resignation. "I always knew Harley would meet a bad end. But you still haven't explained how this affects me."

"In about five minutes, the meeting down the hall is going to fall apart when your CEO threatens to go ahead with the demo, claiming ownership rights without the other members' consent."

Gem's eyes widened. "How in the hell—"

"I've got to hand it to Trevor. It was clever disguising the studio recording as a friendly jam session for old times' sake. And since no one paid for the studio time, he'll use the argument that it is within his rights to claim ownership. Bad move, considering the debt he's amassed with the reconstruction project. I've already prepped Nate to threaten a counter lawsuit. The band members will follow, except for maybe Rocky. They all may be in favor of the album, but no one's on board if Nate isn't."

Gem didn't bother denying it. "Rather arrogant, don't you think? What makes Nate so important?"

"It's not what I think. It's what I know. Shooting Star Records can't afford a lawsuit right now. Trevor's already put company stock up on the open market to cover renovation costs. Even without Rocky's financial support, Nate has more than enough resources to take over controlling interest, destroying Trevor's entire empire if he's in a vindictive mood. Trevor should never have backed my brother into a corner. You want him on your side. You can make that happen."

Gem gritted her teeth. "Oh, goodie. How?"

"He's here at the table, isn't he?"

"That's not answering the question."

"For Nate's cooperation, you will need to come to Williston. "

"Why?"

"If you have a shred of compassion left for your brother, he's going to need you for his arraignment."

Gem reached for the decanter with trembling hands and poured herself another drink. "I—I can't. I have so much to do here with the reconstruction project. I—I don't have the money. And you haven't said one word as to why this is important to you."

"In exchange for your help, F&A Oil will finance Trevor's entire renovation cost. No repayment required."

"Wait—what? Why would you do that? What's the catch?"

"Actually, there are two. First, you will need to decide whether to help or not before I leave town today. This is a one-time offer only."

Before he could continue, the sound of a ruckus broke out in the hallway. Nate could be heard shouting in a loud voice, "You son of a bitch!" followed by a sharp rap on the door. Massey got up from his chair and opened it to find his brother standing outside with Mony in tow. Nate snarled, "Time to leave—now!"

Massey noted Trevor jogging briskly down the hall, crying, "Nate, wait! Don't be like that, man. Can't you see this could be a win for all of us?"

As Nate charged back the way he'd come to confront his friend, Massey looked back at Gem, her eyes wide with shock. "Looks like I'll need your answer right now."

Staring down the hallway, she managed, "What's the second condition?"

"You fly back with us."

CHAPTER 3

NATE

Nate, Massey, and Mony walked to a local bistro, ordered coffee, and took a table in the corner to regroup. Nate's brother seemed pleased with himself. So far, everything was going according to Massey's master plan—but the woman who sat beside him was pissed. She'd been left out of the loop on purpose, which would have certain repercussions.

After the barista delivered the beverages, Mony took a sip of her coffee and demanded, "Is one of you boneheads going to tell me what the hell is going on?"

Nate let Massey take the lead on that one. He'd only become aware of the severity of Trevor's financial woes early yesterday morning, when Massey informed him of F&A Oil's purchase in controlling stock in Shooting Star Records. It had been foolish of Trevor to think that he could pull a stunt like that, claiming ownership rights without repercussions. The behavior reeked of desperation. Nate almost would have felt sorry for his friend if it weren't for the fact that he was going to make a killing after all of this was over. "All he would have had to do is ask. I'd have given him the money. He didn't have to turn friendship into a power play." Turning to face Mony, he told her, "What I said to you in the limo about needing to move forward with the album was sincere. I really want this to work. It seems my friend wants to do things the hard way."

Mony scoffed. "Trevor is no friend."

Nate disagreed but accepted Mony's point of view. Had the situation been reversed, he knew he would have been reacting in a similar fashion. Even Gem had alluded to Trevor's tendency of taking advantage of him. Still, it was a difficult dynamic to concede. Trevor had offered Nate friendship and acceptance when he had needed it the most. Nate had to give his old friend the benefit of the doubt, at least for now. At some point, Trevor would come to his senses.

"It's to our advantage that things played out the way they did," Massey interjected. "It bought us more time to secure leverage on Gem Richards."

Mony choked on her coffee. "What could we possibly need from her?"

Another sore subject. Ever since Gem had verbally accosted her daughters at a concert, Mony had been loaded for bear. She had never accused Nate of it, but he was pretty sure she already suspected him and Gem of having sex. True enough, during his exile, he'd allowed Gem to use her feminine wiles to manipulate him into staying in Vegas. To Nate, it had been nothing more than two consensual adults satisfying a mutual itch—except the scratch marks seemed to have left an indelible mark on his seductress and had shaken Mony's trust in him.

Massey filled Mony in on the Rez shooting and Harland Richards's involvement. "His current medical condition made it possible to obtain a DNA sample—with consent, of course. His prints are all over the toolshed."

Nate blinked in surprise. "Toolshed? You never mentioned anything about the toolshed."

"I'd just learned about it myself before I flew out this morning. Gomez asked Dad and me if she could send her forensic team out to the farm to make another comprehensive sweep of every conceivable surface, on the off chance that they'd find something solid enough to provide a lead. She's suspected Richards's involvement since she took over the investigation, but she needed hard evidence. Now she's got it. His DNA matches prints lifted off the raft out by the pond, on the shabin door handle and in Buddy's toolshed. She's planning to go after him with everything in her arsenal to obtain a confession as soon as his condition stabilizes."

"Wagner should have found that months ago," Mony broke in. "Leave it to detective Gabriella Gomez to get the job done."

Neither Nate nor Massey disagreed. Sheriff Wagner had been shown up at every turn since Detective Gomez's arrival on the Bakken—it had been she who made the connection between his shooter and the white supremacist group back in North Dakota. Nate still didn't know the details surrounding Shannon's death; out of either a misguided sense of protection or just plain decency, no one had regurgitated any of the gruesome detail, not even Gomez. She kept their conversations on the matter nondescript, which suited Nate just fine. Once that story passed his ears, it could never be unheard. He wasn't ready for that. Maybe he never would be.

Gomez had also been the one to confirm that the blow to the back of Shannon McDonald's head, delivered by the lead crystal decanter, had not killed her. It was merely a plant to implicate John Finch, the last person to see Shannon alive. Sheriff Wagner claimed to have known this as well and said that he'd left the implication hanging to create a false sense of security for the real killer. *Bullshit*—the guy hadn't a clue, in the estimation of Nate and Shannon's brother. Wagner had proceeded to ruin Finch's life some more by coercing him into working undercover—a risky venture, considering the lawyer hadn't a clue what he was doing. The upside was that Finch had been pulled from Monroe's legal team in the probate case; the downside was the man was still on the Bakken. As much as Nate despised him for fucking Mony and his murdered friend, it was a relief to know the Chicago lawyer wasn't a killer. Just thinking about the two women Nate cared most about having such erroneous judgment made him ill.

Massey continued, "Finch has been brilliant, convincing the white supremacist he's a *problem fixer* for an infamous Chicago cartel. They've taken the bait hook, line, and sinker. His real-life standing with a prestigious law firm and his work for Monroe Oil have provided the perfect cover."

"And just how is this cloak-and-dagger shit supposed to solve Shannon's murder?" asked Nate.

"We're peeling the onion, so to speak. With the destabilization in oil prices, a power vacuum has been created on the Bakken. All the wealthy conglomerates are scrambling to"—Massey made air quotes— "*diversify* their income. Alliances are shifting between outside powermongers and the smaller cartels conducting illicit activities in the area. The neo-Nazi militia threw in with Mitchell about two months before Shannon's demise, trying to shore up control of the prostitution business. Up until the disappearance of him and his wife, that is."

"Wait, both are missing?"

"Yes, and chances of finding either alive diminish by the day. Dad and I agree with the detective, who believes Dwight has aligned himself with Monroe Oil. Since everyone hates dealing with heir apparent Jason Monroe, the local militia have been shopping around for better options. The verdict is still out on whether Finch and his fake associates can offer better, but they seem to be leaning in that direction."

"Doesn't the fact that Finch used to be Monroe's lead lawyer raise some suspicion?"

Massey laughed. "After Monroe's son-in-law so ineptly lost their case against us in probate court, most of the local militants consider him the next Dave Ramsey of illegal business."

Nate considered the bad blood between F&A Oil and the local real estate broker/business adversary. Dwight Mitchell's attempts at aiding Jason Monroe in usurping

Nate and Mony's inheritance was common knowledge. Was it a stretch to think Monroe was the puppeteer behind Shannon's murder, his shooting, and the attempt on Massey and Mony's life in Arizona, and had hired the militia to do his dirty work? Monroe had been seeking revenge ever since he'd pissed himself in front of the forty-and-over hockey team out on the lake last winter. What the detective needed now was to obtain solid proof there was a connection and shut down Monroe's entire oil operation, banning him from the Dakotas forever.

Mony lamented, "If only Kip hadn't insisted I leave the farm the day we found Shannon. I'd have found the evidence myself." She explained to Nate how the sheriff had shooed her off her own land while he'd still been hospitalized, enlisting Kip's help using her safety as an excuse. "He claimed he wanted me out of the way so he could do his own investigating without worrying about my safety. Very shortsighted, in my opinion. I could have been his eyes in the sky. I could have helped."

Massey's eyes flickered to Mony. "You know there's more to that story—"

"Like what?"

"Jesus, Mony, no one wanted another victim on his hands. Wagner was certain you were the proposed target."

"Conjecture," Mony retorted.

"Is it?" Nate snapped. "Is it conjecture that an attempt on my life occurred within twelve hours of Shannon's murder? A woman known to have spent time with me the better part of the past two years. A woman who'd also recently had been seen consorting with the lawyer for Monroe Oil, much like another certain someone associated with me. Even Gomez thinks you were the intended target."

Mony fell silent, and Nate slid his arm around her, pulling her close. He hadn't meant to be so harsh. They both harbored an incredible amount of guilt over Shannon's death. Logically, he could rationalize that his former lover had in large part brought her fate upon herself by meddling in affairs not of her concern. She'd paid a terrible price for her inquisitive nature. He also had to remind himself that both he and Mony were trying to cope with the whole sordid affair the best they could. He pressed his lips to her forehead. "Sorry. I have to stop losing my shit every time I think about this whole damn mess." To Massey, he asked, "Has Gomez found Shannon's killer?"

"She asked me to procure Gem Richards's cooperation in seeing what we can get out of her brother."

Nate shook his head. "That's a lost cause. She doesn't even acknowledge that her brother's alive."

Massey countered, "They're closer than she lets on, and Richards's testimony is critical. He was at both Shannon's crime scene and the shooting behind the college in New Town. That's not coincidence. He's either the killer or knows who the killer is."

Nate felt the tension ripple down Mony's spine. "What the hell was Richards doing on the Rez in the first place?" she asked.

"After the tornado touchdown in the man camp near Watford City, the region was pure chaos. Hundreds of people were displaced. Some of those people, unhappy with their current living arrangements, just packed up what they could and left. Some tried to muscle in on other people's land."

"What does that have to do with Harland being on the Rez?"

"He was leading a new recruit initiation."

"Meaning?"

"He was looking for working girls."

"Jesus, sick bastard."

"That's not all. The severe weather caused several power outages throughout the area, especially in remote and poorly served locations. The following day, the public health services checked in on all their clients, including Grandma Moonbeam. The woman was found unconscious in her bed."

Mony bolted up in her seat, her face pale. "My God, is she . . . dead? Where's Lil Sis?"

"The prescription bottle found on the bedside stand suggested she may have accidently overdosed on sleeping pills. She is currently being held at Mercy Medical Center for further evaluation."

"Poisoned?" Nate asked.

"Not in the way that you think. According to the pharmacist who filled Grandma Moonbeam's prescription, the pill count was accurate. Poisoning is likely due to a foot injury, probably septicemia. She's a brittle diabetic. The public health nurse was there to do the old woman's sterile dressing changes. Grandmother is scheduled for an emergency amputation, when or if she regains consciousness."

"And what about Lil Sis?" Mony repeated.

"Runaway, most likely."

Mony's eyes lit with fury. "Bullshit. I told Wagner that family needed more protection than my dog. Lil Sis is the only link to her sister. Sissy is a link to the human trafficking that's happening right under his nose. Are you sure she wasn't abducted?"

"There was no evidence of breaking and entering or foul play, and I checked the scene myself. I found footprints below a bedroom window. Both dogs are missing too. The girl either let them loose or took them with her when she ran. I'm leaning toward the latter. The entire Rez community is out looking for them. If the dogs were running loose, we'd have found them by now."

Nate took Mony's hand and locked his fingers with hers. He knew how important both the girls were to her. "Massey, how do you know someone hasn't . . . dispatched the dogs?"

"Possible but unlikely. Eliminating the dogs would have to have been done at close range, probably while in the kennel. It would have created quite a ruckus. The barking dogs would have alerted the neighborhood to approaching strangers. The shootout near the college campus and the missing child and dogs are not a coincidence."

"What makes you think the two are connected?"

"Not too far from the shooting site, trackers found small human footprints followed by paw prints behind the bushes lining a building's exterior wall. The same sets of muddy tracks lead behind a dumpster in the rear parking lot, then disappear completely next to where the school utility vans are parked. It's possible that either someone was there, waiting to nab her, or she met someone intentionally and left willingly."

"Who?"

Mony chimed in, "If she left willingly, it had to be someone Lil Sis knew. I know my dog. Shep would never have let her go with a stranger without putting up a fight."

"That's the sheriff's working theory as well, and why both of you need to come back home to help get things sorted out."

Nate straightened. "What do you need us for?"

"Mony has the best relationship of anyone with Grandma Moonbeam. If anyone can talk with the old woman, she can. If Shep's alive and in the area, he may find his way back to the farm. Someone needs to be there. Besides, Shawn's been asking for you, Nate."

Nate swallowed hard. "Right now? Christ, Massey, I'm not ready for that."

"I get it, Nate, but we're about to stir up a lot of painful shit for Shawn, and he needs his best friend. He hasn't been doing well since Shannon's death."

The rock star felt his shoulders slump. Not a day had passed that he hadn't thought of Shannon or his best friend. Sighing, he replied, "You're right. Every time I talk to him, he sounds deeper in despair. I've been wanting to get a visual on his situation for a while. But why Mony? Aren't we putting her in harm's way just by being there?"

"I'm going with you," Mony retorted. "I—"

Massey held up his hand. "Of course you are. But before we leave Vegas, you need to call Dane and let him know you're on your way back to Williston. Nate, you need to call Gloria and let her know you and Mony will be gone for a couple of days."

Nate nodded and pulled out his cell phone, but Mony balked. "Why do I need to drag Dane into this mess?"

Reaching for his satchel, Massey reminded Mony of Dane's new stipulations. "He doesn't want to be blindsided with news like the last time, especially if things go to shit in a handbasket." He was referring to Dane learning Nate was his biological father through the blood anomaly they shared. The revelation had placed something of a barrier in the relationship between all of them, especially mother and son. Keeping Dane in the loop was a small price to pay if it provided the young man a little peace of mind.

Nate and Mony made their obligatory calls and left the bistro. Standing at the curb waiting for a taxi, Nate looked up at the walkway and recognized a woman from the recording studio as she approached. Gem's assistant Connie didn't even acknowledge Nate and Mony's presence, walking directly up to Massey. Wordless, she handed him a piece of paper and left as quickly as she'd come.

Massey read the note and smiled. "It looks like Ms. Richards has decided to join us after all."

"You mean she's flying with us?" Mony asked.

Massey stuffed the paper in his pocket. "I'm not leaving anything to chance. Gem has agreed to talk with her brother to find out just how deeply he's involved in all this. It's quite possible Harland is a pawn, and not the killer. At a minimum, he'll have insight on who it is. But we can go into more detail about that on the flight back to Williston."

The limo that had brought Nate and Mony to Vegas pulled up to the curb, and the driver hopped out to open the door for Mony. Nate caught her by the arm and said to his brother, "Before we leave Vegas, there's some business I need to attend to."

"What kind of business?"

Nate winked. "You'll see. It's the sort of thing that's straight up your alley."

Nate brushed past the steward's onboard greeting and marched Mony straight to the cabin bedroom in the rear of the plane. Kicking the door closed with the heel of his boot, he pulled her into a tight embrace, pressing his lips hard against hers. She squirmed, caught off guard by his voracity. It made him hot.

"Geez, Nate, take it easy. We need—"

He was done taking it easy. Since his shooting, love-making had been mostly hand jobs and oral sex. Not that he was complaining—he loved Mony's hands and mouth on him—but this time he wasn't settling. Not today. "Mony, the doctor cleared me for sexual activity at my last office visit, and I intend to take full advantage of it."

Mony offered a weak protest, but gradually relaxed into his arms. Confident he had her complete attention, he loosened his hold and brushed a rogue strand of hair from her face. "Two things are going to happen during this flight. Number one, we are not going to let Gem's presence in the main cabin ruin this moment." When Mony opened her mouth to speak, he pressed a finger to her lips. "Number two, I am consummating my marriage, here and now, on this plane. I've dreamed of this moment for as long as I can remember, and I'm not letting anyone or anything deny me. Let this shitstorm come. As long as you and I are united in every way, mind, soul, and body, I can deal with anything. I love you beyond any words I can put in a song, Mony Ferguson. I plan to spend the rest of my life showing you just how much."

"Say that again."

"I love you—"

"No, silly. My name."

He smiled, "Mony—Ferguson."

Nate watched as Mony stood in front of the mirror, making a vain attempt to tame her just-fucked hairdo. Sauntering up behind her, he wrapped his arms around her waist, pressing his naked body against hers. "Let it go, babe. It'll be windy enough when we step outside the plane; no one will know the difference."

After a beat, she gave up and pivoted in his arms to face him. Her smile was radiant. He loved knowing her flushed face and swollen lips were because of him.

Mony lifted on her tiptoes and kissed the crook of his neck. The gentle suction made him quiver between his thighs. Pulling away, she gazed up at him. "I need you to keep what I'm about to say locked in that rock head of yours." She tapped the side of his temple lightly. "We need to stow whatever petty jealousy and insecurities we still have eating at us and call them what they are—irrational and irrelevant. No matter what happens, we are a united front."

"I know. I—"

Mony pressed a finger to his lips. "Shush. I'm not finished. We're going to have to put on one hell of a show, probably the best one of our lives. This time we're both bait. We need to convince our enemy we're divided, let them think we're weak. It will be a tremendous advantage for us."

Nate resisted the instinct to recoil. Didn't she realize he'd been putting on a show most of his life, depicting a happy, carefree, confident man? Now that he'd just secured his greatest desire, she was talking about faking it. He leaned his forehead to hers. "I get it, and I will do my best. I trust you, Mony. I mean that."

"Even if I have to be alone with John."

This time, he couldn't hide the involuntary reflex. He tightened his hold, but replied, "Especially with him. I know it's important you find Lil Sis and the dogs, alive and well. If Finch holds the key, then we need to use every tactic at our disposal to help make that happen."

Pressing a gentle kiss to his lips, she whispered, "I love you madly, Nate Ferguson. Thank you for understanding. Oh, and one more thing." She pulled the wedding band from her finger. "No one can know about this, at least not until I tell the kids. Agree?"

It felt like she'd thrust a knife into his chest. He had

wanted to shout their nuptials from the rooftop. How in the hell was he going to keep this quiet? "All right."

"That was awful quick," Mony said with a hint of skepticism.

Shoving aside his doubts, Nate swept her off her feet. "I aim to please, wife. Now come back to bed—we aren't landing for another twenty minutes. Sex is always better during the descent."

CHAPTER 4

JOHN

A blanket draped over his shoulders, John warmed his fingers and hands over the canned stew heating on the makeshift cookstove. He was tired, chilled, and sick of being held up in the piece-of-shit van, his makeshift home for the past two months. The days were tolerable enough—he could get out in the warm sun, and the humidity had broken after the storm cell passed, making the air dry and comfortable. But the evenings got cool, and sleeping on a thin mat night after night made him unable to fathom the appeal of camping. Adding to his misery, his sinuses were acting up with all the spring mold and pollen floating around.

Augmenting his physical stress was the constant worry that any minute someone would sneak up on him and slit his throat, which made it difficult to get a restful sleep. God, how he missed saunas, massages, and his climate-controlled penthouse overlooking Lake Michigan. It felt like years since he'd slept in his king-size bed. His back was killing him. He needed his chiropractor; he needed a shave and shower. It had been over a week since he'd had a change of clothes, and it was to the point that he couldn't tolerate his own body odor.

"I am so done living like a vagrant straight out of a 1930 Depression documentary," John muttered aloud. The contents of the can began bubbling, and he spooned the pitiful excuse for food into a paper bowl.

Taking a spoonful of the ultra-processed nourishment, he considered the promise Sheriff Wagner had made regarding the imminent end of his limited role in trying to track down Shannon McDonald's killer. John was beginning to realize this had been a bold-faced lie. He felt like Bill Murray's character in *Groundhog Day*, reliving the same hellish day over and over. John mentally kicked himself for so recklessly agreeing to the sheriff's harebrained scheme. It had been a moment of pure catastrophic weakness, a sense of chivalry toward a woman who didn't give a rat's ass about him.

To the best of his knowledge, John had successfully conned all of the low-level foot soldiers of the neo-Nazi organization into thinking he was some vicious hitman, but the knowledge had brought him no closer to finding answers to the questions he was seeking. All parties involved were convinced the young Indian girl was the key, but whether Sissy Moonbeam was even alive—or being held against her will—was anybody's guess. Dwight Mitchell had tried to con John into believing he had her, using the girl as a bargaining chip to get to Ramona. That had gone south quickly when Mitchell suddenly disappeared, bringing John no closer to uncovering the identity of the real piece of human waste pulling the strings of the illicit human trafficking.

And Harland Richards had proved to be a shallow lead. John had undergone dealings with the drug pusher, addict, and pimp several times. A low-rung pawn with a reputation for stupidity, Richards had gotten in over his head the other night when he spearheaded a new recruit initiation, taking on a group of Native Americans on their own turf. As one could imagine, the Three Affiliated Tribes members didn't take kindly to white men exploiting their children. John had yet to meet up with Sheriff Wagner to learn if the idiot had survived the skirmish; if he had, Richards would likely face charges of drug use, statutory rape, pandering, and human trafficking. If he died, well, no great loss.

The sense of urgency in finding and protecting the Moonbeam girls, however, was palpable, thanks to the instigation of Ramona Strong. The story of her confrontation with Grandmother Moonbeam and her willingness to protect the two sisters by any means possible had spread like wildfire on a dry prairie. It seemed she was the only white person who'd ever shown initiative or given two shits about the children. The icing on the cake had been her gift of her beloved guard dog to the family, a sacrifice which had generated considerable respect among the community.

But the bloodbath on the Rez had merely eliminated a few low-life thugs and driven middle-management filth like Dwight Mitchell into hiding. From what John could see, Mitchell was a linchpin holding the entire operations together; all he had to do now was find him.

John's former client Jason Monroe was without a doubt the one holding Mitchell's leash. With oil prices plummeting, Monroe was more determined than ever to hang on to his foothold in the Bakken by any means possible. Aligning with the white supremacist group trying to maintain their power in the Dakotas seemed a practical strategy, but this was speculation from the outside. What John needed to do now was prove it.

Giving up on the food, he peeked out of the cracked window in the cargo door. The moon was almost full, and he was surprised at how far he could make out objects in the distance. It was a sea of barren landscape, one he was sick of looking at. John closed his eyes and imagined sailing under the same moonlit sky heading for the open waters of Lake Michigan, a more welcoming image. He was deep in his reverie when a soft knock at the rear door startled him.

"Finch, you awake?"

Recognizing the voice, John opened the rusted door with a miserable creak. He slid clumsily out of the cargo area and faced his late-night visitor. "For God's sake, don't wake her," he whispered. "She only stopped crying half an hour ago." The two men cast a glance back in the van, where a young Indian girl slept in the reclined seat up front. Lil Sis Moonbeam hadn't moved a muscle. Exhaling slowly, John hiked the blanket over his shoulders and said, "What's up?"

Looking badass in hunting camo from head to toe,

Matthew Ferguson held up a large picnic basket. The odor of fried bread, roasted vegetables, and gamey meat wafted from under the cover. "Poppy cooked up a decent meal for you and Lil Sis," he said, handing the basket over to John. "You'll need the sustenance for the next leg of your journey."

John took the basket, refraining from reminding Ferguson he was a vegetarian. "I'm not so sure the girl will eat," he said, his voice filled with unexpected worry. "It crushed her when I had to let the dogs go." The non-stop wailing still reverberated between his ears. It was a pitiful sound, but he'd had to do it. The dogs had been a benefit for the first twenty-four hours or so; both animals were excellent at keeping a watch out for danger. However, they were also noisy and smelly, and they needed a lot of food. The child had offered to sacrifice her rations as if it were a viable solution, and an uncharitable part of John wondered if it wouldn't have been just as well; she'd stopped eating and drinking anyway once the dogs were gone. "I'm afraid she plans to starve herself."

The attorney was more optimistic. "It's not in a teenager's nature to starve. It's probably the lack of desirable food options. She's used to venison and other wild game. Poppy is very skilled in the preparation of such cuisine, and even though fried bread isn't a true native food, a lot of the people eat it on the Rez. She dusted the bread with cinnamon and sugar. It tastes more like funnel cake from the county fair."

John felt a trickle of drool slipping out of the corner of his mouth and wiped at it unconsciously. "Mind if I eat my portion in your SUV? It's too buggy out here to enjoy, and I can't bear to eat another meal in that reeking van."

"Aren't you going to wake Lil Sis?"

"And listen to her cry some more?" John shook his head. "Let me eat my ration first before you wake her. Then I'll let you coax her into eating."

To his surprise, Ferguson obliged, standing vigil by the van while John wolfed down the homecooked meal. He felt like an animal. He didn't care. Everything was all so wonderful. Even the meat gravy tasted good. He'd had the pleasure of Mrs. Ferguson's cooking once before, a rhubarb pie; Shannon McDonald had it specially made for the dinner they'd shared the night before she died.

John tried not to think about it. Though some of her actions had been misguided, Shannon was a good person. She certainly didn't deserve the fate she'd been dealt.

Matthew caught him licking cinnamon sugar from his fingers when he rapped at the window. "When you and Lil Sis are done eating, I need to get you out of here before Nate and Mony come out to the farm tomorrow."

John looked around for his napkin to wipe his sticky fingers. "I thought you said hiding out at the Altman farm was the safest place for us to be right now." He wiped his hands on his filthy pants.

"Not anymore. Detective Gomez's special ops team will be setting up cameras and patrolling the perimeter in preparation for tomorrow. We're hoping Mitchell will make a move after learning the two are back in town. When that happens, you and Lil Sis need to be as far away from here as possible."

John was acquainted with the "trio of trouble's" method of luring quarry. He'd witnessed the aftermath of their work the past winter, during a friendly game of hockey. Mitchell had ended up a bloody, broken mess for failing to see through an old high school scheme. "I want you to know I despise your use of Ramona as bait—again. You're an asshole for doing it, and you know that asshole Mitchell is expecting it. He can't possibly be stupid enough to get duped again." He shook his head. "You people sure have a peculiar way of protecting the ones you love."

The attorney didn't even bother denying it. "If we can capture Mitchell in an unlawful act, we have greater access higher up the chain."

"I thought that's what the young girl was for, to entice her sister out of hiding. If she's still alive, that is."

"Plans changed—too risky at this point. Better Sissy stay hidden for now."

"You think she's alive?"

"I don't know. I hope so."

Oddly, so did John. He had no emotional attachment to the outcome either way, yet for the sake of the little girl, he found himself concerned for both sisters' well-being. Coming from a solid sibling relationship himself, he believed the younger sibling needed her older sister. Thinking this, John realized he hadn't spoken with his own sister for a couple of months. She too was likely worried sick about him. A pang of melancholy hit him like a sucker punch to the gut. Shaking it off, he asked, "When will we be moving, and where will you be taking us?"

"I'm taking the two of you out of here tonight. I've

gathered your personal effects from the hotel, but I left you on the register and strewed some old clothes and a few toiletries around for show. We want it to look like you're still in the area."

"What difference does that make?"

"If Monroe thinks you're still here, they won't be looking for you elsewhere."

"Ah. Since I won't be here, where am I going?"

"You and Lil Sis will stay at our private hangar until it's clear to fly you out. There's a shower onboard the plane to clean up and change into more comfortable clothes. Wi-Fi is available, and Poppy will keep you well fed. Once you've landed, a limo will be waiting to take you and Lil Sis to an undisclosed location."

"I don't like it."

The attorney brushed the objection aside. "I don't expect you to like it, but you're no longer safe here, and we have a place where you can stay until this all blows over." Matthew held up his hand, waving it to encompass the interior of the vehicle. "Your accommodations will be far more comfortable than your current arrangement."

"I don't care about that," John lied. "Why should I trust you to help me? How is your protection any better or worse than what Wagner can offer?"

Matthew looked surprised. "The sheriff doesn't know you're leaving."

A tingle rippled down his spine. "Why?"

John had begun to question whether he'd developed a peculiar Stockholm-syndrome relationship with the sheriff of Williams County. True, the man had kept him alive so far, despite placing him in highly volatile situations at every turn. But John was growing wary of him, even more so now that it seemed he and the Fergusons were no longer playing on the same team.

Matthew continued, "Dad and I believe there may be an informant within the county department. We don't want to take any chances."

Annoyed, John said, "Not much of an explanation. And since when did you start giving a shit about me?"

For the first time, Ferguson appeared genuinely affronted by a question. "You don't think that I'm aware of what you did behind the scenes to buy us time before the probate hearing? That incompetent jackass stepping in for you knew nothing about the oil industry, North Dakota mineral and land ownership rights, or how to conduct himself professionally. Monroe Oil will be lucky if they can hold onto their existing wells, let alone find a willing seller to purchase more land. Even if they did, I doubt they have the cash flow necessary to drill a new well. No one wants to work with that fucker since he resorted to hiring scabs from the white supremacist camp. Besides all that, you've placed yourself in harm's way more than any of us for Mony's sake. Our family is in your debt. Monroe Oil and your law firm really shot themselves in the foot firing you. It was tremendously shortsighted."

"Suspended with pay."

"Whatever. There are hundreds of companies that would welcome your expertise. I would hire you myself if it weren't for my brother's grudge against you. The least I can do is give you a personal recommendation."

It had been a long while since John had heard any sort of sincere praise. Unsure how to respond, he changed the subject. "You still haven't told me where the girl and I are going."

There was a flash of movement near the front of the old van. Ferguson's eyes darted to the left— "Shit!"—and then he broke out into a run.

It took a beat for John to figure out what happened. "Shit!" He scrambled out of Ferguson's SUV with the finesse of a rampaging bull and followed in hot pursuit. He could hear Matthew shouting several yards in front of him.

"Lil Sis, please come back! I promise not to hurt you."

They sprinted for several minutes before Ferguson stopped and John finally caught up to him. Heaving like a freight train, he leaned forward to rest his hands on his knees, disgusted by his deconditioning. The sound of open water lapping against the shore close by surprised him. He said breathlessly, "She couldn't have gone far."

Ferguson's voice sounded more angry than winded. "I think we should split up, cover more ground that way."

John took advantage of the respite to look around. Water was already seeping into his shoes. "Where could she go? It's dark, she doesn't know the area. Neither do I, for that matter. I think we should stick together."

Ferguson considered, then said, "How about this? You go back to the vehicles in case she circles back. She might think that in our scramble, one of us left the keys in the ignition."

John instinctively stuck his hands in both pockets and felt the absence of the familiar object. "Fuck!"

He tore back in the direction of the van. Spurred on by fury at his negligence, he tried to downplay the threat, then realized, *Of course the girl knows how to drive.* He'd seen kids he swore were no older than ten driving big tractors and towing heavy equipment down the middle of a dirt road, everywhere. *Christ, how could I be so goddamn stupid.*

His pace slowing, John was relieved to see the rickety van and Ferguson's SUV still parked exactly where they'd left them. Taking slow, deep breaths, he walked the rest of the way. His relief was short-lived; when he opened the driver side door, he checked the ignition and found the keys were gone. A flash of irritation rose at how foolishly he'd underestimated the instincts and cunning of his little charge. Even the very young possessed uncanny survival skills out here in the boondocks.

It occurred to him that, from the moment he stepped off the train last winter to his follow-up return, he had failed to understand the inner working of the Bakken people's mindset. They were a resilient, gritty, tenacious clan. It reminded him of a story he'd heard about an animal chewing its leg off just to escape a trap. It reminded him of Ramona. It was a shared motto: survival at any cost. This was a place he didn't belong. Had it not been for the Fergusons' support or the sheriff's protection, he probably would have been dead a long time ago in this wild country. The thought distressed him.

John climbed into the seat and pulled a nearly empty pack of cigarettes from his shirt pocket. His last one. He'd been smoking too much lately. He didn't care. No longer living in the city smog, he figured the fresh air of the wide-open spaces balanced out his lung quality. Taking a long, deep drag, he listened for movement around the vehicles. What he heard was the ongoing chirps and buzzing of night insects and an occasional quack from the waterfowl a few hundred yards away. In the relative quiet, he tried to calm his nerves.

The idea of someone else in charge of his safety pissed him off, but what could he do about it? At least he'd be away from this place soon. Perhaps not having the constant threat on his life would allow him time to contemplate something more meaningful, like restoring a level of normalcy in his life. Maybe he would take his sailboat somewhere south, like the Florida Keys, and live off of the grid for a while until he decided his next course of action. He didn't have the resources the Fergusons and Ramona had, but he was far from poor. The idea sounded heavenly . . . but it would be a life without Ramona Strong.

He'd dropped his grudge toward her for pointing a loaded gun at him and accusing him of murder a while ago. Her actions had been driven by fear after seeing Shannon McDonald's body floating in the water. It was survival instinct. He could forgive that. What he couldn't abide was her unbreakable bond to this place. Despite spending much of her adult existence living and building a life somewhere else, she would always be tethered to this land in history, family, business, and spirit. At first it was something he'd thought he could accept, for in his mind, the only lovable thing about this place was her.

But Ramona was correct when she told him he deserved better, and he knew a lost cause when it was staring him in the face.

Taking the last drag from his cigarette and pitching the butt out the window, John noticed an abrupt absence in nocturnal sounds. Something—or rather some*one*—was outside the van.

Instinctively, he slid down in the seat. *Pointless—you just gave away your location, idiot.* His heart rate kicked up a notch as he considered his options. Slipping out the passenger side and making a run for it wouldn't work. The noise of opening the old rusty door alone would betray that plan. John slunk lower in the seat.

His gut told him it wasn't Lil Sis returning with the stolen key to take the van. He fumbled around the floor, searching for an object to defend himself. Whatever he found wouldn't do him much good if his predator had a gun, but at least he wouldn't go down without a fight. He ran his fingers across a long, thick piece of metal— the crowbar he'd used in the jack to change the tire. He gripped it in his hand.

Several more minutes passed. The chirping and buzzing sounds resumed at their normal nighttime volume. Maybe whoever was outside had moved on. An involuntary twitch began coursing in his leg, and he nervously tapped his foot. If it was Ferguson, he'd have announced himself by now.

A faint sound of nylon fabric slid against the metal exterior. The squish of wet grass under heavy boots moved along the side of the van. John glanced in the broken side mirror and saw a tall, hooded figure creeping up to his open window. He tightened his grip around the piece of steel. If he could see his assailant, the assailant could see him. He lifted the bar to his lap as the hooded figure drew a small handgun to a readied position.

A peculiar trill from a bird halted the gunman's hand in mid-position. John held his breath. *Was someone else out there?*

He didn't have a chance to find out.

The burlap sack came down quickly over his head, blocking his view. A slight metallic odor began to fill his nostrils, and he instinctively held his breath. The cord on the sack tightened around his neck, and he struggled to get his hands inside the closing bag to dislodge it from his head. He gasped, then giggled, feeling a strange sense of euphoria, relaxation, and calmness.

His giggling faded as the world went dark.

CHAPTER 5

MONY

The three spoke little on the familiar drive, each retreating deep within his or her own thoughts. Mony had to stifle a yawn several times. Looking over at her cohorts, it seemed they'd had a hard time getting out of bed this morning as well, evident in the stubble they were sporting. Normally, sitting between the two of them was her favorite place in the world. She always felt safe, protected, and loved. The latter still wasn't in question; it was the former qualities that left her feeling ambiguous.

They parked in front of the private hangar, allowing the least amount of exposure to sniper fire, and slipped inside. Mony was surprised by the transformation in the interior from her last visit. Most of her dad's possessions were gone, and those that were left had been moved into a corner to make room for Detective Gomez's team's temporary base. Spotting them, the detective called out, "Welcome to command central." She approached and reached for each of their hands.

Dispensing with the formality, Nate pulled Gabriella in

for a hug. "Thanks for being here. I know we'll all be in good hands."

Since her assignment to his shooting investigation, Nate had developed the strongest relationship with the detective, but Gabriella was growing on Mony too. She'd offered valuable counsel after Mony shot a man in self-defense, and had also proven herself a formidable force in the search for both the Moonbeam sisters, ranking high on Mony's list as a decent human being.

The detective said, "While the senator dispersed the crop-dusting equipment, it was relatively easy moving in undetected with our large trailers. We've been infiltrating the property over the past twelve hours, entrenching our position. Come on, let me show you what we've accomplished so far." Mony noted the impressive number of closed-circuit monitors lining the south wall. "We've had people watching the monitors around the clock while an elite team canvases the parameter. We've mostly seen birds hatching and deer birthing fawns around the wetland area. These monitors track the day-to-day traffic around the pumpjack and crude oil storage tank at sites one and two. So far, the most excitement we've had was catching a couple of poachers in the wildlife management area. We watched it through the deputy's body cam. You should have seen the look of shock on their faces when they were busted."

Mony gazed into the line of cameras. Nearly every inch of the property seemed to be under surveillance. Even the interior of the shabin was no longer private. She asked the detective, "Was it during the camera setup that you discovered where Shannon had been killed?"

The detective glanced at Nate before responding. "Yes. But when I went back to report the finding to Sheriff Wagner, he claimed he'd discovered the crime scene shortly after Ms. McDonald's body was recovered from the lake."

Mony was shocked. "Why didn't he tell anyone?"

A familiar candy-apple-red Ford truck popped into the monitor screen of sector two, halting a response to her question. Kip was on his way, and he wasn't alone. The remarkable clarity of the camera lens and monitors made it easy to identify the redheaded, red-bearded passenger riding shotgun.

Nate said, "Shawn and I are going to take a walk down to the shabin." He turned to Gomez. "Will that be all right with you?"

The detective directed Nate closer to a monitor. "Sure. We just completed a sweep of that sector. You and your friend will be safe. Let me point out where we have the trail cams located."

As Nate and the detective walked away, Massey said to Mony, "How about you and I walk up to the house and take a look around?"

Outside, Kip joined Mony and Massey as Nate and Shawn headed toward the lake. Mony unconsciously clutched at a tightness in her chest. It was a solemn sight, watching the two friends walk down the familiar path. It grieved her that the sanctuary of her home had been so egregiously violated—not only for her, but for everyone who had spent time there. She felt the anger swelling in her gut. She'd been robbed, invaded, deceived. Nodding her head toward the two men, she asked Massey and Kip, "Do you think they'll be okay?"

Massey's expression matched her thoughts. "Will any of us be?"

As Kip punched in the security code to the kitchen entrance, that ominous feeling prickled down Mony's spine again. Standing on the porch of her childhood home, she felt unnerved by the hidden cameras planted everywhere. The lack of privacy contradicted everything her dad had believed in. His home had always been a welcoming space to all who crossed over the threshold, no matter who they were. It was a retreat house, a place of trust where former combat pilots would drop by day or night, seeking refuge, a beer, a friend, and a listening ear to speak freely of their experiences during the war without judgement.

Mony stood in the middle of the kitchen much the same way she had when she first came to live with Buddy, and felt—lost. Everything appeared exactly as she had left it. The counter space was clean and uncluttered, the refrigerator empty, the space cool and dank with the odor of stale air. She walked to the window above the sink and reached for the sash.

"What are you doing?" Kip yelled.

"I was just going to open—"

"You can't do that. You'll set off the security alarm."

Disheartened, she let her arms fall to her side. She decided to check out the living room.

Rounding the archway, Mony's heart leaped in her throat. She hollered, "Kip!"

Massey came quickly to her side. "God, I'm sorry," he said, throwing his arm over her shoulders. "We had the piano moved to my house in Bismarck. I'm sorry I forgot to tell you. I'm sorry."

She swiped at the sting of salty tears in the corner of her eyes. The piano had been gifted to her by her father and was the birthplace of Nate's musical career. "What the hell was Dad thinking? How are Nate and I ever going to make this our home again?"

Massey gave her shoulder a squeeze. "I don't think Buddy or any of us could have ever imagined the events that have taken place over the past year."

Kip said from the archway, "I did. I warned you as soon as you got off the train, Mony, what you were in store for." He held up a hand to stay Massey's protest. "I'm not saying I told you so. I'm saying this because you and Nate have been gone for too long. You think of life on the Bakken for what it was, not for what it's become. Things are reverting because we're heading for a bust, but that doesn't mean the riffraff have moved on. Some of the transplant workers are returning to where they came from, but most don't even have enough money for bus fare back to wherever. These are desperate times, and it will get worse before gets better. The large conglomerates are biding their time, waiting to scoop up the shattered pieces of people's lives like they've done for decades."

"Goddamn vultures," Mony spat. "This is our home, our land. It belongs to us."

The image of the Moonbeams' small home on the Rez came to mind. She pondered the feelings of anger and despair their people must have experienced watching their ancestral land disappear under the water of Lake Sakakawea. The thought sickened her. It was despicable what wealthy white men did to the powerless for profit.

"I need some air."

Outside, Mony walked around the side of the house to the backyard, where she stood in front of the partially tilled, unplanted plot of dirt that had once been a garden. She had hated working in the garden as a kid, especially when it came time for canning, but she loved the end results. Poppy had insisted she learn the fine art of preservatives along with Nate and Massey. They'd worked tirelessly packing cucumbers in jars, peeling fruit, and shelling chokecherries. But it was so worth it come winter, when she could retrieve a jar of dill pickles or freshly canned peaches from the fruit cellar. The chokecherries were always her favorite.

Kip and Massey came up and stood beside her. She said to Kip, "I see you decided not to use the garden space after all."

"What do you mean?"

Mony thought back to the last time she'd flown over the property, after Shannon's murder. From the air it had appeared someone had left the garden partially tilled. "Didn't you have someone come out and till the garden?" She pointed over the uneven surface, where several large chunks of black soil were clustered in the middle. "It sure looks like it." She walked around the perimeter and was about to step into the garden for a closer look when Massey grabbed her by the arm.

"Wait. Did you say it was like this after we recovered Shannon's body?"

"Yeah. When Nate was in the hospital, I tried to thank Kip for having someone take care of the garden. He looked at me like I had two heads."

"That's because I never sent anyone out here," Kip said. "Didn't your German shepherd retrieve the young Indian girl's jacket out here by the garden?"

A wave of bile bubbled up from Mony's stomach. "What are you implying?"

Kip retrieved the front loader from the Quonset hut and drove around to the backyard, where the forensic team waited at the edge of the garden on standby. Sheriff Wagner and two deputies performed the painstaking task of removing the layers of topsoil with a spade so as not to disturb what they suspected to be a crime scene.

Shawn and Nate had returned to the house, their eyes red and swollen. It killed Mony to see them in such agony. It was like rediscovering Shannon's body all over again. After a while, Shawn had joined the other search and rescue team members standing vigil by the garden. As curious as she was to know what was buried in the middle of her garden, she and Nate decided to wait it out elsewhere.

Walking hand in hand, they started down the familiar dirt road toward the shabin. Her steps felt like boots weighed down with mud. The space between them felt heavier. She broke the silence: "How's Shawn holding up?"

Nate was quiet for a long while before responding. "I don't know how Shawn can stand living here day to day. I've been here barely twenty-four hours and I'm ready to bolt."

Mony squeezed his hand. "I know what you mean. I can't even think beyond what we're about to find in the garden, let alone consider what we're going to do with all this land. As impressive as it is, Detective Gomez's team has barely scratched the surface of this acreage with all her surveillance cameras, yet I feel like we're under a microscope."

"Exactly. I was afraid to scratch my ass when Shawn and I were standing down by the lake for fear of a camera peering up my butt."

Nate said the words so seriously, Mony couldn't help but laugh. The release felt good. Nate stopped in the middle of the dirt road and pulled her in for a hug. Kissing her forehead, he said, "I need you to make me a promise that no matter what we find here, it isn't going to become a wedge between us. I'll do whatever you want regarding Buddy's property. I don't even know why he—"

Mony pressed her fingers gently to his lips. "We've had this conversation. This land is as much yours as it is mine, and Kip and Massey's too. We will decide what to do together. That's all Dad wanted, and I intend to honor his wish. Our fathers have built a legacy from nothing out here in this prairie pothole region, and I for one am not going to throw it away because some asshole oil company is trying to rob us of our inheritance."

"It's not just the land they're taking," Nate replied with irritation, "it's our peace of mind."

"Then we'll take it back. We will find out who murdered Shannon and rescue the Moonbeam girls. I have to believe this." She swept out her arm to encompass the land around them. "This will all belong to our children someday. We'll figure out a way to hold on to it and make it a safe place—together."

Nate kissed the fingers pressed to his lips, then moved her hand to take her mouth. Mony felt her toes curl in her boots. God, how she loved the way he kissed her, like he was a man parched from a long journey and she was a cool drink of water. His hands slid up under her shirt and stroked the bare skin at the small of her back. Her flesh tingled beneath his touch. He needed the physical contact. She needed him too. Nate murmured, "If it weren't for all of these goddamn cameras around, I'd carry you to the shabin and make love into next week."

A shiver ran up the length of her spine at the primal urge. Every part of her body was in a heightened state of response. Nate never minced words when it came to his feelings for her. He reached for the duck-tail strands of hair at the nape of her neck and gave them a tug, reminding her it was time for a trim. What was it about his lips, his touch, the passion of his lovemaking that made her blood run hot?

And yet, despite his attention, she was distracted. "Did you hear that?"

Nate broke off the kiss and immediately took stock of their surroundings. They stood frozen like two deer in the presence of a predator's scent. A light breeze lapped the lake water against the shoreline in quiet waves as the waterfowl carried on their usual noisy, cantankerous chatter. It wasn't what she'd heard.

Mony lifted an ear to the wind and strained to listen. "There it is again. Did you hear that?"

Nate made a shrill, come-hither whistle.

Her heart leaped with hope. Mony began shouting, "Shep, is that you? Come to me, boy, come on."

They both scanned the horizon of the midafternoon marshy glade. The sun was bright, and without her sunglasses, it was difficult to make out fine objects.

Nate's arm shot out, pointing to a dot in the horizon. "Look!"

Mony shielded her eyes, barely making out the two four-legged creatures loping in their direction. Unable to contain herself, she began to run toward them. Moving slowly, the two dogs still managed to bridge the gap quicker than her human legs could carry her. When Shep was within a few feet, Mony dropped to her knees and said softly, "You've come home to me, Shep—good boy, good boy."

Shep stood just out of her reach as Rainstorm cowered next to him warily. The sight of it broke Mony's heart. Both dogs looked like they hadn't eaten in days, their fur matted and full of cockleburs. Instinctively, she reached into the pocket of her work shirt. As a veterinarian, she'd always carried doggy treats with her. Today, all she had was a piece of hard candy. "Sorry, baby, Mommy doesn't have anything for you right now. Come with me up to the house, sweetie, and I'll get you and Rainstorm something to eat."

Shep crouched uncharacteristically on his belly as he approached. It was heart-wrenching to watch such a proud, regal animal assuming the supplicant position. Rainstorm remained a safe distance away, whimpering obsessively, letting Shep take the lead. Mony held out her hand and let her dog sniff it first before reaching to pet him. As soon as her pet recognized her scent, he leaped onto her, knocking her off balance, and pinned her to the ground, licking her face incessantly. Given the all-clear, Rainstorm soon followed.

Nate's approach momentarily startled the dogs, but when Shep recognized him, the joyous reunion resumed. Mony tried to do a quick assessment of each animal, patting down joints, bones, skulls, and palpating internal organs. Except for feeling a little lean in the middle, it appeared they were both relatively unharmed. "They seem to be okay, but we—"

Her cell phone vibrated in her pocket, startling her. She checked the screen, then put the detective on speaker.

"Try not to handle the dogs more than you have to. I want to get any samples from their fur so we can determine where they were and what they've been up to for the past seventy-two hours."

"Sorry—and yes, I agree. But first, we need to get them food and some fresh water right away. I will need to take them to the vet as soon as possible for a more comprehensive exam."

"Fine. Bring them to the hangar; we have water and will find something for them to eat. I will have the forensic team standing by. I also need you and Nate to look at the monitor for sector eleven. There's something not quite right about the picture we're seeing."

"Well, that sounds ominous," murmured Nate.

The two of them walked the dirt road back to the house with each dog close on their heels. The sight of the animals alive filled Mony's heart with such hope it was frightening. She couldn't help but think, *If the dogs are alive, maybe Lil Sis escaped as well.* It was almost too much to hope, considering the current excavation taking place in her garden. But both the Moonbeam girls seemed to possess a formidable aptitude for survival.

Nate took her hand in his and said quietly, "From what I could tell on the monitor, sector eleven is where we kept the beehives."

Mony looked at him. "But the bees are with your mom."

"I know."

"Wait a minute. Isn't that also the section of property where we had the missing deed?"

"Uh huh."

"What do you think is going on out there?"

"My guess is we're about to find out."

CHAPTER 6

MASSEY

Massey waited on the front porch with his dad, watching as Mony and Nate approached. Kip shouted, "I thought hell would freeze over before we'd find those animals alive."

Shep stopped, and the Rez dog cowered at the sound of Kip's booming voice, but then Mony went down on one knee and called both animals to her side. They immediately responded. Not for the first time, Massey marveled at her way with animals. When the dogs were comforted, she came closer to the step landing and spoke quietly. "Nate and I are taking Shep and Rainstorm over to the hangar. The detective has something she wants us to check out in sector eleven. Do either of you have any thoughts about that?"

Kip directed the question toward Massey. "Sector eleven, hmm. Isn't that where the beehives are kept?"

Massey lifted his shoulder in a casual shrug. He knew the answer. "Yeah, I think so. What's up?"

"Not sure. Gomez didn't get into it; probably paranoid

somebody's eavesdropping. Anyway, if you need me or Nate, you'll know where to find us." The dogs trailed behind as the two headed in the direction of the hangar.

Kip furrowed his brow. "Who in the hell would be eavesdropping? No one's out here except for us, Gomez, and her team."

Massey considered his rendezvous the night before. "The detective's just being cautious." No one had been privy to his meeting with Finch or his grand plan, and it was his intention to keep it that way for as long as he could. There was something off in the county law enforcement office, and until he knew what that entailed, the fewer people who knew John was missing, the better. "Do you think the dogs are a distraction to divert us from our primary focus?"

"What do you mean?"

"Maybe we haven't been so covert after all. Look at all of these people milling around on the property. It's unusual timing, the dogs showing up while we're trying to draw Mitchell out of hiding." He ran his hand across the top of his head. "It significantly undermines the efforts to protect Nate and Mony. If Dwight or one of his peons is brazen enough to try something in broad daylight, this would be the ideal time to do it. I'd feel more comfortable if we got Mony and Nate out of here, at least until we've unearthed whatever is in the garden and there are fewer people on the premises."

Kip shook his head. "All of our resources are tied up right here, right now. If anyone were to go after them on the highway, the way you and Mony were chased down in Arizona, there would be no cavalry standing by to help them. I do agree with your idea about a distraction, though. Let's just have them sit tight for now, at least until the excavation work is finished."

Massey wasn't on board with the idea, but he held his rebuttal. "I'm going to tell them to stay in the hangar until we're done out here."

His father snorted. "Good luck with that."

Grateful for the excuse to get away from the digging, Massey headed to the hangar, interested in what the detective had found on the monitor. He was hoping it would offer a clue as to what had happened to John. By the time he'd made his way back to the rendezvous last night, the white van and Finch were both gone.

Finch had expressed his dissatisfaction and desire to leave the Bakken, but this was no time for a pissing contest. If Finch had an ounce of self-preservation, he'd have gone along with Massey's plan regardless. His actions didn't add up. John was methodical in his conduct. It was one of the characteristics Massey admired about him. Perhaps the two of them hadn't been the only ones capable of circumventing the detective's security.

Entering the hangar, Massey saw Mony off in the corner with one of the forensic team members, snipping fur samples from the dogs—or at least trying. Shep was compliant enough, but the young Rez dog was terrified. Even food couldn't motivate her. Recognizing a lost cause, Massey joined Nate and Detective Gomez at the monitors.

The detective tapped at the screen. "Here you can see two sets of tracks," she said to Nate. "This one clearly had the superior traction; the other must have been rear-wheel drive. Look how it got bogged down in the soft ground." She advanced the screen. "This person obviously didn't know where they were going or what they were doing. The other vehicle in the next screenshot here is much better prepared, more familiar with the terrain. My team followed the erratic tracks back out toward the township road. We expected the tracks to go right, the shortest route back toward the main highway. This driver turned left."

Massey jumped into the conversation. "How is it your cameras didn't pick up the vehicles' movement in the first place?"

Gomez turned to look at him. "The activity occurred before we'd reached that sector. It wasn't until we were out there on foot that we discovered the tracks. Anyway, we found a white van abandoned in sector thirteen in the marsh near the dam. That's where the team is now. So far, they've reported finding a set of human tracks leaving the site back toward the township road; then they disappear."

Nate glanced at Massey. "Isn't Finch driving a white van?"

Massey saw the suspicion in his brother's eyes. "Finch isn't playing us. Besides, he has nothing to gain and everything to lose leaving our protection." To the detective: "You said another vehicle was on site. Did it travel in the same direction?"

"No, that vehicle turned right as expected. And I agree with you, Matthew—I don't think Mr. Finch was out there making trouble. I think someone may have discovered his hiding place."

Nate's eyes widened. "Hiding? Why would Finch be hiding on Mony's farm?"

"For starters, who would look for him on the property of a known rival for Monroe Oil? Second, we believe he may have been one of the people who escaped the failed abduction attempt of the young Moonbeam girl."

"Massey told me about that. It doesn't explain why he'd hide out here."

"If Mr. Finch was there during the shootout and witnessed who tried to nab the girl, he'd have good reason to be hiding. Everyone's looking for the Moonbeam sisters, and they're willing to kill to get their hands on them. If Finch is involved in harboring the child, they are both in grave danger."

Nate threw up his hands. "But why hide out here, in this precise location? How in the hell did Finch get back to the apiary in the first place, especially without help? The site is right in the middle of our land easement with wildlife management, between Altman and Ferguson property lines. The only way in is an obscure field road barely visible from the main road. There is no direct field approach. The 'no hunting' sign posted a few feet away is our marker, not the general public's. The only people who knew that information were me and Buddy, maybe Dad and Massey." Nate started to fidget, then seemed to remember a thought. "You said you found poachers in the wildlife refuge. Is it possible they were scouting out the area?"

"I let the sheriff and his team handle that situation. He would have the details. But to address your question, yes, it's possible someone was on a scouting mission and may know of our presence. It's common knowledge that Ms. Strong would offer safe haven for anyone protecting the whereabouts of either of the Moonbeam sisters. If Finch has her, this farm is the first place I would go."

"So you're saying what happened on the Rez the other night was an abduction attempt?" asked Massey.

"I'd bet my badge on it. I've had the Moonbeam residence under surveillance ever since I arrived in North Dakota. Ms. Strong insisted on it. Her intuition was correct. We intercepted someone sending the younger Moonbeam girl written messages."

"Who?"

"One of her friends from the Rez. Said a stranger paid her fifty dollars to stick it in one of the first-floor windows, no questions asked."

"I bet someone was trying to lure her out," said Nate.

"Likely. They were setting up a rendezvous. Two of the men killed in the skirmish on the Rez were part of Harland Richards's crew. Richards was the last known person John had reported meeting before his disappearance."

Nate scratched his jaw, looking puzzled. "If Richards and his posse are one part of the equation, who was shooting at them?"

"That's easy—members of the Rez community, though no one is admitting to it. Two non-Native factions feuding on reservation land is highly improbable."

"Excuse me." Nate abruptly started, making his way toward the door. Massey caught him by the arm.

"Where are you going?"

Nate glanced downed at Massey's grip on his arm, then gave him a cold look. "I want to talk to the sheriff about these poachers."

Massey held on to Nate for a beat before releasing him. "The sheriff wants you and Mony to stay here. I'll bring him to you."

Before Nate could launch into an argument, the sheriff stepped into the hangar, his face grim. Nate and Massey stowed the disagreement. "What is it?"

The sheriff muttered, "We found something."

The mood around the makeshift grave was solemn as the investigation team examined the disinterred remains of Cindy Van Dyke. After the body had been completely exhumed, a deputy roped off the area with yellow tape; the rest of the team packed up their gear and escorted Nate and Mony back to Williston. Massey offered assurance they would be protected within the caravan, and Detective Gomez informed them a grief counselor had been placed on standby. The two were so distraught they didn't even argue with the detail. Mony did, however, advocate for the dogs, and Gomez gave the go-ahead to take both animals to the veterinarian's office as soon as they got into town. It was a wise move—she needed to divert her attention away from the day's gruesome events, as did they all.

With Nate and Mony securely on their way back into town, Massey lingered at the farm, hoping to have a talk with the detective in private. He had an unsettled feeling that she'd been holding something back during their debriefing. Perhaps he was projecting his guilt at his own duplicity; contrary to his professional conduct, withholding information didn't sit well with him.

Before he left the scene, Massey informed the sheriff he would be sitting in on the interview with Harland Richards. Wagner didn't bother to suppress his surprise. On the flight back to Williston, Massey had spoken with Gem and arranged for himself to provide representation during Richards's questioning. Harland had been brought out of an induced coma that morning, and his sister had been sitting vigil at his bedside since her arrival. Hopefully, she'd managed to weave some sibling magic and get him to talk a little. It was a risk to offer defending counsel, but to get a little, they had to give a little. Massey had convinced Gem that his oversight in Harland's case gave her brother a better chance than a public defender would.

Kip stood beside his son, staring at the hole in the garden. Massey muttered, "If anyone would have told me my old high school flame would end up buried in Buddy's backyard, I would have punched them in the goddamn face. Christ."

"No one saw this coming until it was too late," Kip replied soberly. "Maybe I should have been more tolerant of Nathan and Mony staying with your mother in Arizona. They could have been spared all this. At least they'd be safe."

"If Nate and Mony hadn't come home, we'd never have found Cindy. Which begs the question: why didn't the sheriff's team uncover this the day Shannon's body was recovered, and why in the hell didn't he tell us he'd uncovered the murder scene?"

"What scene?"

"Didn't you know? Detective Gomez just told me, Nate, and Mony that Wagner discovered the murder scene inside the toolshed the same day Shannon was pulled from the lake."

"Scott's been lying to us?"

"More like withholding information. Either way, I don't think there will be any place safe for Nate and Mony until we catch this killer and destroy Monroe Oil. This all started when Jason came after your company."

"Our company," Kip corrected. "And not *all*, Matthew. The Mitchells have been troublemaking sons of bitches for years. Dwight's obsession with Mony has gotten bolder since the death of Bob Strong. Plus, Mitchell has a posse."

"Do you think the neo-Nazi group is pulling the strings?"

"That clusterfuck? They couldn't put a two-piece puzzle together. No, they're working for Mitchell."

Massey looked out toward the western sky. The day was almost over; he should be home already, spending time with his wife and sons having dinner. "More hired thugs."

"Exactly. That white supremacist organization north of town hasn't got a pot to piss in. They sure as shit don't have the money to buy Nate and Mony's property. But a powerful oil company can, and anyone working for said oil company could have ample free space to set up a compound. Talk about ruining the neighborhood."

"Are you suggesting we get out?"

Kip snorted. "Did you see the determination in Mony's eyes when she learned the identity of the corpse? She isn't going anywhere as long as there's a chance that we can find either of the Moonbeam girls alive."

Just then, Massey's cell phone rang. He listened, then said, "Yes, I can stick around a bit if someone can give me a lift back into town."

Kip mouthed, "*I can wait.*"

Massey shook his head. He hated to leave his dad out of the loop, but for the time being, it was necessary. He said into the receiver, "I'll meet you in the hangar, Detective."

When Massey and the sheriff arrived, Gem was sitting on a folding chair, facing her brother near the elevated head of his hospital bed. Harland Richards sat with his eyes closed, oxygen, IVs, chest tubes, and whatnot dangling from every orifice. Gem looked in the direction of the doorway; her face was taut, her expression weary. Massey knew the feeling, recalling Nate's condition after his shooting. Her, he felt empathy for—for Harland he did not.

"It's time to talk," he told her.

Sheriff Wagner read Harland his Miranda rights, then launched into his series of questions. "Where were you the night of Shannon McDonald's murder?"

His eyes closed, Harland muttered, "I was at my trailer."

"Were you alone?"

One eye opened, and his gaze slid to his sister. "I had—company."

"Anyone willing to bear witness to that?"

Harland didn't answer immediately. "That Van Dyke bitch stopped by looking for Mitchell."

"What was she driving?"

The patient shrugged his stiff shoulder. "How the fuck should I know?"

Gem touched her brother's IV hand. He gritted his teeth. "Truck. Don't ask me make or model. It was dark."

"What time—approximately?"

Richards lifted his non-IV hand slowly and scratched his chin. "Not sure. Might have been around one o'clock."

"Was anyone with her?" Massey interjected.

Both eyes opened, and Harland fixed a foggy glare on Massey. "Who the fuck are you?"

Gem prodded her brother. "Answer his question, Harland."

He was silent for a moment, then growled, "Yes."

"Male or female?" the sheriff asked.

"I told you it was dark," Richards snapped. He took a couple of deep breaths, exhaling as if he'd run a race. In a less defensive tone he replied, "Female, I think. I don't know no man who'd wear their hair bushy like that."

"So two women came by around one o'clock looking for Mitchell. How long did they stay?"

"I told them he wasn't around and to get the fuck off my property. Ten, fifteen minutes, tops."

Sheriff Wagner continued his probe, rephrasing the

same four questions. It was like pulling teeth to establish a consistent timeline for Cindy Van Dyke's whereabouts. Massey had already determined Richards was splicing truths. Shannon McDonald's timeline and whereabouts prior to five o'clock in the morning were well established—Harland was making a grave error by implying both women had been together. "Was anyone else with the two women?" Massey asked.

"That cocksucker Finch might have been with them," Richards lied.

This time the sheriff called him out on it. "Either you're feeding me a line of bullshit about Cindy Van Dyke showing up at your trailer, or you're lying about the timeline. Which is it? If you can't tell me something useful, I'll arrest you right now for murder."

"I'm not—you got nothing on me," Richards sputtered. "I'm the victim here—bunch of goddamn Indians. I'm lucky I wasn't scalped."

"Harland, I swear to God, if you don't stop your trash talk and come clean right now, you're not seeing a dime of my money for your defense," Gem shouted. "Am I making myself clear?"

The threat got Harland's attention. "All right, all right. I'll tell you—but first, you're going to promise me some sort of protection, Sherriff. There're spies everywhere." He looked around the room and whispered, "Might even be some right here in this hospital."

Massey hated the thought that anyone of the decent staff members working at his local hospital would get mixed up with a piece of scum like Harland. But hard times and the promise of easy money had a way of corrupting even good people—Cindy Van Dyke, for one.

In an ominous tone, the sheriff said, "You tell me what you got, and I'll tell you what I can offer for protection—otherwise you're on your own."

"Doesn't sound fair to me. What if he has people already in your office—I—"

"Harland Richards, you're under arrest for the murder of—"

Harland's face turned fire red. "You got no proof I murdered anyone."

The sheriff removed a plastic Ziploc bag from his pocket and casually tossed it into Harland's lap. "Do you recognize this?"

Fumbling to pick it up with his IV hand, Richards examined its contents. His eyes lit with recognition. "Looks like a rag to me."

"It was found at the crime scene. Your DNA is all over it."

Richards shook his head. "Not possible. Wasn't at no murder scene. Besides, how do you know it wasn't planted, huh? How do *I* know you didn't go into my trailer and grab one of my wife-beaters off the floor to pin this all on me?"

"Are you saying it's yours?"

Harland dropped the bag on the floor like it had burned him. "You said it, not me, and how the hell did you get my DNA? Isn't that illegal or something?"

"Shows what you know about the law," said the sheriff coolly.

"I know my rights!"

Massey brought the conversation back on topic. "Which is it, Harland—someone planted your shirt, or it was stolen out of your trash heap?"

"I don't have to answer. I want my lawyer."

Gem abruptly shot to her feet. "You stupid son of a bitch, your lawyer just asked you a question."

Sweat beads collected along Harland's receding hairline as the color drained from his face. "Why didn't you say he was my lawyer?"

"I just did, you asshole."

Massey raised his hands. "You have an opportunity, right here and now, to have any false charges dropped, or you can take your chances in court. Either way, the lack of evidence supporting your innocence greatly diminishes any appointed defender's chances of winning your case. The choice is yours."

Harland glanced up at his sister as she loomed over his bed, her arms crossed over her chest. He looked like a kid who'd been caught with his hand in the cookie jar. "Harland, please," Gem implored. "There's enough evidence to lock you up for life. If there's a deal to be made, I suggest you get on with it."

What little defiance had been left in the invalid deflated in a long, deep exhale. "I didn't kill the redhead. She was already dead when her body was thrown in the water."

"How do you know?" asked the sheriff.

"Because they made me help get rid of her body."

Massey leaned closer. "Who's 'they?'"

Harland hung his head. "If I tell you, I'm a dead man."

Gem reached for her brother's hand. "You'll rot in a prison cell if you don't."

"At least I'll be alive."

"But for how long?" Massey said. "Do you really believe you can't be reached in prison?"

"That miserable cunt," Harland spat. "I had everything under control until Mitchell fucked everything up, flooding the market with that social worker's girls. We had enough girls working the man camps; we didn't need any more. But no, he had to get his old lady involved. The stupid bitch. All her little twats had families. I told him—it never works when they have families. They've got to be runaways, looking for a way out of a bad situation or to make money. I take care of my girls, I do. Sure, I need to rough 'em up now and then. You know—to keep them in line. But they know it's for their own good. Now Mitchell's got all my girls mixed up with his, and most have run off. It's what they do, you know, when there's no one's keeping 'em in line. I should have dumped her body in the lake when I had the chance."

Gem stared at her brother, horrified. "What do you mean, dump her? Dump who?"

Harland lifted his shoulder in an insolent shrug.

Massey struggled to maintain a civil tone. "We're not talking about your human-trafficking ring. We're talking about your involvement in murder."

"Like I said before, I didn't kill the redhead, just helped her over the edge of the boat."

"Did I accuse you of killing Shannon McDonald?" the sheriff broke in.

Harland's eyebrows furrowed. "Then what the fuck are we talking about?"

"I'm not placing you under arrest for the murder of Shannon McDonald. You're under arrest for the rape and murder of Cindy Van Dyke."

CHAPTER 7

NATE

Nate pulled up behind a white utility truck parked beneath a blooming crabapple tree. Shawn McDonald stood beside the driver's side door, a slight sway in his balance. A knot clenched at Nate's gut and, unbidden, the words of an old song came to mind: *O Death, no wealth, no land, no silver, no gold, nothing satisfies you but the soul.* Staring at Shawn, he wondered if the words pertained to the soul of the deceased, or the ones left behind to grieve.

He approached his best friend and extended his hand. "Thanks for meeting me here, man. I don't think I could have done this alone."

As Shawn took his hand and pulled him in for a shoulder bump, Nate caught the strong whiff of Irish whiskey. "No problem," his friend slurred. "I haven't been by to visit Sis for a couple of days now. Your call reminded me to get my ass over here. Besides, I need to give her the 411 about her friend."

The two men walked silently among the dead toward the McDonald family headstone. Not far away stood the

Altman marker. An overwhelming sense of sadness consumed Nate. Two friends gone in less than a year. He gazed up into the cloudless sky, where several songbirds tweeted joyfully, oblivious to the solemnity of their surroundings. *And why not?* It was a beautiful sunny day, with temperatures predicted to reach the high seventies—a picture-perfect day in North Dakota. Hell, if it weren't for Buddy's passing, the two of them would have been on Lake Sakakawea right now, enjoying a beer and catching walleye. It was depressing the difference a year made.

As they neared an upturned plot of dirt, Shawn called out, "Hey, Sis! Look what the cat brought home. It's our old friend Nate."

The levity in the ethereal greeting was apropos despite the setting; as Shawn settled in, he conversed with Shannon like they were standing around a bar. "I'm sorry to tell you, I have some really bad news about Cindy."

He proceeded to share the details of the previous day's awful events. As Nate listened to his friend's one-sided conversation, he mulled over what he might say. Before he could figure it out, Shawn abruptly stopped talking, nodding his head toward the grave. Reaching back into old dynamics, Nate tried to sound casual. "Hey, Shannon—long time, no s—"

He choked. *Long time, no see* had been his and Shannon's usual greeting since forever. It didn't matter whether it had been a couple weeks or just a few hours since they'd seen each other. He pushed down the tears that clogged his throat. "Sorry about what I said the last time we talked at the bar. I know you were only trying to look out for me. I want you to know I appreciated that, even though your information was bogus."

His words piqued Shawn's interest. "What did you say to her?"

Nate felt his cheeks flush. "She accused Mony of sleeping with my brother."

"Oh, that." Shawn pulled a flask from his coat pocket and took a big swallow. "So you're saying they didn't?"

Bewildered, Nate jerked his head up. "You believed that shit?"

His friend gestured his flask toward the gravestone. "My sister did. Said that Cindy Van Dyke learned the information from an eyewitness to the account."

"Who?"

"Her husband."

Fury filled Nate's eyes. "Mitchell? You both know better than to believe anything coming out of that cocksucker's mouth."

Shawn spoke without judgement: "You must have believed it yourself. Otherwise you wouldn't have beaten the shit out of Massey, then hightailed it to Vegas."

Nate's flush of anger turned to shame. Shawn was right—he'd been there to pull Nate off Massey as they scrapped in Poppy's kitchen. It had been a massive lapse in judgement, one he would forever regret. "What happened between me and my brother had been brewing for decades. Overreacting to a lie was just the catalyst. I made a huge mistake taking it out on Massey."

"I get that. I have five brothers myself, and we all have Irish tempers. We don't see eye to eye on things half the time. Personally, when I come across a bit of gossip, I take it with a grain of salt. Still, no matter how unreliable the source, there's always a thread of truth dangling somewhere in that web of lies. Plus, you have to ask the question, why would Cindy lie to Shannon? They were best friends, for Christ's sake. It would be like you lying to me."

There were many reasons Cindy Van Dyke would have lied—revenge, to name one. None of them mattered anymore. Nate weighed his next words carefully before he spoke. "Your sister . . . didn't always have the best judgement when it came to her source of information."

Shawn showed no offense at the remark. "That is true." He took another swig from his flask before handing it to Nate.

Nate accepted the offer. After a long sip, he said, "Mony wasn't fooling around on me."

"How do you know?"

"She told me."

"Yeah? What's her story?"

He felt like a traitor for sharing Mony's horrendous experience without her permission. She'd kept the secret for so long. But in the absence of truth, rumors and lies replaced fact, the downside of keeping silent. Now that Mony had exposed her nightmare to the light of day, Nate felt compelled to set the record straight.

Shawn was taken aback by the story. "Well, shit. I had no idea. So what about Strong? She must have been fooling around with him to marry him so quickly."

Nate clenched his fist, resisting the urge to blacken his

best friend's eyes. "Do you remember Dane telling the story of how his parents met after a wild night of partying?"

Shawn snorted. "Sure. The kid would tell it during our hunting trips to Montana all the time. What about it?"

"Mony wasn't hungover when she ran into Bob Strong that morning in the dormitory bathroom. She'd just survived a brutal rape, and Strong had helped care for her in the weeks that followed. I guess they'd developed feelings for each other during that time. Anyway, when Bob learned she was pregnant, he offered her child legitimacy by marrying her."

Despite his well-inebriated state, Shawn assembled the pieces of the puzzle swiftly. "Are you implying Dane's not Strong's biological son?"

"Correct."

"Then if Dane isn't Bob's kid, whose is he?" Shawn's watery eyes widened. "Did one of those bastards knock her up?"

"He's . . . he's my son."

Shawn stumbled back. After a few moments of silence, he asked, "I suppose Mony told you that too?"

"Yes and no. I mean, she finally admitted it after I'd already learned the truth anyway."

"How?"

"Remember my blood anomaly?"

Shawn grunted. "Remember it? How could I forget? Massey was always nagging us about how we had to 'watch out for his little brother Nate,' because you had some weird blood thing and it would really be bad if you got hurt or something."

Nate remembered it too. As a kid, it had been embarrassing to be treated differently than the rest of the fellows. It must have been the same for Dane when he was growing up. "Right. Well, I had lost a lot of blood after being shot and needed a transfusion before they could take me to surgery. The problem was the hospital couldn't find a donor match, not even my dad or Massey, because of my blood anomaly. I was in dire straits. Lucky for me, Dane happened to be along with Massey when they found me in the desert. He saved my life—my son."

Reaching for the flask Nate still held in his hand, Shawn tossed back the last swallow and wiped the dribble from his beard. "Well, fuck me." He stepped closer and pulled Nate in for one of his grizzly bear hugs. "Christ, I'm sorry. I didn't really buy that bullshit about Mony sleeping with Massey. But running off with Strong—" He pulled back abruptly. "Wait. If Dane was—is—your son, why didn't she tell you? I mean, aren't you pissed? I know you were still in high school and all, but—"

"I was seventeen when Mony and I made love. In a week she'd gone back to college—a week after that, she'd been raped. How could she have known for sure who fathered her child at the time? She probably hadn't even missed a period yet."

"Couldn't she have done a paternity test or something?"

"You watch too much Springer. I was a minor, remember?"

"Yeah, yeah, right. But so what? No one would have cared. Maybe Kip would have been pissed for a while, but he'd have gotten over it. Did Massey know any of this?"

"Again, yes and no. Massey found Mony shortly after

her assault. He knew something was wrong, but Mony wouldn't say what. He wanted to take her to the ER, but she wouldn't consent. He did the best he could to take care of her. She snuck out of his apartment the next morning and stopped attending classes after that."

"Ah . . . well, that explains the rumor."

"Right. She never returned to her dorm, according to her roommate—Cindy, of course. Massey was in the middle of hockey season and didn't see her again until she came home to visit with baby and a husband."

"Jesus. Couldn't he have gone to the police or something?"

"And do what? You know how they are. A college co-ed makes a bad choice, gets in a car with an acquaintance, gets raped. Not much to do except maybe some vigilante justice."

Shawn nodded. "And your brother would have gone after the asshole who'd done it, for sure. Probably would have killed them. I know I would have." Tears suddenly began to well in his eyes. "If only I hadn't stopped for gas that morning, and those goddamn donuts she always insisted we have at the bar. Maybe I could have stopped all this. Maybe I could have saved her."

"What the hell are you talking about, man?"

Shawn hung his head. "Shannon always opened the bar, you know—started the coffee and the grill. If I'd have been there earlier, noticed her gone, maybe I could have stopped all this from happening."

"This is not your fault, Shawn. The killer is to blame."

His friend wasn't listening. "I knew it was a bad idea

for her to invite that asshole lawyer to her place. Saw the cocksucker walk up the back stairs that night like his dick was too big for his britches. Should have beaten the shit out of him when it would have made a difference—when I could have stopped things before it was too late."

Nate placed a hand on his friend's shoulder. "If I knew anything about your sister, it was that no amount of reasoning would change her mind after it was made up. Shannon was going to do what Shannon was going to do."

"I should have seen it coming," insisted Shawn. "I could have stopped it."

The two friends settled on the ground near Shannon's footstone. The upturned soil hadn't completely settled from its unearthing; it would almost feel like Shannon was there beside them in quiet contemplation, if it weren't for the quiet. Shannon had been anything but quiet. She loved to talk and loved gossip. Nothing happened in the tri-county area without her making it her business. She'd have made a terrific blackmailer. Maybe that had been her intent—pursuing Mony's past, spinning lies into truths to ruin her reputation. Shannon had always been jealous of Mony.

As if reading this thought, Shawn put a hand on Nate's shoulder. "She really did love you, you know," he said with a big sniffle.

"I know—I cared about your sister too, a great deal."

"But you didn't love her."

Nate had always considered Shannon a good friend, despite her antagonism toward Mony, and he'd valued their relationship. But Shawn was right; aside from the casual sexual benefits, for Nate, the relationship had only been a friendship. "I was always straight with Shannon where I stood regarding Mony, no matter how much she tried to alter or influence those feelings."

Shawn blew out a heavy breath. "I said as much to her myself when she start talking trash about Mony. I guess that's why she took that trip to Cozumel. Must be true what they say, about love being blind and the heart wanting what it wants and all that shit." He looked at Nate pointedly. "You need to remember something too: You're no more responsible for my sister's death than I am."

Nate appreciated the sentiment, but when he opened his mouth, he couldn't bring himself to acknowledge it. "Tell me more about her trip to Cozumel."

Nate left the cemetery with a heavy heart. It felt like he was abandoning his best friend, but no amount of coercing could dissuade Shawn from remaining at his sister's grave. As Nate drove away, Shawn walked back to his truck and retrieved another bottle of whiskey.

Sighing, Nate placed a phone call. The favor he asked didn't surprise the friend at the other end of the line.

"Sure, I'll see to it Shawn gets home safe," Virgil Sanquist assured him. "Don't worry, Nate. This is a good thing. Shawn's been waiting for a sit-down between the three of you for a while now. Maybe he'll get some closure."

But will he? If the roles were reversed and it were his brother planted in the ground, Nate knew he would never have closure until the killer was brought to justice—perhaps not even then. A loved one's death had a terrible way of changing a person's life forever. It was how things had been for him after Buddy's and Shannon's deaths.

Suddenly, anger replaced his sadness. Why hadn't Sheriff Wagner established a clear murder suspect yet? If that prick Finch wasn't the killer, who the fuck was?

Nate met up with the family at his parents' house in Williston. Entering through the mudroom, he was greeted with a hug from Mony and a yippy little ankle-biter named Ava. She was the newest addition to Massey's family; they'd acquired the dachshund from Mony, who'd been gifted the puppy by Finch to win her heart. Nate didn't hold it against the animal; bending down, he scratched behind the ears of the little dog, who barked with joyous delight.

The family crowded around the kitchen table over one of Poppy's amazing pot roast dinners. Despite the wonderful food, however, Nate couldn't help but notice his stepmom lacked her usual vim and vigor. Cooking was one of her greatest pleasures, as well as a major stress release. She hadn't been herself since his shooting. It worried him.

After dessert, they discussed the family business. Despite the tumbling oil prices, Kip swayed them to forge ahead with drilling. Established prior to horizontal drilling, Oil Well Number One was close to forty years old and had been decreasing in production for the past five years. Circumstances being what they were, the timing was right for a temporary shutdown and retrofit of the outdated equipment. Mony reluctantly agreed to use eroded limestone from the gravel pit on her property in Minnesota, significantly reducing the cost of drilling to the next fracture line of shale. The decision in no way satisfied her environmental concerns, but at least drilling in an existing site left the landscape of the perimeter leases unsullied.

With the Ferguson and Altman homestead standing unoccupied, Kip chose to rent out the tillable acreage for planting sunflowers. Because of its proximity to the wildlife refuge, it would provide a welcoming apiary environment for honeybees returning to North Dakota.

With things copacetic in the realm of business, Mony gave Nate a kiss and grabbed a dish towel. "I'm going to help Poppy with dishes."

Nate and Massey retreated to the backyard, sitting around the firepit with a beer and a soda. As they drank, Massey shared what he could from Harland Richards's interview. "I think Richards realizes the safest place for him right now is in custody. He's already admitted to helping dispose of both Shannon's and Cindy's bodies, but claims both were already dead—"

"Do you believe him?" Nate had formed a significant hatred toward Gem's twin brother, and he'd never even met the guy.

"No. His timeline of events is way off. He's hiding something, but at least we have proof he was at Cindy's murder scene."

"And Shannon's."

Massey didn't answer.

"Did he say anything about the lead crystal decanter?"

"Only what we already know—that it was a plant to incriminate Finch."

Nate huffed in frustration. "So in other words, his information is completely worthless."

"Not entirely. He claims to know who killed both women, but he wants to strike a no-contest plea agreement to the lesser charges of attempted kidnapping, aiding and abetting, covering up a crime scene, and human trafficking."

"Is the prosecution on board with that?"

"Prosecution and defense attorneys plan to meet tomorrow morning to discuss it before the arraignment. I'll know more then."

"Is there enough evidence for a conviction?"

Massey heaved out a deep breath. "The evidence shows Richards was at the crime scene, but it doesn't prove he committed murder, which he of course adamantly denies. He was merely a pawn following orders, nothing more."

"Orders that included killing. There's your motive."

"Yes, but that wouldn't stand up in court. If I were prosecution, I'd pursue Richards's strong hatred toward Cindy and Dwight for messing with his prostitution business."

"How about fear for his life? Kill or be killed."

"Yes, that's possible. The mere fact he's afraid to be released from custody supports that hypothesis."

Nate rubbed at his temples. "Man, this is giving me a headache. Can we talk about something else?"

"As a matter of fact, I have some news."

"All ears."

"Detective Gomez has Lil Sis in protective custody."

He sat bolt upright. "Holy shit! When did she find her?

"Early this morning."

"Where?"

"Hiding in Finch's white van, out by the dam. Gabriella's team was pulling it out of the marsh this morning. Apparently, the girl had been sleeping there."

"Why didn't she tell me? And how in the hell did the kid get there in the first place?"

"Gomez didn't tell you because you were attending to other matters. As for how she got there, Finch must have had her all along."

"I bet that asshole abandoned the kid and hightailed it back to Chicago."

Massey shook his head. "I called his sister Lyn. No one's seen or heard from him, not even Wagner. I'm worried someone may have found his hiding spot and nabbed him, or worse."

Nate laughed. "Nab him? Who would want him? Murder, sure. He betrayed Monroe, and he's lost his foot-hold with the white supremacists now that Richards is in custody. If he truly kidnapped the girl, he's going to be in some major-ass trouble with the Three Affiliated Tribes. I think he's on the run. Does Mony know about all this?"

"She does. She agrees with my theory about John—"

"Of course she does."

"She met with Lil Sis this morning while you were

visiting with Shawn. Mony and I have a plan for keeping the girl safe."

"Which is?"

"I doubt you're going to like it."

"Probably not. Those Moonbeam girls attract trouble like no one else I know."

"Except for maybe you and Mony?"

Nate took a long drink of his soda. "As long as we're sharing information, I have something to tell you about Shannon."

"Oh, and what is that?"

"What do you know about Shannon's trip to Cozumel?"

CHAPTER 8

JOHN

John opened his mattery eyes to distorted darkness. At first, he thought the stuff clogging his vision might be blood, but the irritation tickling in his nose and the snot draining like a sieve from his nostrils reminded him of a sinus infection. His impaired sense of smell did nothing to disguise the offensive dust and chemical odors triggering his allergies. The nasal discomfort was nothing compared to the massive migraine headache pounding in his skull. He attempted to wipe the obstruction in front of his face and discovered his hands were bound behind his back. It took a beat for his senses to sharpen before he realized a burlap sack covered his head.

Brushing his fingers across the surface, John padded the area where he lay, picking up a tiny splinter in his finger. He winced. The last thing he remembered was being in the van—a distant memory. Honing in with his other senses, he strained to listen for any sound or movement that would lend a clue to his location. Except for the occasional chirp of a songbird and the sound of wind leaking through a narrow passage, there were none. He couldn't hear the lake or the waterfowl that loitered on the banks near Ramona's farm. At least he was out of the elements in a relatively cool, dry place—for now.

Rolling onto his side, John clumsily brought himself to a sitting position and assessed himself for other injuries. His every bone, joint, and muscle ached. He was stiff as a board, but nothing seemed to be broken or out of place. Stretching his legs out in front of him, he discovered his feet were bound as well. All in all, other than the sinus congestion and the migraine, he was relatively intact. Still, it was grievance enough. For him, without his medicine, a migraine was as incapacitating as any gaping wound, injured organ, or fractured extremity.

He drew his knees to his chest and tried to rub his snotty nose on his kneecap. The gesture didn't improve the situation. Dust mixed with the solidifying mucus secretions, effectively plugging his nostrils. He coughed and tried to force an exhale through his nose by breathing in through his mouth, but the dust and seed particles trapped in the burlap fiber caused him to spit and sputter. Between his spastic coughing fits, he heard someone laughing.

"Who's there?"

Silence hung in the air. The strong breeze outside whistled between cracks in the structure's walls, lending a menacing quality to John's roommate's guttural response. "You should have brought me Altman when you had the chance. Now you're a dead man."

Mitchell.

Judging from the proximity of his voice, John's

adversary was only a few feet away. *Is my roommate captor or fellow prisoner?* John chose his next words carefully. "I got her to North Dakota, didn't I?"

Mitchell snorted, the sound of gurgling fluid in his throat muddling his tone. "You had nothing to do with that. Richards going after the kid sister is what brought her back to Williston." He gave a wet cough. "That stupid motherfucker couldn't even kidnap one bratty kid without getting himself and half his crew killed. Worthless bastard."

"It's what happens when you put your stock in a bunch of harebrained Nazis," John said coolly.

There was a swipe of movement near his feet. John retracted his legs quickly and took painstaking effort to roll his body away from the motion. Butting his back against the wall—as far away as he was going to get—he added, "Guess if you want a job done right, you have to do it yourself, eh, Dwight? Is that why you're here, to finish the job?"

Mitchell evaded the question. "Neither one of us would be here if you hadn't fucked up on one simple task."

"Which was?"

"You stupid ass, I told you, give me Altman."

John recalled the note left in his van by the Sissy imposter. "I told you she's here, yet you don't seem to be in any position to do anything about that. What do you want with her anyway?"

"None of your goddamn business."

"Did you piss off someone higher up on the food chain? Monroe, perhaps?"

John heard shoes scuffling on wood, and then a massive shadow loomed over him. He assumed a fetal position and braced for impact, but then, as a sudden thud reverberated off the wooden floor, the shadow disappeared. Mitchell groaned, "I told you, I wasn't the one who fucked up."

John was tired of the bravado. "Cut the crap, Mitchell. You'd have kicked the shit out of me by now if your own ass weren't in a wringer. If things are as dire as you imply, we'll need to work together if we're going to get out of here alive."

Mitchell was quiet a long time—longer than John would have liked. He had no idea what sort of shape Mitchell was in, or if he'd been trussed up too. If Mitchell were in a similar predicament he'd be of little help, except for maybe information.

Finally, his adversary said, "What do you have in mind?"

"First off, I need to know who our captor is."

The sound of Mitchell's maniacal laughter was disturbing. "For being a lawyer, you're dumber than a box of rocks."

The mocking laughter came to an abrupt halt at the sound of rattling keys and a clattering padlock. Remaining in his protective position, John fell silent.

The rusty door's hinges creaked ominously as it swung open, letting a gentle breeze sweep through the dust-filled space. A beam of bright light illuminated two figures in the doorway, one massive in size, the other petite by comparison. The floorboards groaned under the weight of the larger person, obliterating the lighter footfall of the other. A deep, husky voice said, "Well, what is my favorite cocksucker doing lying on the floor with his ass up in the air? I may have to help myself to a piece of that. What do you think, cousin?"

John lay still as death, imagining the scene. The natural light filtering through the burlap sack offered enough illumination for him to make out Mitchell's silhouette lying in the supplicant position on the floor. The massive figure stepped between John and Mitchell and kicked him in the rib cage. The submissive response confirmed Mitchell's defenselessness. He made a weak, pitiful plea for help. Even if John had wanted to, things being what they were, there wasn't a damn thing he could have done to abet the brutality.

A young female voice said, "Sure, why not. It ain't any worse than what he done to me and the other girls. But wait until I'm done with this other wasicu before you do it. I want to look at his face while you're fucking him in the ass." John's gut roiled. Mitchell was in deeper shit than he thought.

He sensed the petite female come near and squat directly in front of him. "You made me miss my rendezvous with my sister, Mister Lawyer. Now you're going to tell me where you hid her."

"And who might your sister be?"

The large figure broke off his assault on Mitchell and was on top of John in a millisecond, pummeling his ribs like a punching bag. John tightened his fetal position. It was a wasted effort.

"Ayustan yo," the female shouted. "I need to talk to him."

The beating stopped, and the weight lifted off his chest. The stealthy young figure moved closer, crouching down on her haunches. John maintained his protective position as best he could, anticipating another assault. She hissed softly next to his ear, "He'll leave you alone if you tell me where she is."

If only he knew. Given his current predicament, the knowledge of the younger Moonbeam girl's whereabouts would be useful information. The obvious conclusion was that the young female in front of him was Sissy Moonbeam, alive and well. Obvious, John thought, except for the fact he'd been tricked by a decoy once before. The intensity of the interrogation led him to assume that neither this one nor her massive helper had a clue, buying him some latitude in fabricating a convincing truth. "How do I know you won't have your thug over there kill the kid like he did the older sister?"

The giant straddled over him. John stiffened, bracing for the provoked assault. He cried out as the steel-toed boot jabbed into his right kidney.

"I can make you answer, wasicu."

"Cousin," the girl yelled, "I told you, this one is the white woman's lover. I need him alive."

In a fog of pain, John searched his clouded memory, trying to recall which white woman Sissy might be referencing. Shannon McDonald and Ramona Strong were the only two who came to mind. He considered where Sissy may have seen him with either, then remembered the denim jacket discovered in the garden the day Shannon McDonald was pulled from the lake. *Did Sissy have something to do with Shannon's death?*

"Killer," he rasped. "I'll never tell you where the little girl is."

The open-handed slap across the side of his head triggered a high, shrill ringing in his ear. "Why would I kill my own sister?" his tormenter snapped.

"How do I know you're Sissy Moonbeam?"

The hood was yanked from his head, and John gasped at the uncontaminated air. Bright sunlight poured in through the open door; blinking several times to adjust his vision, he made a quick assessment of his surroundings. The room he occupied was no bigger than an eight-by-ten shed. In the opposite corner, Mitchell was not only bound, but chained by his ankles to a stake driven into the floorboard, his head covered with a stained burlap sack.

"As you can see, you have no place to run. I am Sissy Moonbeam. Now, tell me what I want to know, and I promise to let you go."

It was a lie. If there had been any plan to let him go, his hood would have never been removed. "I've never met Sissy Moonbeam. For all I know, you're just another indentured subjugate doing what she's told."

The closed fist across his cheekbone lacerated his skin, sending blood trickling down into his mouth. Sissy's male sidekick, towering over six feet above him, was poised to inflict further damage.

"I've been tricked before," John shouted, and jerked his chin toward Mitchell. "By that asshole. He tried to pass off one of Richards's runaway girls as Sissy Moonbeam. She passed a note to me demanding I bring him Ramona—Mony Altman."

Mitchell was incensed. "What the fuck are you doing?"

Saving my ass. He understood now why Mitchell was a prisoner. Their captors must have assumed he'd know the whereabouts of the younger sister. Unfortunately, Mitchell didn't have that information either, rendering him as useless as tits on a boar. John looked at the stained burlap sack. Judging from Mitchell's appearance, he was getting payback for his atrocities. The probability of Dwight leaving this place without being debased was marginal at best. Sissy's thug had even used Mitchell's own words against him: "My favorite cocksucker."

Revenge was all he was good for. John hoped to fare better. To accomplish that, he needed to sever any association between the two of them quickly.

"Just like a white man, thinking all Indians look alike," the big man scoffed.

"What does the cocksucker want with the white woman?" Sissy demanded.

"Wealth, land, revenge. She's humiliated him countless times in front of his peers and community. He hates her."

Mitchell screamed, "Shut up."

John ignored him and spoke to Sissy. "Don't you know this white woman, Ramona Altman, is trying to protect your little sister? She gave up her guard dog to watch over your family. She is trying to help all the young girls being used as sex slaves. She abhors male cruelty."

Mitchell's continued attempt at protest was silenced by

a debilitating blow to the head, and he slumped to the side. Sissy scrutinized John. "I trust no white person, least of all a two-faced one like you."

"Are you denying your own eyes? She tried to help you when she found you hiding out on her farm."

Sissy's resolve wavered a little. "I've heard lies like that before. How do I know she won't betray me like that other white woman?"

"Other white woman? You mean Shannon McDonald?"

A puzzled expression spread across the big man's face. "The redhead," Sissy told him. To John, she said, "No, the social worker."

Cindy Van Dyke. "Did you kill her too?"

"The redhead should have picked better friends," the big Indian grunted.

It wasn't a confession, but it could be misconstrued as one. *Jesus.* Not only was Sissy linked to, possibly involved in, Shannon's murder—she may have also been responsible for Cindy Van Dyke's disappearance. "Shannon McDonald was a good friend of Ramona's," John told her.

"It didn't look that way to me," the big Indian said.

"We didn't kill the redhead," Sissy snapped. "She was already dead when Mitchell had Richards and his Nazis dump her in the lake. We were there for the social worker."

"To do what?"

Sissy and the big Indian exchanged a subtle look. John knew right then and there, the next words from the young girl's lips would be another lie.

"We didn't do anything to her."

"Liar."

All eyes turned to Mitchell. He had regained consciousness and managed to pull himself to a sitting position, leaning against the side wall, his chest rising and falling erratically. "You're a liar," he repeated.

John hollered at Mitchell to shut up. To Sissy he said, "You'll need Mitchell—he's the only witness that can back your claim you had nothing to do with McDonald's murder. You killed all the other witnesses in that little ambush on the Rez."

Sissy reared her head back. "What do you know about that?"

"I was there."

"You lie," the big Indian shouted.

"Really? Then why am I here?" When neither responded, John forged ahead. "You claim I know where your sister is. How would I know that if I hadn't been there? It's why you followed me to the Altman farm and nabbed me. You knew I had her."

Sissy stood and nodded toward the open door. Wordless, she preceded the big man out. John heard the door lock behind them, plunging the small shed into darkness.

He waited for the footfalls leaving the shed to disperse before whispering to Mitchell, "You planned to kill Ramona, and you killed Shannon McDonald by accident."

Mitchell was silent a long while, leaving John to wonder if he'd lost consciousness again. Perhaps he was unwilling to admit to his guilt. He finally said, "She should have never gone looking for Cindy after you left her apartment. The Indian was right—McDonald was collateral damage."

"And your wife?"

John heard Mitchell breathe a ragged sigh. "She was already half dead when I got there."

"What do you mean?"

"You dumb fuck, you still don't get it. If Altman would have sold to Monroe and kept her nose out of that little cocksucker's problem, this situation could have all been avoided."

"If you know Ramona Altman at all, you know she would never go against the Fergusons, or allow that child to continue being your victim."

"Victim," Mitchell snorted. "Is that what you believe? And since when has a Ferguson done anything to help Mony?"

"I don't understand."

"God, you're stupid. She married Strong, didn't she? Why do you think she did that?"

John had no idea what Ramona's past relationship with her deceased husband had to do with the present. "If you're planning to enlighten me, best get on with it."

"Her son isn't a Strong."

"Jesus, what's that got to do with anything?"

"Everything. Her son belongs to one of the fellows who took her for a little car ride after a beer party and had their own little party."

"How do you know this?"

"Because I was there."

"Bullshit."

"Ask her. She didn't want Ferguson to know what kind of a slut she really was."

"Christ, Mitchell, now I know you're lying—"

Then it dawned on him why Shannon was so hell-bent on finding out the truth about Ramona's son. Mitchell had it all wrong. A kid would seal the rock star's relationship with his one true love. But in addition to the child's uncertain paternity after her rape, she'd kept silent out of fear of retaliation toward the men who'd violated her. "The lot of you would be dead by now if Ferguson had found out," he told his fellow prisoner. "That's why she never told Ferguson. She didn't want her baby daddy going to jail. She saved your sorry ass, Dwight. Too bad you've wasted the munificent gesture, you piece of shit. You're the one who could have avoided the mess you're in."

"She's a whore."

"Yeah, a whore you're in love with."

The sound of the key rattling in the lock silenced Mitchell's rebuttal. This time Sissy led the way. She stood next to Mitchell and pulled off his hood.

His face was barely recognizable. The right side of his skull was enlarged from massive swelling, his right ear a lumpy mess of broken cartilage. It was nothing compared to the grotesque disfiguration of his shattered eye socket and broken nose. There was bruising and dried blood everywhere. If he didn't have a massive concussion, it would be a miracle.

"Here's what's going to happen," Sissy said, looking him square in the eye. "I'll keep you alive like the lawyer suggested, but you're not going to like it very much. I have a friend outside waiting, and he doesn't care what kind of hole he fucks." She bumped Dwight's shoulder.

"It will be like old times, you and me. Only this time my friend will be you, and I will play Hitch." She held up a cell phone. "I even brought a camera. Don't worry, I'll leave your hood off. I know how you love to watch."

She turned her attention to John. "As for you, Mister Lawyer, you're going to have a talk with Miss Mony and tell her to bring my sister to me. If she does that, maybe I'll let you live. If she doesn't . . ." Sissy pointed to Mitchell, whose face was pinned down on the floor under the boot of his dominant. "Take a good look at your fate."

Sissy aimed the camera lens in Mitchell's face. "Now, let's see how your Nazi friends enjoy watching one of their own taking it up the ass, especially Richards. If he's still alive, he'll be next."

CHAPTER 9

MONY

Amid considerable protest, Mony and Nate chose to spend the night out at the Ferguson farm. Lord knew there wouldn't be any privacy staying at Nate's parents' house, and they needed time alone. The truck cab was pleasantly crowded for the ride. Mony sat cuddled under her husband's arm, the two dogs on the other side of her. Shep assumed his usual position perched on the seat, watching intently out the window, while Rainstorm lay curled on the floor; both were calm so long as they were near her.

Nate drew the line, however, when it came to the bedroom. As he closed the door with his foot, Rainstorm immediately began to whimper just on the other side, pawing at the door.

Mony sat on the bed, pulling off her boots. "Aw, do you have to do that?"

Nate sauntered toward her with one of his roguish smiles and tackled her to the mattress. Pinning her arms above her head, he planted a long, lush, open-mouthed kiss on her lips. "Yes, I do. I don't need an audience while making love to my wife." Mony returned the kiss, but she could feel the lackluster quality of her own passion.

Releasing her arms, Nate brushed his fingers across her cheek. "Don't worry, the dogs will be fine. I left blankets and pillows for them to lie on in the hall. They'll settle down in a few minutes." As the two lay on the bed, his assertion came to pass. The whining and clawing were eventually replaced by the sound of paws scratching fabric. Point made, Nate resumed his seduction.

Mony couldn't help but notice a slight disquiet in his approach, affecting his usual finesse. She wondered if it had anything to do with his obsession with making up for lost time, or maybe he was avoiding an argument. What she did know was that neither one of them had the stamina for the sort of lovemaking he seemed to be contemplating in his pretty little head. They both were running on fumes. The past forty-eight hours had taken a toll on her homeostasis as well as her emotional stability.

Nate cupped her breast, fingering her nipple through the soft fabric of her tissue tee. "Can we make love first, then talk? I really need to be inside you right now."

Tilting her head back, she offered her mouth. Unable to resist, her lover took it greedily. Nate fell into a comfortable pattern, and she was his emotional fix. Sex was like a sedative for him, his remedy to insomnia, anxiety, depression. Despite feeling somewhat objectified, Mony felt her skin temperature respond to the stimuli. There was something aggressive yet gentle in the way he pressed his lips against hers.

"I love kissing you," he whispered between breaths. "When we're together, I feel content, restored, wanted. I wish I could be the same for you right now."

Mony frowned. *Am I that easy to read?* "I'm with you," she said, hoping to sound convincing. She slid her hand around the back of his neck, pulling his head toward her. Heat rushed through her veins, her heart pumping faster. Perhaps she could use sex too, to quiet her restlessness. *Would a brief moment of pleasure betray the commitment I made to Lil Sis and Sissy?*

Pulling his T-shirt loose from his waistband, Nate broke the kiss long enough for her to take it off over his head and begin working on his jeans. A bead of precum had already moistened his boxers. She stroked him through his shorts. *This is going to be quick.*

Nate's hands fell to his side, clenching the comforter. "God, I love it when you touch me."

To Mony's surprise, they climaxed together—a rarity, especially considering how preoccupied her mind had been. Typically, she needed to be a little more focused to feel an orgasm. Laying her cheek against Nate's naked chest, she listened as his heartbeat's rhythm slowed. Drawing little circles through his chest hair with her fingers, Mony said, "I love you madly, Nate Ferguson."

He breathed a contented sigh. "Mony Ferguson, I've loved you since the day we met." He pulled up the sheet covering their naked bodies, and his eyes drifted shut.

Oh, no you don't. Mony lifted herself on an elbow. The

two had unfinished business, and no one was getting any sleep until they'd talked it out. "Are you okay with us taking Lil Sis back to Vegas tomorrow?"

Nate kept his eyes closed. "It seems Massey's already made the arrangements. If that's what you want, we'll make it work."

She kissed his cheek. "Thank you."

Nate opened an eye. "For what?"

"For understanding."

He turned on his side to face her. "Taking Lil Sis to a safe place is a no-brainer. It's clear no one can keep her safe here, including her own people. As long as no one knows where she is outside of you, me, Massey, and Gabby, she should be relatively safe until this shitstorm blows over. It was taking Finch with us that I wasn't on board with. Now that he's gone, it's a nonissue."

"I don't understand why he would just leave without an explanation."

"I don't understand why everyone is so worried," Nate grumbled. "He's a grown man, he can make his own decisions. Let him crawl back into that hole, Chicago or wherever he came from. He had no business being out here in Williston in the first place."

Before Mony could formulate a rebuttal, her cell phone vibrated on the nightstand.

Nate plopped his head back on the pillow. "Ugh, let it go."

Accustomed to late-night calls, Mony reached for her phone. "It might be word on Lil Sis." She checked the number and frowned. *Unknown*. She answered with her perfunctory "Hello, Doctor Strong."

As the person on the other end of the line began to talk, Mony felt the color drain from her face. Nate sat up and watched her intently, mouthing, "*What is it?*"

Mony shushed him with a silent glare and placed the call on speaker. The caller said, "Do as I say, and no one will get hurt."

"I want proof of life," she demanded, but the call had already been disconnected.

Visibly shaking, Mony resisted the urge to scream. Nate put his arm around her, his expression both pained and fearful as she struggled to regain her composure. He waited quietly for an explanation.

"He says he has John, and there are *terms*."

There was a mix of annoyance and relief on her lover's face. Nate pulled Mony into an embrace. "Tell me everything word for word. Then, we call Massey."

Mony made her way to the kitchen and started a pot of coffee while Nate hopped into the shower. They spoke very little after the call, each unwilling to instigate an argument that was certain to spiral out of control. They were already entrenched in their positions, and it ate at her like acid. Past experience had taught her a valuable lesson on the destructive effect of pent-up emotions. Nothing killed a relationship faster—but so could rushing a conversation if neither party was ready. It was a hell of a way to start their marriage, especially when factoring in their history. The two of them carried enough baggage to sink their fragile union before they could leave on a proper honeymoon.

Movement caught her eye, and she looked out the kitchen window just as Kip's truck pulled into the driveway. Poppy dropped out of the passenger seat, laden with an oversized picnic basket. Massey and Kip retrieved a large cooler from the back. It appeared her mother-in-law had pulled an all-nighter—no surprise. What was astonishing—and a relief—was that Sheriff Wagner wasn't with them. Ever since Massey and Mony had found Sissy hiding out in the shabin, she'd had an uneasy feeling about the man and the way he was handling the entire situation. His excuses about not being able to meddle in Indian affairs were a complete and utter cop-out, and she couldn't shake the sense he was hiding something.

Despite everyone's overwhelming fatigue and palpable tension, they ate breakfast like it was their last meal. It wasn't until Poppy started gathering the dishes that Nate decided to kick off the discussion. "I have to say, a lot of things don't make sense about that call last night, Mony."

"What parts?"

"For one, how did the kidnapper get your personal phone number? Second, why would the abductor expect you to hand over money for John Finch?"

"I was thinking some of that too, Nate," Massey said. "Plus, why would they deny proof of life? No one knows of Mony's relationship with John outside this circle, and no one knows John's working with the investigation except for Wagner. We left the public believing he's still an adversary working for Monroe. It doesn't add up."

"There is no relationship between Mony and the lawyer," Nate interjected, his voice rising, "and since when did he become an ally? He's still working for that blood-sucking law firm in Chicago, and for all we know he still works for Monroe. As for the phone number, anyone can call Mony's clinic for her cell phone number. I agree with you on one thing, Massey. It's stupid to think any one of us would allow Mony to just fork over the money, with or without proof of life."

Mony felt her skin bristle at the first shot of the morning. Nate was completely ignoring the fact that John had rescued most of those young girls trapped in the prostitution ring at Richards's trailer, and his working with the sheriff basically translated to his working for them. With a conscious effort, she held her tongue. "My office doesn't give out my personal phone number, only my emergency—"

Massey cut across her. "Nate, you're missing the point. I'm asking *why*—why would anyone think Mony cares what happened to Finch or that she would be willing to invest that sort of money in his well-being, unless they had inside information as to their relationship?"

"There is no relationship!" Nate shouted.

Massey leveled his eyes at Mony, then looked at his brother. "Like it or not, there *was* at one time."

Nate clenched his jaw, his hands turning to fists at his side. Steeling herself for the blowback of past indiscretions, Mony forced herself to don a placid expression.

She was spared the confrontation when a black SUV sedan pulled into the driveway. A petite woman with a lush, thick mane of jet-black hair braided down her back stepped out of the vehicle. Detective Gomez had arrived just in time.

They stowed the conversation long enough for Gabriella to enter the kitchen. She took one look at Nate and told him, "If you're not going to be part of the solution, Nathan, I'm afraid you can't be a part of the conversation."

Nate's face flushed with fury. It was brutal to witness the internal conflict on public display. Part of Mony wanted to rush to his side and apologize for her involvement with Finch. The logical side of her brain prevailed. Detective Gomez put her logic into words.

"You can't change what's happened, Nathan. You can only use the hard-earned truths of the past to make positive change moving forward." She turned to Mony. "Where are we at?"

Mony released the breath she'd been holding. "The caller said he would contact me this morning at six forty-six sharp with further instructions." She pointed to the clock on the stove. "We are clearly past that. Do you think the kidnapper is having second thoughts?"

"Williston is on central time, correct?"

"Yes," Massey confirmed, "but Dickenson is on mountain time. You don't have to travel far to be off by an hour. What are you thinking, Detective?"

"Either the kidnapper is not a local and is unaware of the time difference," Kip put in, "or they're unconcerned about it."

Gomez agreed. "Making the probability that Finch is being held hostage in the vicinity slim to none. He's out of Williams County."

"And Wagner's jurisdiction," added Massey.

Mony took a sip of her cold coffee, irritated by the situation. "It was Wagner's job to protect John."

The detective said without sympathy, "Mr. Finch understood what he was getting into. No one's had contact with John in over three days. I find it odd the kidnapper is first making contact now."

Nate threw up his hands. "There's no mystery. It's what Monroe has wanted all along: lure Mony back to Williston so he can have another shot at her." His gaze met hers. "He didn't succeed in killing me in Arizona, and he's failed to capture the little sister, so he's using the only other pawn at his disposal—the fuckin' lawyer."

Mony rubbed her forehead. No one knew the details of her relationship with John, not even her family—not really. No one had ever seen them together, except for her friend Juanita in Chicago. That meeting had been confrontational. She and John had spent time in public on Navy Pier, but no one had been watching.

Then she recalled waiting for a water taxi out to the sailboat mooring. Three of John's male colleagues had been watching them intently. She'd recognized one of them as Ethan Rice. He'd taken over for John during the probate hearing and lost the case miserably. *Could this all be some ploy for revenge?*

Mony tried to concentrate on her memory of the kidnapper's voice. Addressing the detective, she asked, "Hypothetically, do you think anyone from the Indian community would be working for Monroe?"

The detective gave her a puzzled look. "Unlikely. Word

on the Rez is that if any of Monroe's people approach their people for work, they're to run them out with a shotgun. Why do you ask?"

Thinking better on her feet, Mony stood from the table and began pacing. "I can't say with certainty, but the kidnapper's voice sounded . . . Indian."

Kip's brows shot up. "What makes you think that?"

Mony stopped in front of the sink, thinking back to college and her study of the Lakota language. "The kidnapper's speech pattern was very . . . distinctive. Not like a Southern twang, or a Bostonian accent dropping the 'r' in the word, or even a Norwegian accent emphasizing the 'o' sounds. It had more of a . . . sing-song rhythm."

"Say more about that," Gomez urged.

"I'll give you an example. When he said, 'Bring it'—referring to the money— 'and I will let him live,' it sounded more like, 'Brng t, nd wll lt m lve.' All the words ran together without any vowels. There was a . . . shortening or reduction of words, if you will. It reminded me of the way Grandmother Moonbeam spoke during our conversations."

Poppy asked, "So, you think we're dealing with someone from the Rez? Why?"

"Maybe an arms buildup," Massey cut in. "The shooting on the Rez left a pile of dead Nazis. Maybe they're refortifying weaponry in case of another attack."

Nate scoffed. "That still doesn't explain why they'd contact Mony. And all this jabbering is pointless. She is not getting involved—period!"

This time, she couldn't hold back. Mony opened her

mouth, ready for a full-on argument with her significant other—only for her wrath to be interrupted by her ringing cell phone.

The room fell into silence. She glanced down at the *Unknown* appearing on her cell phone screen. Seven forty-six exactly. The detective nodded the go-ahead. Taking her cue, Mony answered on the fourth ring and immediately placed the call on speaker. "Doctor Strong speaking."

"Do you have the money?" the male voice asked without preamble.

Mony counted in her head—*one Mississippi, two Mississippi*—up to five before responding. "You didn't give me enough time. Don't you know the banks don't open until nine?"

"An excuse," the male voice snapped.

Again, she counted to five. It did nothing to contain the anger filling her voice. "For Christ's sakes, money doesn't grow on trees. I don't have a cool million dollars just lying around in the mattress. I need more time."

A horrendous pause followed. Sweat beaded around her forehead. Had she provoked her antagonist?

His voice finally came back over the receiver. "You have two hours. I'll tell you then where to bring it. No cops, or I'll have to start cutting off body parts."

"I want proof of li—"

The call ended before she could finish her sentence. "Goddamn it!"

The detective spoke into her mic. "Do we have a location?"

Not privy to the response, everyone in the room

watched Gomez listen without expression. Mony's gut roiled with fear. John's location was key in the next phase of the detective's plan. After a couple of minutes, Gomez signed off and acknowledged the waiting room. "It seems our hypothesis about the kidnapper being outside the central time zone is correct. The closest we can pinpoint, the call came from in or around Wolf Point on the Fort Peck Indian Reservation."

"Christ. That's in Montana." Nate ran his hand through his hair. "They have no intention of an exchange. Monroe's using him to lure Mony away from Williston just like he did when he had me shot in Arizona. He plans to isolate her, hope that we'll follow, and then either kill us all or wreak some form of havoc on the business or land while we're all away." He looked at Mony with desperate, pleading eyes. "I'm begging you, do not tell me you are even remotely considering falling for a trap this obvious."

Mony walked to Nate and wrapped her arms around his waist, holding him tight. His returning squeeze took her breath away. He was clinging for dear life—hers.

She tightened her grip and looked up at his beseeching face. This was no time to lie. "You and I need to take a walk."

Nate closed his eyes, his face wrought with agony. A bead of moisture escaped from the corner of his eye, a telling sign that he understood he wasn't going to like what she was about to say. Exhaling long and slowly, he brought his lips to the crown of her forehead and kissed her gently. In a placid voice he said, "There's nothing to discuss. You've already made up your mind."

And with that, he released his hold and walked toward the outdoor screen like a man on his way to his execution.

Mony started after him. "Nate—please—wait."

The detective took a firm hold of her arm as she passed. "Let him be. You both need to cool off before you talk. You are not opposites, but of equal mind, entrenched so deep in your own viewpoints that a discussion would be pointless. Negotiation requires listening and concession. Neither of you is in the right headspace for that. He has every right to be afraid for you. We're all afraid. You need to honor that."

Mony's self-righteousness deflated in a breath. Detective Gomez was wise beyond her years. But what she didn't understand was that for most of her life, Mony's role had been to lure quarry by playing the lame duck. Reprogramming that mindset wasn't going to change with one brisk scolding.

Finally, she gave a nod, and the detective released her arm. "Good. Now let's focus on the kidnapper's next call. We need to be ready. This time we've got to hear from John. It needs to be clear—nothing moves forward without that. If they are indeed halfway across Montana, we'll need to be prepared to mobilize."

"Wolf Point is right on US Highway 2," Massey said. "Is there any way for the phone you traced to have been dumped in an over-road truck, with someone else either making the call or activating the phone remotely?"

"I know what I heard," Mony insisted. "The voice was the same on both calls."

"There's technology making that possible, but it's

highly sophisticated and outrageously expensive. Let's focus on simplicity," Gomez suggested. "We've been scouring the surrounding fifty-mile radius since John went missing and have come up empty. Going back to Indian involvement, it is fact that the Tribal Nations have been unsettled since the Moonbeam girl's disappearance. I've done a background check on the girl's father. He was a decorated war hero, garnering immense respect from his people in and outside of the Three Affiliated Tribes. It may be the kidnapper is finding immunity through the father's connections."

"That would make sense; military folk tend to band together, especially in times of trouble," said Kip.

Mony saw an idea light behind Massey's eyes. "Could this kidnapper be working on the Moonbeam family's behalf?"

Detective Gomez was curious. "Explain what you mean, Matthew."

"Mony, you gave your personal phone number to Sissy after Wagner had her taken into custody, correct?"

"I did. I gave it to both Sissy and Lil Sis."

"Since John interfered with Lil Sis's abduction on the Rez . . . could the kidnapper have followed John to the apiary hoping for a second chance? When the girl wasn't there, they took him instead."

From beyond the screen door, Nate called, "It still doesn't answer why the kidnapper would think Mony would give money for his ransom."

Grateful for his return, Mony went to him. "Please come inside. You need to be part of this."

Nate entered and immediately wrapped her in his arms. "Sorry I lost my shit. Just needed some fresh air to clear my head and think." As Mony took his hand and led him to join the others, he asked, "What are you thinking, Massey?"

"Process of elimination. If Finch no longer has Lil Sis, Mitchell doesn't have her, and Monroe and the white supremacists don't have her, who would be the next in line concerned about the child's welfare?"

All eye's fell on Mony.

"I suppose us," Nate concluded. "But why is the kidnapper asking for money and not the child?"

"Not the kidnapper—her older sister."

"You think it's Sissy behind all this? Why the cloak-and-dagger routine?"

"Simple. Sissy wants to stay hidden, and this is only phase one. The kidnapper knows Mony well enough to understand she would easily part with money, but not the child—ever."

"Why kidnap Finch? Why not one of us?"

"Access," the detective said. "Assuming Mr. Finch did indeed have the child, they were there for her. When they couldn't find her, they took him instead."

"So, not only are Monroe and his flunkies making trouble for us, but we have the entire Three Affiliated Tribes against us as well?"

"Not the whole thing, just a faction."

Nate scratched his chin. "I know I'm going to be gutted for saying this, but wouldn't it be simpler to give the younger sister to her older sibling?"

"It would," said Gomez, "if we knew for certain the older sister was calling the shots. The male voice making the demands tells me otherwise."

Mony didn't care for the direction of the conversation—plus, they were wasting valuable time. "You all seem to be forgetting, Sissy's still a minor, not to mention her poor track record making good life choices. None of this changes the fact that Lil Sis's life is still in danger. She needs our protection. At least until we know who's pulling the strings on John's kidnapping."

"Agreed," said Gomez.

Mony sighed inwardly. At least she had one person on her side. "So what's our plan moving forward?"

CHAPTER 10

NATE

As the third ransom call came in, Nate felt nowhere near invested in the detective's plan. He kept to himself, watching the scene unfold as Gabriella readied her recording device and speaker. Mony engaged the caller.

"You got the money?"

"I want to hear from John before I answer," his wife demanded.

"I'll kill him if you don't give me what I want."

Mony's voice oozed with venom. "You're a liar. You don't have him—either that, or he's already dead. Why would I pay money for a corpse?"

The kidnapper laughed. "You gotta smart mouth. Good thing you weren't in the military. Hard to know how many soldiers you'd have left behind. Hold on, you can talk to the windbag."

Nate had always been indifferent to Finch's well-being, thinking his and Mony's lives would be better off without the man—until he saw her expression. In that moment, he'd have given every dime he owned to remove the look of trepidation from her face.

It took a long while before Finch's voice came on the line. "Hello? Ramona?"

Jesus. The guy sounded like shit. Nate could hear the audible wheeze from across the room. The congested gurgling in Finch's throat made him sound like he was talking with a mouth full of marbles. Mony's voice cracked under the duress. "It's me, John. I'm coming for you. Just stay alive, please stay alive. I'm coming."

"Ramona, don't believe this bullshit—Sissy's—" John's voice broke away, replaced by the kidnappers.

"You can hear he's still alive. Now, what about my money?"

Mony completely lost her equanimity. "He's worth nothing to me half dead. I pay for a whole person, alive and well. That's the deal. You don't poison him, torture him, or cut off body parts. Now, when and where for this exchange?"

"Not so fast." There was a pause over the phone, followed by the sound of scuffling and a sudden scream of pain.

"You son of a bitch!" Mony shrieked. "I swear to God, I will hunt you down like a rabid animal and kill you."

The kidnapper's voice was filled with a humorous inflection. "Do you think you are the first person to threaten me? You needed reminding—I'm calling the shots."

Gomez gave Mony a reprimanding stare. Nate's wife

humbled her tone. "I have the money. Where and when for the exchange?"

"Much better."

Nate helped Mony load and secure the dog kennels in the main cabin of the company's private jet, grateful for the distraction. He needed all the busywork he could conjure if he was to delay the inevitable.

"They won't be any trouble if you leave them in the kennel," Mony said with an exhausted breath. "The crate is like a den, a place of safety. Shep is used to it. I think Rainstorm will follow his lead." *Not likely*, Nate thought. Sure enough, as soon as he and Mony left the cabin, the Rez dog began to whimper. Nate shared the sentiment. He could have gone for a large crate just then, one big enough to hold him and Mony—a place where they could be relatively safe and weather this shitstorm together.

The two stood on the tarmac, waiting for Gem's taxi to arrive. A surge of anxiety wedged itself into Nate's throat, and his heart raced as if it were a horse being whipped. Mony wrapped her arms around his waist, offering reassurance, but it didn't take. He hated everything about this plan—hated that his wife had made a conscious choice to rescue Finch, hated that he had to return to Las Vegas without her, hated the responsibilities being thrust upon him. The entire drive to the airport, he'd argued for a better way of retrieving Finch, to no avail.

Mony squeezed him as if she'd read his mind. "You'll be in the loop the entire time. The jet will remain on standby at VGT for you to get back to me quickly after your re-cording session. But by then, it will be all over. Please try not to worry. Massey and Gabriella's team will be with me every step of the way. Trust them. They'll keep me safe."

Nate choked on his words. "I—I'm supposed to keep you safe."

Breathing a sigh, Mony told him, "You are, Natty. Just not in the way that you want. What you're protecting is my sanity, the things I love, my peace of mind. It will help keep me focused on the task at hand. This is an in-and-out operation."

Her use of his pet name had a soothing effect. He wasn't sure if she'd meant to be patronizing or comfort-ing, but his racing heart slowed a beat and the lump in his throat loosened.

"I need to know you're my backup if things go south. Assuming Monroe is behind all this, there's no telling what he'll do. We cannot make it easy for him to take us both out with one shot."

"Christ, Mony, don't say that."

She squeezed him tighter. "Sorry. Bad choice of words. But you know what I mean. You and me in the same place is exactly what our adversary wants."

"No, Mony, they want us divided."

"Then let them believe they've succeeded. We know different. We can use their hubris to our advantage."

It wasn't his enemy's hubris he worried about. His inse-curities were getting the better of him, the words spilling out of his mouth before he could stop it. "Are we united?"

"Natty." Mony pivoted to face him. "I understand trust

isn't easy for you, but we've weathered far worse separations than this. No one, not one thing can put a wedge between us, except ourselves. Since the moment we met, everything I've done has been out of my love for you, Nathan Ferguson—that, and my own survival. It will be that way until my last breath. But you have to decide for yourself whether you believe me or not, my love. Our relationship has no room for doubt. It all boils down to a matter of trust."

A quarter past the hour, Gem arrived in a black SUV chauffeured by Detective Gomez. Her expression sullen, she dispensed with any greeting and boarded the jet without a word. The detective stood next to Nate on the tarmac. "I know that look, Nathan Ferguson. You have to believe we'll keep Mony safe for this to work. I'm giving you my word on that. Is the cargo secured?"

It was a struggle to minimize the frustration in his voice. "I know you mean it. I just want this to be over and Finch and Monroe out of our lives forever."

Mony maintained her hold. "We all do, baby. And yes, Detective, the precious cargo is secure."

A mile above the ground, the dogs settled in their kennels. Reclining her seat, Gem Richards donned a black eye mask and earplugs and pulled a blanket over her head. Alone with his thoughts, Nate started humming to himself as lyrics began forming in his head. He took out his portable roll-up piano and began playing around with his newly created melody.

Mony's words kept ringing between his ears like clanging bells. God, that woman knew exactly the right buttons to push, quoting lyrics from one of his favorite musicians. He had to keep reminding himself that though she held on to her secrets, whenever confronted, she'd always told him the truth. Now, more than ever, he needed to believe that. If his lifelong journey had taught him one thing, it was that believing in others required trusting himself. That was a major stumbling block in his life. For as long as he could remember, Nate had always relied on others to assign him value, setting the standard of whether he was worthy of love—or not. It was a habit of self-deprivation he had to stop.

Focusing once more on his music, Nate began singing softly, building the verse and chorus, working his way into a crescendo when his voice cracked at the pinnacle of his arc. He laughed out loud, embarrassed by the novice mistake. Clearing his throat, he restructured his lead-in using a lower chord.

"Leave it."

Nate looked up from his sheet music to see Gem sitting upright, watching him as he worked. Her disheveled hair and sleepy eyes made her look vulnerable and sweet. She repeated her comment.

Annoyed yet intrigued, he asked, "Why?"

Gem leaned forward in her chair. "Your natural break adds to the anguish of the lyrics, highlighting the internal conflict. Very powerful, and . . . relatable. The question you pose is the same one I asked myself before flying to that godforsaken shithole to help my asshat brother. That son of a bitch has let me down more times than I can count—certainly more times than your girlfriend, I suspect—and yet we still love them."

Nate had been preparing a snarky comeback, but he let it go. There was sincerity in Gem's words, a logic he wanted to explore. Grateful for someone to talk with, he set aside his keyboard. "It kills me that I'm never there to protect her when she needs it most. It's always someone else who gets to be the hero."

Gem snorted without derision. "Protecting her is your need, not hers. Anyway, I don't think your woman is looking for a hero. She seems like a person who can take care of herself. What she needs is someone she can rely on to take care of the other things that are important to her, someone she can trust."

Mony had said as much before he left. Nate was well aware of the tight inner circle of friends she kept—when she did let someone new into that circle, the process was like a captain picking a team during tryouts. Massey was always her forward, aggressive in both offense and defense situations. Nate, on the other hand, was a winger, someone there for the assist, her backup, her last line of defense protecting what she treasured. Even Finch had a role on her team, though Nate couldn't for the life of him imagine what that might be. Whatever it was, it had to be important enough for Mony to put herself in danger.

A thought suddenly occurred to him: perhaps the rescue had nothing to do with her feelings for Finch at all. All her life Mony had assumed the role of *bait*, a position she'd taken seriously. Was she putting herself out there because she was protecting someone else, relying on the rest of her team to follow through with their roles? It was clear she trusted wholeheartedly they would all come through when she needed them. Finch was merely a means to an end.

Nate put his personal angst aside. "Are you going to help your brother?" he asked.

Gem was surprised by the change in subject. Lacking her usual guarded response, she said, "I think Harland is beyond my help. It looks bad for him—really bad. If it weren't for his injuries, he'd be rotting in a jail cell right now. The sheriff has him dead on human trafficking, and that's the least of it. His DNA is all over the murder scene of some social worker, providing ample evidence to charge him with murder, according to your brother. He's admitted to being involved in disposing your friend's body, then foolishly thought the confession would exonerate him from that mess. When that didn't pan out, he simply denied killing anyone, as if the word of a convicted felon matters." Gem shook her head. "The evidence against him is too damning. Anyway, why do you care?"

"Do you believe him?"

"I—I don't know. I want to believe him. Harland's not a violent man by nature. He's more a gluttony and self-gratification sort of guy. Sure, he roughs up his whores—"

"Underage victims."

"—but he's not a killer." Gem threw her blanket on the floor. "It pisses me off that he keeps defending those cocksucking Nazis like they're coming to his rescue. He's being a chump. He should be looking to me for help. I'm the one with the bail money, but all he does is lie."

"He wouldn't give any clues on who the murderer or murderers might be?"

"Oh, he gave me plenty of information, but no one's going to believe it."

"Try me."

Gem eyed him skeptically, deliberating. Finally she said, "He says that Mitchell guy was working with the sheriff."

Nate suppressed the surprise in his expression. "Are you sure he's not trying to throw the sheriff under the bus?"

"It's possible. I mean, who'd believe a bullshit story about some upstanding businessman in cahoots with the local law, murdering a couple of women? Where's the motive?"

Clearly Gem didn't know Dwight's history. Considering the number of people Mitchell had swindled over the years, Nate suspected there were plenty of people willing to reap a little payback. "There's nothing noble about Mitchell, and if anyone had the means of destroying him, it would be his deceased wife. She knew all his dirty secrets. I just can't see him pulling the trigger, though. He's not only a fraud, he's a coward. What I'm curious about is, why drag the sheriff into this? What's his angle?"

"I know, right? Though even a coward will come out with claws and teeth to protect himself when backed into a corner. But the sheriff—who would believe that? Certainly not your brother. He was sitting right there when the sheriff questioned Harland in the hospital. The way I see it, either my brother's lying, or you're all

156

involved in one massive clusterfuck. If the latter is the case, my money won't help a damn thing—my brother's a dead man."

Nate considered what Shawn had shared with him regarding Wagner. "I know someone who would listen to your story."

Gem's brows shot up. "Who?"

"Someone with money, power, and enormous influence."

"Yeah, yeah—who?"

"Mony Altman."

Gem snorted. "You're kidding, right?"

"Do you want to help your brother or not?"

"Why would the high and mighty Ms. Altman give two shits about my brother? Besides, she hates me."

"She doesn't hate you. It's more like she's pissed you decided to mess around with her daughters. Do you want to hear what I have to say or not?"

Gem made a zipping motion across her lips and sat back in her chair.

"Mony's been suspicious of Wagner for months, ever since she found Sissy Moonbeam hiding on her farm and the sheriff failed to protect the family."

"Who's Sissy Moonbeam?"

"One of your brother's trafficking victims. The girl's disappeared. Mony believes Sissy knew all the players in the illicit activities happening on the Bakken, including who's behind the murders of Shannon McDonald and Cindy Van Dyke. John Finch was set up as the fall guy until the case lacked evidence; then he agreed to go undercover to help discover the truth. Now Finch has been kidnapped—but why? Who's pulling the strings behind the ransom? Why is he even important? Few people knew Finch's whereabouts—the sheriff, and maybe Detective Gomez."

"Do you trust your brother?"

"With my life."

"That doesn't really answer the question. As I remember, this is the same guy you beat the shit out of, then fled to Vegas because you thought he slept with your girlfriend."

Nate felt the flush of shame on his cheeks. The event seemed a million years ago. "Massey has always protected the family—protected me. He and I might not always agree on the method, but I trust him explicitly."

Gem nodded. "Fair enough. So what's Mony's theory on the sheriff's motive?"

"She believes the sheriff is hiding something—maybe he's getting a cut in the drug and human trafficking business, or someone could be blackmailing him. He's been a lifelong friend to F&A Oil, but allegiance can change when the payout is big enough. Shannon always made everything her business. Hell, she probably had dirt on just about everyone in the tri-county area. My suspicion is she was on to something, something she ended up dying over. We know she'd been associating with Cindy Van Dyke, a woman with enough dirt on Mitchell to build a new mountain range. That these two women would end up murdered is not a coincidence. If your brother didn't do it, but was still involved in disposing of the bodies, he knows who did. Who told him to get rid of Shannon's body?"

"He says Mitchell, plus some mercenary working for a guy named Monroe."

"How did he know the mercenary was working for Monroe?"

"Mitchell told him. Said if he knew what was good for him, he'd cooperate or he'd be next. Harland claims Monroe's mercenary organized the white supremacists to do a few side jobs until the oil business started taking off again and promised them a plot of land to establish a proper compound."

"What land?"

"Yours and Altman's; he said anyone who sympathizes with an inferior race doesn't deserve to own land."

"And which 'inferior race,' pray tell, are we supposed to be commiserating with?"

"The Indians."

That struck a chord of truth. Mony was doing everything within her power to help the Indigenous community to retrieve and protect the Moonbeam girls. Nate was about to elaborate on that point with Gem when the jet did a violent shimmy.

The kenneled dogs woke from their slumber and started to whine. Gem instinctively fastened her seatbelt. Nate leaned over to look out the window. They were flying low—low enough to make out the topography below, a maze of sandstone spires, red rock cliffs, canyons, and plateaus. The cabin shook again, and the pilot's voice came over the intercom.

"This is your captain speaking—we are experiencing slight turbulence, and I'm asking you to please fasten your seatbelts. We seem to be flying through an air pocket. I'm going to increase altitude and see if I can get above the jet stream and out of these strong winds."

Having flown in small aircraft most of his life, Nate was relatively accustomed to turbulent flights. This felt *different*. He thought about the preflight check. As an on-the-job trained aeronautical mechanic, he'd often helped Buddy ready Mony's Piper or Buddy's crop-dusting planes preflight. For this flight, however, he'd left that responsibility to the Sloulin Field mechanics.

The plane shook again. This was more than just an air pocket. Nate stood.

"Where the hell are you going?" Gem gasped.

"Cockpit," Nate said evenly. "I want to see what's going on."

"You need a front-row seat to our crash?"

Nate heard the fear beneath the sarcasm. "Don't be dramatic. Just sit tight. I'll be back."

The dogs began to whimper louder as Nate made his way to the cockpit. An uneasiness settled over him. The flight attendant met him partway down the aisle.

"I'm going to have to ask you to return to your seat, Mr. Ferguson. It's not safe walking about the cabin during turbulence."

Judging from the look of concern on the flight attendant's face, she didn't believe it was turbulence either, particularly when the next shimmy made both their knees buckle to the floor at the same time. Nate didn't have to look out the window to confirm what he already knew. "We're losing altitude."

He found it darkly humorous when the flight attendant looked out the window to verify. Her eyes widened with horror.

The pilot's voice came over the speaker. "Camilla, I need you at the cockpit now. Everyone else, buckle in quickly. I am preparing to make an emergency landing."

"Lilly will need to move into the cabin area," the attendant told Nate.

"I'll get her."

He gazed out at the horizon as the jet's flight path closed the distance between sky and ground. In the jump seat next to him, the young Moonbeam girl sat in stoic terror. The pilot, a former Air Force comrade of Nate's father, spoke quickly into his mic. "I feel like I'm back in Nam and we're coming in hot. It's the rate of descent I can't control, like something is blocking the fuel line between the fuselage to the engine. No—there's no way I can override or correct at this point." The pilot glanced up, noticing Nate standing over his shoulder. "Take our young passenger back to the cabin and buckle in. I can't keep this bird in the air much longer."

Wordless, Nate unbuckled the girl, snatched her up in his arms, and made his way to the main cabin. She offered no protest. He glanced out a window as he passed, noticing the flaps in an upright position. He hurried to his seat, dropping the girl in the seat closest to him, and fumbled with her seatbelt.

"I can do it," she said. Nate's head reared back, surprised at the young passenger's calm behavior. He let her complete the task, then strapped himself in.

Gem glanced at the girl, then at Nate. "Who the hell is this?"

It was Lilly who answered. "If we live through this, I'll be sure to introduce myself."

CHAPTER 11

JOHN

Mitchell had been carried out of the shed some time during the night. John had been too preoccupied with a coughing fit and wheezing brought on by bronchial spasms to ask questions or formulate any sort of protest. He'd have felt guilty about that, if he hadn't been so focused on his own survival.

Shortly after sunrise, Sissy came to the shed unescorted. She carried a plate of fried bread and a glob of something that looked like dehydrated meat and dried berries glued together with lard. John retched at the sight of it. As she set the plate and a bottle of water on the floor next to him, he considered asking about Dwight's fate, but the effort seemed too great.

Squatting onto her haunches, she looked at him from eye level—assessing. This close, it would have been easy to grab her wrist and force her to let him go. If only he had the strength. The problem was, where would he go? After what he'd overheard last night, he'd started to wonder if she was being used as well and didn't know it.

The teenager must have come to some conclusion; she handed him a small leather pouch. Moving with caution, John took it. "Thank you," he said without checking the contents.

In his moments of lucidity, he'd spent part of the night hatching a plan to convince the young girl that she, too, was a prisoner, but timing was everything. Sissy already struck him as a *show me* sort of person. Poorly timed words would only bounce off her like toy arrows against a plate of armor. Better to wait for the right moment to present itself before broaching the subject.

Sissy glared at him with disdain. "Don't look so ungrateful. This food will be your last chance to eat for a while. The pemmican has good protein and will give you strength for the journey. I told one of our healers about your breathing problem, and she made you a medicine bag. Wear it around your neck and rub it under your nose and mouth from time to time. It will help your allergies." She pulled out a glass mason jar from a deep pocket in her jacket. "This herbal tea will help. The honey will suppress the cough."

She set the jar on the floor and stood. Making her way quickly to the door, she stopped mid-stride and reached into her other pocket, pulling out a small cylinder and tossing it at him. He caught it clumsily against his chest. "I found this," she said, "It's the best I can do for now."

John looked down at the object cradled in his hand and almost wept: an inhaler.

The combination of food, hydration, and medicine improved John's condition greatly. He didn't know the contents of the pouch, but at least he could breathe without wheezing and coughing up a lung. Despite his recovery, however, he decided to play the crippled captive for the time being. It seemed advantageous to let his enemy believe he'd been beaten into submission.

His ruse seemed effective. When the big man came for him again, instead of a burlap bag over his head, John was given one made of freshly washed cheesecloth. Though the recent demonstration of kindness in no way diminished the clear and present danger he was in, he accepted it gratefully.

Grabbing him roughly by the upper arm, the Indian escorted him out of the shed into the sunlight. Warmth radiated against his back. It felt good, despite the menacing shadow next to him. Air moved freely through the cheesecloth, which was sheer enough that John could see objects illuminated by the sun. Thanks to the inhaler, he could smell that rain had fallen during the night. Despite the daylight and the thinness of the veil covering his face, there wasn't much to see. Barren of trees or structures, the topography looked much like the surroundings of Ramona's farm. It would have been easy to think he was still in North Dakota, if it hadn't been for the long drive suggesting otherwise.

Behind him, a friendly female voice called out in a native dialect, "You two be careful among the white men. I'll watch for this white woman you speak of. See if she comes alone."

John turned his head toward the voice long enough to catch the silhouette of a thin woman standing in the doorway of what looked like a run-down trailer home. The big Indian slammed his hand between his shoulder blades, knocking the air from his lungs. "Eyes forward, asshole." John obliged. His survival depended upon his perceived cooperation.

The Indian loaded him into the bed of a camper top truck—alone. Again, he considered asking about Dwight. He didn't. What he didn't know wouldn't come back to bite him in the ass later, allowing plausible deniability if he were ever questioned about it.

John settled his back against the cab wall and took stock of his surroundings. The windows on the topper were blackened, blocking out light and view. Save for a ragged foam mat, the bed of the truck was empty. The smell of diesel and dust filled the confined space as the truck rumbled to a noisy start and bounced along a dirt road for several miles before reaching an asphalt surface. There was a hint of moisture still lingering in the air, and he was grateful for the protection from the elements were it to rain again.

Despite the truck's poor suspension, shortly into the drive, John dozed off to sleep. He'd lost track of the travel distance when they made their first pit stop. It was Sissy who'd come to retrieve him, leading him to believe he must not have presented much of a threat. She hadn't even bothered to bind his hands or place the hood over his head. Allowed the minor freedom, John took stock of his surroundings.

They'd stopped at a poorly maintained rest stop somewhere off the main road. Sissy walked behind him toward the cinder-block bathroom, then directed him around back. She stood—waiting. "Go ahead. Ain't like I haven't seen a cock a hundred times before."

He believed her. It was easy to see from the young girl's hardened appearance that she'd been used and abused—frequently. Still, though it may have been no great shock to her, he'd never been deprived the privacy of taking a piss before. There was something perverted about having a teenage girl for an audience. Sissy read his thoughts. "It's no skin off my nose if you sit in your own piss the rest of the ride."

It took him several minutes of straining and passing flatulence before he could get a steady stream going. When he was finished, Sissy led him back to the waiting truck. The surrounding landscape was hillier than where they'd come from, with sporadic vegetation scattered across the horizon. There was a pungent smell of refuse mixed with the distinct odor of fried food coming from somewhere nearby. Dark storm clouds loomed on the skyline ahead of him—west, most likely—lending a sense of foreboding. Williston was at the far western reach of North Dakota, leading John to presume they were now somewhere in Montana. The landscape remained sparsely inhabited. A sound of traffic passing along a highway indicated they were near the outskirts of a small town or community.

Then he heard it—the familiar lonesome sound of a train whistle. His eyes narrowed in that direction when the sharp blow of an open hand smacked between his shoulder blades.

"Head down, asshole, and keep moving."

They left the familiar pavement after the stop and began traveling backroads. The dust was so thick that John felt the beginnings of another asthma attack coming on. To distract him from his misery, he started planning out his escape. There was much to consider—Sissy, for one. It was too early to know where she fit into all this; she was a variable that presented a high risk. Still, an hour into the drive had him reconsidering.

A cell phone rang inside the cab. It was the big Indian who engaged the caller.

"The bitch is smarter than I thought," John's male captor grunted to the girl.

John was only able to catch every other word, but he got the gist of the conversation. The big man was pissed, and switched to his native tongue. He was clearly referring to Ramona.

"I told you," Sissy scolded. "Her dad's former military, a Nam vet."

"Her old man is dead."

"She can fly her own plane, stupid. She would know how to handle a drone."

The sound of a sharp crack against bare flesh ended the conversation. John held his breath, waiting for a rebuttal, but Sissy spoke no further. An hour passed before the big Indian said in a repentant tone, "Don't call me stupid."

It was oddly comforting yet disconcerting to know Ramona was on her way. It seemed Attorney Ferguson had indeed been a man of his word when he said he wanted to help. Ramona would never have made such a bold move alone without Ferguson's approval or support. John wondered briefly if the rock star was in support of the rescue mission. He doubted it. The last time he'd spoken with the attorney, the plan had been to stick him and the younger Moonbeam girl on a plane back to Vegas. *Wouldn't that have been a trip!* John was well aware of the rock star's animosity toward him—the last time he and Nathan Ferguson had met, he'd gotten his ass handed to him.

The way he saw it, Ferguson didn't deserve a woman like Ramona Strong. The man was nothing more than an overgrown bully with an inflated ego, shielding his insecurities under the guise of love and protection—quite at odds with his music, which conveyed a message of love and acceptance. It was of no consequence. Ramona clearly believed she was in a healthy relationship and seemed determined to make it work. To John, it seemed Ramona was no different than his young captor sitting in the cab of the truck. Both were blind to more viable options.

Humidity was replaced by an arid heat that beat against the topper. John had worked up a powerful thirst. He considered tapping on the window between the camper and cab and asking for some water when a sweet scent accompanied by a hot metallic odor gave him pause. Their caravan of one veered onto a paved highway. There was a distinct bustling of cars and trucks rumbling next to his prison on wheels. Bumping over a couple sets of railroad tracks, the driver made a series of left and right turns before coming to a stop. *We must have pulled into a gas station or garage,* John thought. It had been clear for several miles that there was an issue with the engine.

The passenger cab door opened with a rusty creak, and Sissy slid open the window between the cab and the camper. She spoke in an ominous tone: "You'll keep quiet and stay put, if you want to live." John glanced through the opening. Another rundown trailer. His hope deflated, he nodded. Sissy closed the window.

Outside the truck, John heard the steady thrum of traffic passing over concrete and steel. The big Indian greeted another man with cordial levity in an unfamiliar language. They laughed—frequently. The word *wasicu* was mentioned more than once. Their laughter was followed by the sound of rusty metal as the two men opened the hood of the truck. The tone became serious. A woman's voice, sweet and motherly, called from a distance, "Where's my niece? She must be thirsty. I've made her some lemonade."

Sissy shouted something back in her native tongue, then said softly without opening the window, "You be quiet and maybe I'll bring you some too." With that, she exited the truck.

The promise of something to drink lifted John's spirits, until an abrupt exchange of hostile words between man and woman rent the air. The kindly female voice took on a sharp, don't-give-me-any-of-your-bullshit tone. The argument ended, and the two men resumed their engine analysis. Sissy didn't return to the truck.

With his captors occupied, John considered the opportunity presenting itself. He had no idea where he was, but the bustling sound along with steady traffic suggested commerce in the area. A sudden boom of two large objects colliding shook the truck. *Is there a train yard nearby?* It was the break he'd been waiting for.

The sound of metal smashing on metal from the front of the truck distracted his thoughts. A flurry of curse words suggested repairs were not faring well. The two men's voices faded as they walked away from their project. Wasting no time, John eased himself toward the tailgate of the truck. He felt bad for what he was about to do. He was about to betray the kindness Sissy had shown to him. The thought was fleeting.

Hunched next to the tailgate, John tested to see whether the topper had ever been locked. He gave it a jiggle. *Nothing.* He tried again, this time using more force. Still nothing. Unwilling to accept defeat, he tried again, each attempt more aggressive than the last, until he heard the satisfying rusty *click.* Gingerly, he opened the camper hood.

For all he knew his captor could be standing right outside the hatch, ready to shoot him as he tried to escape. But what choice did he have? The big Indian was probably going to kill him anyway, or worse. The piston hinges moved with significant resistance as gravity worked against him. Each time he let up on the pressure, the hatch began to close. At least it didn't squeak. With the door mostly open, John took a quick survey around him. Thank God no one was watching him.

Using his back, John propped up the hatch and slithered awkwardly out of the truck bed over the tailgate. Feeling with his right foot, he searched for the bumper only to discover there wasn't one. He sat straddled on the tailgate, using his head to prop open the heavy hatch, his neck and balls taking the brunt of the pressure. His body slid halfway down the back end of the truck before the tips of his toes reached the ground. The hood of the topper responded in kind as he lowered his body over the edge, closing with twice the speed. Despite his deconditioned state, his martial arts practices gave him the flexibility to make the necessary straddle. However, his agility didn't stop the heavy topper from crashing down against the lower part of his left leg, leaving a gash and pinning him against the tailgate. John imagined the sight he might have presented to an unsuspecting observer watching the whole fiasco, and despite his pain he managed a laugh.

Extricating himself from the metal trap, John planted both feet firmly on the ground, crouched low behind the truck, and took in the lay of the land. He was in a trailer park located close to a row of warehouses near the edge of town. There was a highway overpass less than a block away, near the front of the trailer park. For the second time that day, he almost wept at the sight of the railroad tracks behind him.

Crouching low, he made his way swiftly across the street, heading for the shelter of a row of storage sheds.

His confidence surged until, halfway through the street intersection, he heard someone shout, "He's getting away!"

He broke into a dead run. The pursuit of heavy footfalls gained on him quickly as he wove in between the row of storage sheds. John reached the end of the row only to discover he'd also reached the end of the block. With no place close to hide, he ran toward what looked like a saloon on the next block. He had no way of knowing whether it was open; the best he could hope for was someone to witness his plight. Then the sudden sound of a train whistle rent the air, and he lurched into a new direction.

The glorious sight of a familiar arrow of blue and red shimmered on the body of silver as the western sun struck against the metal surface. The word *Amtrak* came into view. It spurred John on, but the sound of his captors was closing the gap. He tried to ignore it. There was one thought in his head: *Get across the track before the train blocks your escape.* The problem was, if he crossed the track at his present position, so would his enemy, who would easily overtake him on the other side. He needed a different strategy.

Launching a petition skyward, John altered his direction, setting a collision course with the train.

Quick-twitch muscles and sprinting had never been his strong suit. Endurance, however, was. John kept up his dash for as long as he could before settling into a long-distance running stride. He had a distance to go, and he prayed his pursuers would run out of steam before he did.

The train whistle gave a long, insolent warning,

sounding angry against the still afternoon air. The menacing sound drowned out the shouts from his captors as well as the pounding heartbeat in his chest. A muscle cramp took hold in his calf, brought on by dehydration and hours of sitting in cramped quarters. He pushed through it. Sucking dry air deep into his lungs, he hoped to balance his inspiratory/expiratory ratio to maintain his speed. Unfortunately, every inspiration was laced with diesel fumes and other toxic chemicals from the train yard, making him cough and wheeze. A full-blown asthma attack wasn't far off.

As the train slowed for its stopover, John realized he had critically misjudged his timing. To make matters worse, his energy was nearly spent. He considered crossing the track, but the moment was still wrong. John fought the onslaught of his pending respiratory shutdown as best he could and continued running toward the train yard.

His only saving grace was that his pursuers were tiring as well, unfortunately not as quickly as he. John fumbled in his pocket for the inhaler. *Would it give me the breathing capacity I need to escape?* He couldn't risk it.

The wail of the train whistle pierced his eardrum as a cramp seized in his calf. Like an offensive wide receiver preparing to intercept the catch of the season, John made the decision and darted right, cutting in front of the train. With his last burst of strength, he lunged forward. The train whistle's scream sounded like it was coming from inside his head. Barely able to lift one foot in front of the other, he stumbled—the heel of his shoe caught on the steel track, and he was hurtling toward the ground.

Dirt pressed against his cheek and mouth. John made a half-hearted effort to untangle his leg, but it was no use; his energy was completely depleted. Rolling onto his back, he stared at the partly cloudy sky and smiled. It seemed fitting that his old friend the train would be responsible for his demise. At least he wouldn't suffer. At least it would be quick.

A scramble of commotion surrounded him, and John wondered if the angel of death had come to carry him away. He felt his whole body being hauled across the gravel as if it were being drug by the train. Was that it? No piercing pain, no anguish and suffering? *If that was death, it wasn't so bad—I didn't even feel it.* His body abruptly shifted to an upright position. Was his angel going to make him walk? All right. He took a step forward but immediately fell. *Do I still have legs? Or were they cut to ribbons by the steel wheels of an iron horse?*

Someone yelled in his ear, "Move, you stupid son of a bitch."

John heard the shrill cry of the train whistle, or perhaps it was the people standing on the platform waiting to board the train. Rising awkwardly to his feet, he lunged like a baseball runner sliding into second base, headfirst. His head hit the ground in a cloud of dirt and oil. Sharp stones shredded his hands and face. A ripping feeling of pain tore at his knee, and the warm smell of salt and iron made him retch. This was the death he'd expected—pain, violence, misery.

A vision of Shannon McDonald flashed through his mind. Wouldn't it be nice if she were sitting on a cloud with a decanter of Irish whiskey to share while they laughed, watching the world floating by beneath their feet. No longer able to move, John lay where he'd landed, waiting for his guardian angel to take him to the redheaded beauty.

When nothing happened, he opened his eyes to a growing circle of people standing above him. The look of concern on their faces varied from shock and horror to pure outrage. John reached down to feel for his legs and realized he was still holding onto the inhaler. He took in a gasping breath and began coughing uncontrollably.

"What in the hell were you thinking?" an angry voice shouted. A man wearing a dark blue Dickies work shirt and pants parted the small crowd and reached down, grabbing John by the scruff of his shirt. "No suicides on my watch."

John tried to put the rescue inhaler to his mouth. There was no way he would be able to answer anyone's questions until he got the asthma attack under control. A woman wearing a cowboy hat and boots recognized the small handheld device. Crouching next to him, she helped hold it to his mouth. "On the count of three, sweetheart, take in a deep breath."

As John sucked in the life-saving medicine, he remembered his last-ditch effort to clear the tracks and looked for his captors. Had he been successful in creating a barrier between himself and his enemy? If so, not for long. That train wouldn't sit there forever.

The symptoms of relief from a rescue inhaler typically took fifteen to twenty minutes to kick in—he needed to be long gone by then. John grabbed onto the woman's arm and pulled her close to his lips. "I—I need to get out of here. Tw—two men are trying t—to kill me. I—I have money. I can pay you."

The woman narrowed her gaze, assessing him. Reaching in her shirt pocket, she pulled out a cell phone. "Yeah, Krystal, this is Caldwell. Send the rescue unit to the Amtrak station, quick. We have an asthmatic on the platform, probably needs an ER visit. No—absolutely no lights or sirens, just get here."

She clicked off the call and dropped the phone back in her pocket. Leaning close to John's ear, she whispered, "You're going to have to play out whatever little drama you've got going here to ensure transport. Can you do that?"

John didn't have to pretend. "I can do that."

CHAPTER 12

MASSEY

Massey checked the mileage range on the RV. He said to his passenger, "Check the navigation map for the next town. We need to stop for gas."

Mony did so without comment. He could tell she was still stewing about the failed rendezvous near Wolf Point. He was trying to make sense of it himself. But they had no choice but to follow the old woman's instructions and continue west if they were to retrieve Finch. They were within twenty miles of Shelby when Mony's cell phone rang. She'd synced it with the Bluetooth so that Massey could listen in. There was a noticeable change in the tone of the kidnapper's voice.

"Head to the Glacier Peaks Casino. Wait at one of the quarter slots furthest from the main door for more instructions. No bullshit this time. The old woman nearly died of a heart attack when you flew that drone into her kitchen window. You wouldn't want her death along with the lawyer's on your conscience, would you? I expect you within the hour."

"That's impossible," Mony said. "I just passed through Havre and I need to stop for gas."

"Not my problem."

"It is if you want my money. I don't even know where Glacier Peaks Casino is located."

"It's on the Rez."

"Yeah, which one?"

"Blackfeet."

"Western Montana? Christ, I'm over three hours away."

None of that was true. Massey had made considerable effort to close the gap once they'd hit the open highway after leaving Wolf Point. One nice thing traveling west across Montana was that the traffic was less dense, and with no daytime speed limit, he could push the RV's Mercedes diesel engine to its limit. The other nice thing was having the law to clear a path for you.

"I'll give you three hours."

"Shit, you gonna provide a magic wand with that demand? I want proof of life. I want to hear John's voice."

The kidnapper found her vehemence amusing. "Just like a privileged white woman. You misinterpret my understanding of travel distance for clemency."

"You know nothing about me."

He laughed. "I know plenty, rich oilman's daughter. You fly your own plane and got a smart mouth. That's all I need to know."

Massey made a rolling motion with his finger, encouraging Mony to keep him talking. He took the opportunity to listen for what *wasn't* being said. He noticed the distinct sound of an engine revving—diesel, most likely—and an overstressed transmission stuck in a low gear. There was the familiar road sound of rubber rolling over uneven asphalt. A train whistle blared out a warning somewhere off in the distance. The male kidnapper cursed.

"Three hours. Not a minute more."

"I want to talk to John."

He disconnected the call.

"Damn it."

Massey reached for Mony's hand, holding it tight. "He's messing with you, showing who's in charge. Don't worry, John's still alive."

Mony dialed Detective Gomez's number per instruction. Gabriella answered on the first ring. "What do you got?"

Massey relayed the next rendezvous point.

"Were you able to talk to Finch?"

Mony was too despondent to answer. "No," said Massey.

There was a weighty silence.

"East Glacier would have been nicer," Massey interjected, "more touristy. We could've blended in better."

"He might think you're flying, not driving. We can work with this. Stick with the plan. The kidnapper is playing it safe, staying close to reservation land. It makes sense; local law intervention would be limited. He must be unaware that John's kidnapping is a federal case. It can play in our favor."

Massey concurred. "What's our next move?"

"Are you close to a town? We need to get the two of you wired."

"We have to stop in Shelby for gas. Will that work?"

"I'll make it work. There's a diesel stop near the western edge of town. You should be able to get the RV in and out easily. I'll have someone waiting for you. They know what you're driving, so let them approach you."

"We'll be there."

One of Mile High City's ballads began playing on the radio—tension permeated the chassis of the RV. At last, Mony broke the silence. "What are we going to do when we get there?"

"The casino? Too many moving pieces. We need to take one thing at a time."

She stared out the window. "Patience was never my virtue."

Massey couldn't help but laugh. "I know."

She gave in and joined him, providing much-needed relief. "Why do you think the kidnapper wouldn't let me talk to John?"

"I think it's just to keep you on edge. I'm guessing Browning may have always been the intended endpoint. It makes sense if our assumption the kidnapper is Indian is correct. The Rez would be a haven. Much more so than traveling through Glacier."

"I don't know about that," Mony countered. "There are thousands of acres of remote wilderness to hide in the park. They could easily get lost in the backcountry." A frown marred her face. "That would be rough for John. He's a city dweller. His respiratory condition alone would be a huge handicap."

"Exactly. Finch would be a liability in that scenario. Too

risky. Unless there was never a plan for him to be exchanged in the first place."

"Jesus, Massey, don't say that."

"My theory is that he's bait for a much bigger prize."

Mony looked at him with a puzzled expression.

Massey rolled his eyes. "You, Mony. You're the prize. Why settle for a paltry few thousand when you can acquire millions for a wealthy heiress?"

"They get my money either way. Besides, I would draw too much attention, and I get the sense our man is trying to fly under the radar as much as possible. You can do that with a couple of thousand and blend into the backcountry. Dealing on a level where millions of dollars are at stake, you would have every mercenary in the country chasing you to the ends of the earth. For a racist, it would be just another excuse to kill an Indian."

"Unless you have someone securing an escape plan. Someone with money, like Monroe Oil."

Mony waved it off. "Monroe's too volatile. He would just eliminate the guy and save himself the headache and money. I get a sense our kidnapper is smarter than that."

Massey considered the assertion. "I'm not sure why, but I'm inclined to agree."

Shelby's population was a little over three thousand, yet it had a courthouse, police station, post office, and hospital—important amenities when living in a remote rural area. A block off the main drag, Massey noticed the Amtrak stopped at the depot.

They found the gas station Detective Gomez had suggested. Before exiting the cab, Mony slipped on her wedding ring. "What are you doing?" Massey asked.

"If we're pretending to be married, I thought it would be good to look the part."

Massey had begun fueling when the person pumping gas beside them struck up a conversation. "Nice rig. I've been meaning to get one myself. Mind if I ask you a couple of questions?"

Mony indulged the woman's questions, and they were still jabbering when Massey went inside to pay. He wandered around the store grabbing water, soda, and snacks while waiting for the detective's agent to approach him. After ten minutes, he paid for his purchases and left.

Still talking to the woman, Mony reached out for him and said, "Would you mind if Dara took a peek inside the RV, honey? We could pull over to the overflow lot and let her look around."

Massey lifted an eyebrow at the term of endearment. He was even more surprised when Mony took the water jugs and locked an arm with his. She told Dara, "We're on our way to Glacier to celebrate my husband's retirement."

He didn't need to be hit with a two-by-four to understand what was happening.

Dara's team fitted each of them with a wire and ear mic. Mony mentioned Massey's theory regarding Browning being the endpoint. It piqued Dara's interest. "In that case—" She pulled out an injection gun. Massey felt like one of his hunting dogs when the technician inserted the microchip in his arm. "Don't look so glum, Mr. Ferguson. This may well save your life."

Later on, Massey was grateful for the extra time Mony had negotiated. He was cracking open a soda and negotiating the RV under the I-15 overpass when the wailing sound of sirens caused him to pull over. A rescue unit came whizzing past from the east and shot up the I-15 on-ramp.

"Wonder what that's all about?" said Mony.

Massey was waiting to pull back into traffic when the unexpected ring of Mony's cell phone startled them both.

The kidnapper's voice crackled against the background noise. "Change in plan. When you get to the casino, go to the buffet and wait for more instructions." Before either of them could say anything, the caller had hung up.

Mony furrowed her brow. "Well, that's worrisome. Our kidnapper changed his mind—again. Things must be falling apart. I've got a real bad feeling—"

A moment of clarity hit Massey square between the eyes. "Well, I'll be goddamned. Get the detective on the phone, hurry."

Mony gave him an annoyed look, but did as he asked. When the detective answered, he shouted, "They're here—here in Shelby. Have your team keep their eyes peeled for an old run-down truck, likely diesel, possible North Dakota license plates."

"What's this all about, Matthew?"

"Mony just got a call. I heard the train whistle and the ambulance siren over the phone. They're either in the vicinity of the hospital or maybe further up the road, but they're close."

The detective didn't question his hunch. "I'll get my team on it."

Mony began scanning the horizon. "Should we turn around? Maybe they're behind us."

Massey shook his head. "No, let's keep moving forward for now. At least we know they're not in Browning waiting for us, but they're still heading in that direction. I want to get there before them, if we can."

Mony pulled up the map on the navigation system. "Shit, Massey, we've got a problem. There's a fork up ahead. They could either take I-15 or stay on US 2 to get to Browning. I-15 is actually a few minutes shorter."

Massey considered the options. "I-15 is faster but longer in distance. If the truck is as bad as it sounded over the phone, there's no place for service. Let's stay on the highway."

They'd reached the edge of Cut Bank when Mony said, "Massey—check your side mirror. Is that a truck with a North Dakota plate behind us?"

Massey eased up on the gas and took a long look in his side mirror. "It's a diesel all right, and it sounds like the transmission may be going out."

"Any sign of John?"

"No, but the truck's got a camper top. Maybe they've got him in back."

"Maybe he's not there at all."

"Don't be pessimistic. We have to believe he's still part of the equation. And you were right about the kidnapper. He's Indian, and a bruiser of a fellow at that. We'll need to be careful. It looks like someone is riding shotgun with him."

"Male or female?"

"I can't tell. They're slouched down in the seat."

"Do you think it's Sissy? John mentioned her name when he was allowed to speak to me. Maybe she's been kidnapped as well."

"I didn't get the best look, but I suppose it's possible."

Mony clenched her teeth. "So what we're dealing with here is an Indian using one of their own as a human shield in their moneymaking scheme. The dirty bastard."

"Don't go jumping to conclusions. I do agree with the person being in on the caper. Whoever it is, they seemed pretty comfortable riding in the cab."

"A child will do whatever it takes to survive."

"I don't disagree, but maybe kidnapping John is part of her survival."

Massey let the truck pass and fell in three vehicles behind. It seemed a good strategy, until the faster drivers kept passing the old truck, exposing the large RV's generous view of the windshield. He let a semi pass in between them to maintain their cover. It would be awful to be recognized now that they were this close.

Mony addressed the obvious. "He's going to blow that engine or drop the transmission on the highway before he reaches Browning. We'll be the first in line to pick them up."

Massey notified Gomez of the predicament. She went to work, setting up a relay of unmarked cars stationed along the route in anticipation of this inevitable factor. They seemed to have a viable plan. All he and Mony had to do was monitor the situation.

The two pseudo-retirees caught up with destiny just west of Blackfoot. Coming over a slight rise in the highway, they'd just crossed Willow Creek when Mony said, "Massey, isn't that our truck?" Off on a gravel side road, an old truck sat with the hood open, smoke billowing over the top. "Now what do we do?"

"Did you bring your dad's gun with you?"

She looked at him with surprise. "'Violence begets violence,' Massey, you know that."

He was relieved. "Just checking." A gun could turn this situation ugly very quickly, and he didn't need any surprises from his partner. "I want you to sit tight here in the RV. I'll see if I can distract the big fellow."

"What about backup?"

Both Massey and Mony's earpieces crackled to life. The detective informed them, "I dispatched the Browning unit to your location as soon as you mentioned the truck on the roadside. ETA in five, six minutes tops. My tracker shows you're stopped near Stone Ranch Road. Take your time slowing the RV, then pull up behind him as close as you can. When you've come to a stop, I want each of you to leave the RV at the same time. Massey, you approach first, drawing the driver's attention. Do it slowly. Wait until the driver sees you before you move closer. No need to spook him. Try to stay toward the rear of the truck, at least until Ms. Strong's in position."

"Mony, you will come up quickly on the passenger side and stay toward the back of the truck. The satellite image shows you don't have much for cover, so slip on the tan hooded sweatshirt Dara gave you and crouch close to the ground. You'll blend in with the landscape. You stay put and listen for Matthew to engage the driver in conversation before you go any further, then see if you can check out the passenger. Look—but try to stay out of sight. If it is Sissy Moonbeam, she might get out and make a run for it. If she doesn't have a weapon, stall her. By the time this all plays out, the team will be on site. Good luck to you both."

Massey slowed the RV per instructions, leaving no space between the nose of the chassis and the bed of the truck. He glanced over at Mony, who'd already crouched down in her seat. "Ready?" Eyes wide, she nodded.

The beauty of owning a newer rig was that it didn't have all the little creaks and crunches an older one had. Without a sound, Mony slipped out the passenger door seamlessly and disappeared into the ditch. Massey started toward the truck. He waited until she was in position behind the right rear wheel to shout out, "Hey, do you need some help?"

The big Indian poked his head from around the hood of the truck. His eyes filled with suspicion, he glared at Massey. "Not sure. Know anything about engines?"

Massey lingered near the rear of the truck, torn about his next move. When the Indian said no more, he moved the narrative forward. "Mind if I take a look?"

The big man shrugged. "Suit yourself."

Taking it as an invitation, Massey advanced, praying the promised cavalry was on its way.

CHAPTER 13

MONY

Crouched in the ditch, Mony watched Massey's feet from under the truck as he unhurriedly walked past the camper top. She wondered if he'd heard any sounds of life as he passed. She hadn't heard anything herself, but tried not to worry. Maintaining her sanity at this point was paramount. She simply had to believe John was somewhere alive and safe; the alternative was too much to bear.

As Massey reached the front of the truck, Mony crept forward. Just behind the passenger door, she caught sight of the young girl through the side mirror, sitting with her shoulder propped against the window and texting on her phone. Mony recognized her immediately. She heard the kidnapper say, "Can't tell if it's the engine or the transmission."

Massey engaged in conversation: "What year's the truck?"

"Ninety-three, 7.3-liter—best diesel engine Ford ever made."

"Damn straight. Ah—but no turbocharger."

"You know engines?"

"Not as well as my brother, but I know my way around. Ninety-three, you say? A 250, right?"

"Yup."

"Does it stall now and again?"

"Like now, yeah."

"Is there a shift delay, like it bangs into the next gear?"

"It shifts rough."

"Hmm—hard on the engine."

Tuning out the conversation, Mony focused her gaze on the side mirror. It took a beat before the teen finally looked up from the phone screen. The kid all but rolled her eyes. She had the nerve to mouth, *"What are you doing here?"* Mony wanted to slap her.

She made a motion for Sissy to follow. The teen glanced at the front windshield, the view obstructed by the raised hood, then back to Mony. Slowly, she eased the door handle open. Mony held her breath. So far, so good. Up until the young girl leaned her weight against the door— the rusted hinge groaned mercilessly.

Both Mony and Sissy froze, then looked toward the obstructed windshield. Mony strained her ears, tuning into the conversation at the front of the truck. *Still engine talk. Jesus—Massey's a good bullshitter.* But he wouldn't be able to keep up the pretense indefinitely.

Mony glanced back at the RV, then looked beyond. A semitruck was about to pass their roadside emergency. If the driver stopped, it would throw a wrench into the entire plan. Pointing to the door handle, she mouthed to Sissy, "*Try again.*"

That was when everything went to shit.

The scuffle that broke out in front of the truck grabbed Mony's attention just as the door flung open, slamming into her head. She fell backward into the ditch, stunned and confused. Scrambling to her feet, Sissy jumped out of the truck, pushing Mony to the ground, and kicked her in the side of the ribs. Air left her lungs. She didn't even have time to catch her breath before Sissy kicked her again, this time in the pelvis. Searing pain shot down Mony's leg. *What in the hell is she doing?*

The kidnapper shouted, "You got her, cousin."

Sissy yelled back, "Don't worry about me, worry about him."

Mony looked up in time to see Massey's large frame hit the asphalt, blood oozing from the side of his head. She screamed, "Son of a bitch, I swear to God, you won't live to see the sunset on this day."

The kidnapper laughed as he came around the truck. "Always the smart mouth. Cousin, shut her up."

A roll of duct tape materialized in Sissy's hand; she tore off a piece and stuck it over Mony's mouth. Her muffled screams of anger had no effect on the teen, who stared at her with cold, dark eyes.

Leaving Massey where he lay, they grabbed Mony by the arms. It took both Sissy and the kidnapper's strength to pull her dead weight off the ground. When that didn't keep her anchored, she flailed, kicking and thrashing. Sissy lost her grip, and they both fell. Mony scrambled to use the ditch slope to roll over on top of the teen, pinning her to the ground. *Where in the hell is Gomez's team? They should be here by now.*

Sissy's wiry frame wriggled out from under Mony, then stood and kicked her in the gut. Doubling over in a fit of coughing, Mony tried to wrap her head around the insanity of it all. *What the hell is wrong with this kid? Don't you know I'm trying to help you?* She stayed on the ground and began crawling back to where Massey lay. She could see his boots from her vantage. He wasn't moving. A wave of nausea threatened to overtake her.

The kidnapper grabbed Mony by both arms, lifted her feet off the ground, and stared her in the face, then shook her until her teeth rattled. "If you puke, you choke. If you choke, you die. You're worth nothing to me dead."

Mony's eyes welled with tears at the taste of bile in the back of her throat. She didn't give a damn what she was worth. She looked away to Massey.

"He's all right. He'll just have one hell of a headache when he wakes up. Now stop fighting. My cousin is a sore loser when it comes to a fight. She's liable to beat the shit out of you next time."

Mony was nowhere near done fighting.

The kidnapper must have come to the same conclusion. To dissuade her efforts further, he bound her at the wrists with duct tape and threw her over his shoulder like a sack of flour, then carried her to a waiting truck that was hidden behind the RV. He dropped her in the truck bed, climbed in, and closed the tailgate, then set to work groping at her jeans.

She kneed him in the groin. The man let out a howl and backhanded her across her cheek. "Cell phone—now—or the rest of the drive you'll be riding naked."

If she could have projected venom from her eyes like a lizard, he'd have been dead three times over. He pointed a finger in her face. "You cooperate, and I won't come back and finish what I started on your old man. Do you understand?"

Relenting, Mony rolled onto her side just enough to expose her right hip pocket. He grabbed the phone and threw it over the side of the truck. After he'd thumped his fist on the cab window, the truck backed up, flipped a U-turn, and headed back toward the town of Blackfoot.

Mony tried to regain her equilibrium and concentrated on what was happening. *Why are they heading east if they were supposed to meet in Browning? And what about John?* The thought had barely entered her brain when the truck made a sharp left turn onto gravel road, heading north. They were moving fast, too fast for the rutted dirt road. She bounced around in the bed of the truck as if she weighed nothing more than a kitten, while her nemesis sat with his back resting against the wheel well, like a man without a care in the world.

As she tried to sit up, he pushed his foot against her chest, shoving her back to the floor. "Nah-ah. You need a sack over your head for that. Just relax. We'll be on smoother roads soon enough."

Mony rolled onto her side to face him, using her bound hands to cushion her head against the pounding. Her ribs hurt, her cheek stung, and her gut ached. She'd have killed for a drink of water just then. Pushing primal needs aside, she focused on details imperative to her survival. Her captor had been lying in wait, and he had a plan. Sissy's bizarre actions confirmed Massey's suspicion—she was in on the caper. It made Mony both angry and sad. If Sissy wanted to buy her way out of a life of prostitution, Christ—all she needed to do was ask. Mony would have given the kid the world, without all this drama.

The truck's sharp, jarring movements over an uneven surface snapped Mony from her introspect. There was a sweet, mildly pungent odor mingled with nitrates. Less than a mile later, they crossed an even rougher surface. An image of the RV navigation map flashed in her mind. The train tracks and Willow Creek each ran parallel north of the highway. They were heading deeper into reservation lands, away from the main road, civilization, and federal agents. She thought about Massey. *Has the detective's team found him yet? Is he all right?*

Looking up at her nemesis, who sat with his eyes closed, she wished she'd have brought her gun. Nothing would have given her more pleasure than to pop a cap in the big Indian's groin right about then. She despised his cold arrogance. God only knew what he'd done to John or Sissy to be wearing that smug expression.

It wasn't long after they'd crossed the tracks that Mony sensed a gradual turn in direction. Despite the overcast sky, there was a definite breakthrough of sun at the twelve o'clock position. They were heading west, probably toward Browning. She listened for any sort of sound that might give a clue as to whether they were getting closer to town. Aside from a brief stint crossing asphalt, all she heard was crushed dirt beneath the wheels.

The truck continued along the dirt road for a good hour before it stopped. Mony was eager to sit up and stretch. Her hips and back throbbed with pain. She had a killer headache and a powerful thirst, but she waited for her captor to tell her what to do. It was best to let her enemy think she'd been beaten into submission.

The big Indian jumped nimbly over the side of the truck, walked to the back, and lowered the tailgate. Nodding the go-ahead, he let Mony struggle on her own into a sitting position. Her head began to spin, and a wave of nausea was about to engulf her. Taking a couple of deep breaths, Mony suppressed the urge to vomit and took stock of her surroundings. The low-hanging sun pointed out the westerly direction, but the mountain ranges in the not-so-far-off distance would have sufficed. Having only flown into Kalispell during a visit to Glacier National Park, she hadn't driven through this part of Montana much. Typically, when entering the park, it was through West Glacier, driving Going-to-the-Sun Road from west to east all the way to St. Mary and East Glacier. Once, they'd taken US Highway 2 around the southern tip of the park to the Two Medicine entrance and Running Eagle Falls. Beyond that easterly point, the mountains abruptly ended, turning into rolling prairie land.

"This isn't a sightseeing tour," the big Indian scoffed.

Mony did what she could to slither her ass across the truck bed with minimal success. Her body simply wasn't cooperating. It felt like she was stuck in a vat of tar. She looked at her adversary and held up her bound hands. He eyed her suspiciously, then glanced around at the environment before pulling a buck knife from an ankle holster. He pointed the tip an inch from her face. "Don't do anything stupid." Mony held out her wrists, and he sliced the duct tape like butter.

She immediately ripped the tape from her mouth, her eyes welling with tears as the adhesive tore the top layer of skin from her lips, leaving a burning like fire. "Please, I—I need water."

Sissy and the mystery driver had exited the cab truck and stood next to the big Indian. Looking at the three of them side by side, it was clear they were in solidarity. Mony didn't know what to make of her situation. They didn't look like murderers. They looked . . . desperate. The driver, a woman of Indian heritage in her mid-forties, climbed into the truck bed and handed her a bottle of water. Mony accepted it gratefully. "Pilamaya." The woman stared at her, but didn't respond.

They walked single file along a dirt trail to an elongated cabin made of weathered timber, tucked against a mixed coniferous forest. There was a small lean-to along the side, where a pile of wood stacked for winter had been almost entirely depleted. Oddly, there was a fragrant odor of smoky pine in the air. The interior was stark but quaint. The smoke Mony had smelled came from a fire burning in a stone fireplace nestled in the corner of the cabin, lending a cozy feel to the open living space. Worn furniture surrounding an equally worn rug made of fur and hide defined the living room.

The big Indian sat Mony down—hard—in a chair next to an old red Formica table and stood over her. She glared up at him. "What's the plan?"

He took one of the mismatched chairs next to her, turned it around, and straddled it backwards. Leaning on the back rest, he crossed his muscular arms and flashed a smug grin. "That depends on your cooperation."

Mony crossed her ankles. "Oh, that's all." She looked at Sissy and the woman, who stood next to a work counter. "To gain my cooperation, you need to earn my trust. Forcing a vulnerable child to be your accomplice after the abuse she's survived only shows me you're just some spineless mercenary who blindly follows malicious orders for a paycheck."

"Sized me up with your bias and prejudice, have you?"

"I know what I see. John's not here. I can only assume you've either killed him or left him for dead like my brother on the highway. This in no way motivates my cooperation."

"I could kill you, you know." The big man reached over and placed his massive hand around her throat, applying pressure. "I could snap your scrawny neck."

Mony's eyes began to water at the mild constriction on her airway. She instinctively grabbed his arm and tried to wrench away from his grip. "Enough," shouted the woman from across the room. "No man wants damaged goods."

He released his grip with a laugh. "You should know." To Mony he said, "You think you know me?"

Mony was too busy coughing to answer.

"If the lawyer's dead, it's because he lost at a game of chicken with a train, not because I killed him. And I told you, your brother's alive. His head will hurt a little bit, that's all. As for my cousin—" He gestured toward Sissy. She obediently walked to his side, and he wrapped his arm around her waist. "How do you know she's not the one calling the shots?" He reached in his pocket and handed Mony his cell phone. "Now call your people."

"My what?"

Her captor looked at her with frustration. "Your family, people—business associates. We need to talk terms."

Mony took the phone from him, then handed it over to Sissy. "I gave *you* my number because there is no one else to call. I've already told you I would help you. If it's money you need, all you had to do was ask without all this bullshit and death threats. But that arrangement is between you and me. This pimp and his bottom bitch over there are not part of the agreement."

The big man lurched to his feet and backhanded Mony across the face again. "You forget: what I say goes."

The blow was hard enough to turn her head—tears welled in her eyes—but she ignored the pain and his outburst. "I don't know them, and I don't trust them. I don't trust you either, but I can excuse your bad choices based on the knowledge you've been badly influenced and horribly abused." She turned her attention to the man standing over her. "My authorization is the only thing that will ensure any money exchange. You deal with me directly—and I promise that you, a murderer, pimp, and child molester, will never see a dime of it."

The woman intervened. "Sissy, Todd, come outside."

"Don't call me that," the big Indian muttered. Then the three walked out of the cabin, leaving Mony alone in the quiet with her thoughts.

It surprised her that no one had bothered to bind her. They hadn't even locked the door, leaving a gaping opportunity for her to escape. *But escape to where?* She had to be deep within the boundaries of the Blackfoot reservation, which would make her stick out like a tornado on the prairie landscape. Besides, she was in no physical shape to endure a night alone in the wilderness. Her muscles had already begun to seize and cramp due to limited activity and restricted movement. Her cheek was bleeding again. She had no water supply. Sure, they'd crossed over a running creek nearby, but even if she had a receptacle to carry it, the potential for the water to be tainted with either Giardia or E. coli diminished its viability significantly.

Accepting the foregone conclusion, she resigned her rescue to Detective Gomez's capable team and focused on her conversation with . . . *Todd*. What the hell did he mean, "lost at a game of chicken?" Mony thought back on the course of her travels, to the place where John may have encountered a train. She remembered the ambulance coming from the direction of the train depot back in Shelby. Drawing an unsettling conclusion, she cast her eyes upward. *Dear God, protect him from doing something stupid.* Mony had come to think of John as a logical, sensible man, but lately his actions had pointed to something more emotionally driven.

Her consciousness was pulled back to the present when her ears detected the welcoming rhythmic *whop—whop—whop* of whirling blades. A moment later, however, the hum was disrupted by the unmistakable sound of gunplay just outside the cabin.

A spatter of bullets dropped Mony to the floor like a stone, taking out the two windows in front of the cabin. She screamed at the ensuing shouting and gunfire. Pinned to the floor, she attempted to use her forearms to belly crawl toward the door, but the searing pain in her right arm halted her in her tracks. Looking down at her shirt sleeve, she saw a red bloodstain begin to bloom. "Damn it!" She rolled to a sitting position, assessing the damages. Bright red blood oozed from under a shard of glass that protruded from her deltoid. "Goddamn it!"

Frantically, Mony looked around for some sort of fabric. All she found was a tattered towel hanging from a drawer handle near the kitchen work counter. It would suffice. Unable to use her arms, Mony tried butt-walking toward the intended goal. It was not only undignified, but extremely difficult to navigate an unpolished wooden floor among a minefield of broken glass. Twice she stopped to pull a wood splinter from her butt and thigh. With each jarring movement, the glass piece protruding from her arm bored a bigger hole. By the time she'd reached the towel, the side of her shirt was completely saturated with blood. She pulled the glass from her arm and wrapped the wound as best she could. Her screams of pain were drowned by the noise of chaos outside.

Eventually, the gunfire was replaced by angry shouting.

The quieting thrum of whirling blades indicated that the approaching helicopter had landed. Two men dressed in camo fatigues burst through the door, holding a battering ram between them. Two more flanked them, approaching locked and loaded with semiautomatic rifles.

"Clear," one of them shouted. The two carrying the battering ram dropped it to the floor, and three of the four men fanned out through the small cabin. One came to her aid.

"Can you walk?"

The camo gear and blackened face obscured the identity of her friend—or foe. "Who are you?"

The reply didn't lessen the ambiguity of his status. "Someone who's hauling your sorry ass out of here."

CHAPTER 14

NATE

Nate looked back at what appeared to be an abandoned airstrip. Despite the runway landing, he knew it was a miracle they had arrived in one piece. He joined the pilot in performing a walk-around of the grounded aircraft. "I gotta hand it to you, Jerry, you sure have a gift for crash landings."

The pilot scratched his head. "Yeah—well—lots of practice. Fortunately, this isn't Nam. Though landing on someone's private property is heavily frowned upon."

Nate scanned the rugged terrain. "Considering the circumstance, I think you'll be forgiven. Do you know where we are?"

"We'd just entered Utah airspace over the Dixie National Forest when I started having the engine trouble. I reduced my altitude as soon as I realized we weren't going to make VGT. I kept us aligned with I-15 hoping we could glide into St. George airport. That plan went to shit when the second engine failed."

"So where are we?"

"I believe this is Hurricane Mesa. The Virgin River's in that direction. This, I think, is the abandoned supersonic military air research track facility. It's where they tested ejection seat systems after World War II."

"Well that's a lucky break."

"But by the grace of God. A little further west and we would have been in the Red Cliffs National Conservation Area; east, we'd have been in Zion. There would have been no place to land in either."

Nate nodded. "Were you able to radio in a mayday?"

"Yup. They dispatched a search and rescue team from St. George as soon as I told them about the engine trouble. ETA should be less than an hour."

"What do you suggest we do in the meantime?"

"As soon as I determine it's safe, we'll reboard the plane and sit tight. We've got ample food and water. Even so, we'll initiate desert survival protocol. We might not be very far from civilization, but it's no time to get cocky. People have underestimated the desert environment before and died under better circumstances than ours."

Nate agreed. "I'll be back to check out the engines in a minute. First, I want to let the women know the plan and check on our little stowaway."

Jerry held up his hands. "Why all the secrecy about the kid anyway?"

"Her life's in danger. The fewer people who know her whereabouts, the safer for the people involved."

"Well, that cover is about to be blown. As soon as the SAR team gets here it'll be headline news. How do you propose we keep her safe from the media?"

"First things first. Let's get the jet stabilized, then I'll figure it out."

Gem, the flight attendant, and the young girl sat with the two dogs a few hundred yards away in the blistering sun. The lot of them looked like wilting flowers in a ceramic pot left too long in the August sun. Perhaps it was stress from realizing they'd just survived a crash. In any case, reboarding the jet had become the ultimate priority. Nate checked his watch, his mind drifting to Mony and Massey. How close were they to accomplishing their mission? He cast his eyes upward. "Please, let one of us be successful."

"What did you say?" Gem asked, mopping her forehead with the back of her arm.

Looking at her, Nate couldn't help thinking that for a woman who lived in a desert climate, she looked the worst of any of them. "I said, the captain is doing his visual safety inspection as fast as he can. He'll cue us when it's okay to reboard."

"And then what?"

"Then we wait until search and rescue gets here from St. George."

"St. George? That's two hours from Vegas. I'm supposed to be in Vegas within the hour."

Ignoring her, Nate turned to the young girl. "Where am I supposed to be taking you?"

The girl simply sat quietly, petting her dog.

"Hey, be nice," said Gem. "Don't take it out on the kid."

Nate softened his tone. "You're Sissy Moonbeam's little sister, right?"

The girl stayed focused on her dog, who now traded affection back, nervously licking its human protector's hand. "I'm Lilly, but people who know me call me Lil Sis. Did your brother drive the white van or the nice truck?"

Nate was confused by the question. "My brother doesn't own a white van."

"Oh, then he was the one with the nice truck. He said that Finch and I were going to stay with a nice lady who has a ranch and horses."

"When was the last time you saw Finch?"

"Two nights ago, by the lake."

Nate rubbed his hand through his hair. *Jesus Christ.* "Do you know what happened to him?"

Gem butted in. "What's wrong with her coming to Vegas with us? I'm sure Trevor can find a safe place for the girl to hang out for a while."

"The last thing I need is to drag Trevor and the rest of the band into the middle of my mess."

"Middle?" Gem snorted. "My brother is mixed up with a bunch of murderers, I know about your little stowaway—and I'm a passenger onboard your sabotaged jet. That already qualifies being in the middle. Besides, you know Trevor can help you."

"We don't know that it's sabotage, and . . . it's complicated."

"Well, uncomplicate it."

Nate and Gem looked over at Lil Sis, who'd taken an interest in the conversation. "Why can't I go to Las Vegas with you?" she asked. "As long as the dogs can stay with me, I don't mind."

A smirk bloomed across Gem's lips. "I'm liking this girl already."

Having neither the energy nor the mood to argue, Nate walked back to the jet. Unless he found a direct flight from St. George to Parker, any way he looked at it, Gem would likely get her way. Any flight would have to pass through Las Vegas in order to get to his mother's ranch. It was either that or drive—though he had to admit, having just survived a crash landing, driving was looking more like a viable option.

His exterior inspection of the turbines revealed no significant evidence of uncontained engine damage. Perhaps it was because the pilot had decreased his altitude and managed to successfully land the aircraft, averting further disaster. Turbine engine failure typically occurred with an unexpected stop in rotation, usually due to a malfunction or fuel exhaustion. Nate had checked the fuel gauge when he was in the cockpit before the crash, and its readings were on point—that narrowed the cause to an interior mechanical failure. He called to the pilot, who'd been inspecting the landing gear below him. "Hey, Jerry, before the second engine failure, didn't you say it seemed like something was blocking the fuel flow?"

"Yeah, I tried to gain some altitude and my forward speed just choked. I started gliding at that point."

Nate grabbed a tac light and mirror from the tool chest and opened the hatch to the engine chamber to get a closer look. He was immediately accosted by a distinct odor of chemical contaminant. Sure enough, there was evidence of an oil leak and a damaged fuel pump. Nate shook his head in disgust. This was a huge miss, even for a rookie on a preflight visual inspection.

"Was Karl hungover this morning when he did the pre-flight visual?" he hollered. Karl Lindgren was a former Air Force pal of Buddy and his dad's. After his discharge, they'd hired Karl as a mechanic. He'd been on the F&A payroll for years and was a trusted friend.

Jerry stuck his head through the engine chamber door. "Karl didn't do it."

"What do you mean?"

"Didn't you hear? Karl's wife was in a bad accident on her way to her shift at Mercy Hospital early this morning. Some asshole sideswiped her passing on the highway, then ran her into the ditch. Thank God she was driving the truck. Anyway, she was airlifted to the trauma center in Bismarck. I'd heard she'd been taken into surgery before takeoff. I don't know her condition."

"Well, shit. Why didn't you tell me?"

"You seemed pretty preoccupied with your own issues when you boarded. I figured I could tell you about it after we'd landed in Vegas, since there wasn't much you could have done about it anyway."

"Who the hell did the preflight visual?"

"You'll have to check in with the ground crew at Sloulin. And before you get your underwear in a knot, everyone knows you like your own people taking care of the jet, but on such short notice, I'm sure they grabbed whoever was available."

Not only did the narrative read like sabotage, but there was objective evidence to prove it. Gem's assertion was spot-on. "Do we have electrical power back up in the cabin?"

"Not quite. I still have a few things to check out before I bring the power back online. Why?"

Nate pulled out the cell phone in his pocket. "I need to tell Dad to find out who serviced the jet." He climbed back out of the cramped engine chamber and held his phone in the air, looking for a signal. *Nothing.* He scanned the nearby terrain. "I'm going to try to get on top of those buildings over there and see if I can get a signal."

"For Christ's sakes," Jerry protested. "I'll have the power back up in fifteen minutes tops. Can't it wait?"

"I wish it could, but every second counts. We're going to have company soon, and not just the SAR team. As soon as the media catches wind of this, the place will be crawling with reporters. Lilly and I need to be long gone before then. Besides, I promised Mony I'd check in the second there was trouble. If I fail this time, she's liable to kill me."

"Here." Jerry tossed him his water canteen. "Take that with you. It would be embarrassing if you became dehydrated before the rescue team arrives."

Nate had hiked the quarter mile toward some concrete buildings when he heard the dogs barking. He turned around and saw Shep and Rainstorm coming up fast on his heels, with Lilly chasing from behind. "Wait for me, Nate."

He stopped to let them catch up. "You should stay with the others near the jet. It's the safest place to be right now."

Lilly bent forward and rested her hands on her thighs, catching her breath. "I go—where the dogs—go."

"Fair enough. Take the dogs with you back to the jet."

"They want to follow you."

Nate was in no mood to argue with a tween. "But you're not. The dogs will be fine. They'll come back when I come back."

"Where are you going?"

"Just over to that building. I want to get on top of it. I'm trying to get a signal so I can make a call."

As Nate started walking, his three companions followed. He stopped and spun to face them. "No, really. I promise to bring the dogs back. They can keep up with the pace. This may be too much for you."

The defiant tween crossed her arms. "That's what Finch promised—then he left them loose and abandoned them. He told me we couldn't keep them. Said we didn't have enough food to feed them."

Nate tried not to smile at her obstinance. "If it's food and water you're worried about, there's a fifty-pound bag of dog food back on the jet. Besides, had I been in the other guy's shoes, I'd have probably done the same thing." As Lilly glared at him with disdain, he sighed and held up his hands in surrender. "Look, I don't know your dog, but I know Shep. He's a guard dog, fiercely loyal and protective."

"A warrior."

Her description made him chuckle. "Yes, you could

say that. But he also has an uncanny sense of smell. I've gone hunting with this dog. He can sniff out prey a couple hundred yards away, and he's a terrific tracker. That nose led him and your dog straight back to Mony's farm."

Lilly scratched Shep behind the ear. "Mony said he was smart."

"He's very smart. So you don't have to worry about me running them off. They're both loyal to you now. They'll come back."

"If they are loyal to me, why are they following you?"

The hairs prickled on the nape of his neck. *Good question.*

Shielding his eyes, Nate scanned the horizon. It felt like they were out in the middle of nowhere. Located on a flat-top mountain, the airstrip seemed to have no clear way on or off except by plane. There wasn't much for sound, except the occasional screech of a predatory bird and insects buzzing. But when he listened closely, he could hear a thrum of traffic from somewhere below the mountain. He couldn't see beyond the rock formation east of the valley. To the west lay the Virgin River, and a mountain range beyond that. The community of St. George was south, the direction their rescue team would approach.

Lilly's hand shot out in front of her. "What's making that big dust cloud over there?"

He stared long and hard in the direction the girl was pointing. Something was moving fast just below the rim of the mesa out of visual range. "Fuck me." He got down on one knee and grabbed Lilly by the arms. "Listen. You take the dogs and keep going to that building over there." He pointed. "See?"

Lilly dumbly nodded.

"I want you to hunker down—you know, hide and keep the dogs quiet. I don't know if these guys are friend or enemy, but I'm not taking any chances. You stay put until I come and get you."

He stood, and Lilly grabbed his hand. "No. Your brother said you have to stay with me. They're bad people. I know it. The dogs know it too."

"I have to warn the others. I—"

"It's too late for that. Look."

Two Humvees painted in desert camouflage had crested the rim of the mountain and were heading toward the jet. It wasn't search and rescue. SAR would approach from the air.

"They'll see you coming," Lilly cried. "You can't help the others if they see you."

"I can't just leave them."

"You have to. Look, the two girls are already running toward the jet. Captain Jerry will protect them."

Nate's conscience wouldn't allow it. "If I don't come back, head toward the river. The pilot said there's a town nearby. Take my phone and the water canteen. If you get a signal, press the name that says Kip."

"Who?"

"Kip, Kip. That's my dad. He'll know how to get you to safety."

"But I don't want—"

"This is nonnegotiable, Lilly. You go. Now."

The girl broke out into tears. "Massey promised you

would protect me, whatever it takes. Are you making him a liar?"

God, this kid sure knows how to play hardball. Nate looked back across the airstrip at the scene about to unfold. The girl was right. Not only was Jerry a decorated Vietnam combat pilot, he was an active member on the SAR unit back home in North Dakota. If anyone could help them, it was him. "All right, stay low. Let's go."

Nate wished he'd have grabbed a set of binoculars and more water before leaving the plane. As it was, the van-tage point on top of the building was over a mile away. Angry shouts echoed as men exited the Humvees, carry-ing what appeared to be assault rifles. *Where in Sam Hill is search and rescue?* The jet had to have been grounded for over thirty minutes by now—surely they couldn't be too far off.

The shouting continued, followed by the unmistakable reverberation of a semiautomatic round. No movement came from in or around the plane. More shots rang out as five men fanned out around the aircraft. Nate wanted to look away, turn and run. He couldn't.

Lilly whispered to him, "I think I hear a helicopter coming."

There came the sound of a handgun firing off six rounds. Two of the five men immediately fell to the ground. Nate's jubilation was short lived, as two more men exited the Humvee. "Christ, how many of these fuckers are there?"

The helicopter Lilly had heard came into view, flanked by two single-engine Cessnas. The siren system echo-ing off the mountain walls was deafening. Despite the altitude, the rescue crew had to be in visual range of the ambush waiting on the ground. Nate saw three of the five men running for cover near a shroud of shrubs. The two remaining made their way toward the right turbine engine. *What the hell are they up to?*

Nate's question was answered by the sound of semi-automatic fire peppering the left side of the jet commanding all the attention. Lilly sat beside him with her hands clasped over her ears. From this distance, the noise wasn't so much loud as it was menacing. The two rogue assassins continued to creep closer to the starboard engine.

The alpha helicopter blared over the PA system. "This is commander Santana of the Nellis Air Force Base, escorting the Utah Civil Air Patrol search and rescue. Cease fire. I repeat: cease fire. We are responding to a distress call. We have no hostile intent. We will, however, retaliate if fired upon." The commander repeated his warning several times before the Cessnas broke formation.

Advancing from the north, the Cessnas aligned with the fallen craft and made their approach while the helicopter rained down a round of cover fire upon the assassins. It was like shooting fish in a barrel. No further activity came from the three men hiding in the bushes as the jet fired shots at the two rogue assassins. Nate couldn't be sure the two approaching Cessnas had been aware of the splintered faction, but he wasn't going to chance it.

Taking the mirror he'd used to examine the engine chamber from his pocket, Nate flashed it at the helicopter. His Morse code wasn't worth shit, so he simply covered and uncovered the surface of the mirror. The tactic must have gained the pilot's attention. The Cessna approaching the starboard side of the jet broke off its landing approach as more gunfire erupted, this time from a semiautomatic handgun. *Someone else besides the pilot has a firearm.* Whoever it was found their target, as one more assassin fell to the ground.

With flaps fully deployed, it took several hundred feet before the second Cessna came to an effective stop. The helicopter rained down additional gunfire as the rescue team deplaned and made their way quickly to the main cabin door. Flanked by the flight attendant and Gem, the pilot stood at the main cabin hatch. Even at a distance, it was clear their family friend was in trouble. "Jerry's hurt," Nate told Lilly.

The girl chose to rejoin Nate in watching the rescue. Unyielding in duty, the flight attendant supported Jerry, letting Gem slide down the emergency chute first. She waited at the bottom, but one of the rescuers whisked her off and hurried toward the Cessna. Camilla moved Jerry into position next. An explosion in the starboard engine catapulted Camilla and Jerry forward, sending them into a free fall halfway down the escape shoot. They tumbled the rest of the way to the ground, where Jerry lay unmoving. Gem screamed as she boarded the Cessna.

Gunfire broke out in the direction of the cluster of brush. Both the rescuer and Gem fell to the ground. Nate shot up from his hiding place, and Lilly grabbed his arm. "Don't leave me," she screamed. Another explosion rocked the jet, this time severing the wing from the fuselage.

Nate fell to his knees, horrified by the sight he was

witnessing. Good people were dying. Dying because of his cowardice. "This is all my fault. If I'd have been there, no one would have had to die."

Lilly squatted next to him. "You don't know your friends are dead. And even if you had turned yourself over to those bad men, how do you know they wouldn't have killed all of us anyway?"

This child was wise for her years. Nate took his last look at the disaster. "Come on, Lilly, we need to move."

CHAPTER 15

JOHN

His condition upgraded from critical to serious, John had been cleared for questioning. He'd just finished a nebulizer treatment when Detective Gomez pulled back the privacy curtain to his ER cubicle. The emergency physician had reiterated his recommendation that John should be sent to a higher-level critical care facility and receive proper medical attention, but John had informed both the doctor and the detective he wasn't going anywhere.

He'd brought the detective up to speed on everything he remembered about his captivity. Gomez had showed no emotion when she learned that Sissy Moonbeam was still alive and in on the caper; nor had she batted an eye when he told her Mitchell had been severely tortured and likely left for dead somewhere. It was also during their discussion that John learned too late of Ramona and Matthew's failed rescue attempt on his behalf. Their actions confounded him. Everyone involved should have known it was a blatant trap. *Why would they risk their lives—for me?*

John had been moved to a recovery suite by the time Matthew Ferguson's rescue chopper arrived in Shelby. The senator was there too, having flown in from Williston just minutes before his son. John was shocked by the lawyer's appearance as the rescue team wheeled him to the critical care unit. His head and face were covered in blood from an apparent blow to the head, and an angry contusion bloomed over his right eye. John glanced over at the senator, uncertain who would require more immediate medical attention, father or son. The elder Ferguson had an unhealthy, sallow sheen to his skin, and his breathing became erratic as he followed behind the gurney.

Despite his appearance, the gods had been smiling down on Matthew Ferguson that day. A passing semi-truck driver, Gomez informed John, had glanced in his side mirror just as the lawyer hit the pavement. He'd slammed on the brakes and run back to help the detective's team as they arrived on the scene. However, help had come too late for Ramona. The semi driver had reported finding Ramona's cell phone smashed on the ground as an unidentified truck fled the scene into the backcountry. The only silver lining in any of this, according to the detective, was that Matthew and Ramona had been microchipped just prior to the event in preparation for worst-case scenario.

She wasn't fooling John. He knew a tracker wasn't protection—only a means of finding a body, alive or deceased.

As if none of this was bad enough, John completely lost

his shit when rescuers wheeled his tormentor through the bay doors of the ER. He had a large gauze wrapping on his leg, oozing bright red blood. Consumed with fury, John approached the invalid, ready to kick the living shit out of him. A security guard intervened.

"I swear to God," John hissed at the Indian, "if you've harmed Ramona in any way, it'll take more than paltry hospital security to stop me from killing you."

The big Indian looked up at him and laughed in his face. "You and Miss Smart Mouth must be a couple. If she's hurt, it's because her own rescue team opened fire on the location where she'd been safely secured."

John wanted to punch the fucking liar in the teeth.

Detective Gomez came up to the security guard. "Can you direct us somewhere private? I need to speak with Mr. Finch."

The rehashing of events did nothing to diminish John's anger or anxiety regarding the botched rescue attempt. "This is bullshit. You mean to tell me no one saw who took her? How the fuck does that happen?"

Despite her youth and beauty, it was easy to read the detective's anguish. Marred with stress lines and darkened circles around her eyes, she looked as if she hadn't slept in weeks. John tempered his anger—he knew Gabriella was doing everything humanly possible to find Ramona. In a softer tone, he asked, "Do we at least know if she's alive?"

"Nothing is for certain, but we believe so. We're tracking the signal from the implanted device. They're presently following an abandoned in-road that parallels Highway 89 going north into Glacier National Park backcountry."

"What about communication?"

She shook her head. "The kidnappers found the wire plant and neutralized it with extreme prejudice."

"That's not what I meant. Has anyone tried to contact you?"

"No."

"How do you know they're not hauling a corpse?"

The detective bristled. "She's worth nothing to them dead."

"That depends on what they want—money, revenge, all of the above."

"We know what Sissy wants—"

"Yeah, her little sister. Ramona can't help with that. The kid ran off the night I was abducted."

"Not exactly." The detective informed him how the sister had been found the next day, camped out by the lake.

John felt a glimmer of hope. "Well, then hand her over in exchange for Ramona. Everyone wins."

"It's. . . complicated." The detective proceeded to bring him up to speed on the F&A plane crash and ground attack. "We've been informed that the pilot's in critical condition. Gem Richards and the flight attendant, Camilla Barnes, are being held overnight for observation for injuries sustained during the engine explosion."

"Well, shit. What happened to the little sister and Ferguson?"

"Those two and both dogs are missing."

John's brows shot up. "Dogs? What dogs? And what do you mean, missing?"

"The usual. Gone—vanished—not at the crash site—missing." She let out a deep breath, tempering her own anger.

No wonder the senator looked like hell. His entire family has been taken from him in the span of a few hours. John genuinely felt sorry for the guy. He changed his tone as well as his attitude. "What can I do to help, Detective?"

Matthew Ferguson was lying on a gurney in the radiology waiting area, a mummy-like gauze dressing encasing the crown of his head. John walked over to him and said, "You and I need to talk."

The orderly standing cross-armed beside Ferguson looked at John like he was a bug. "Beat it, asshole, before I call hospital security."

Ferguson raised his hand. "It's all right, Alex. This is my friend, John. He's been working with us to rescue my sister. Can you take us somewhere private?"

John and Matthew exchanged their respective accounts of chasing Sissy Moonbeam across the state of Montana. When each had finished, John said, "You realize if the kid hadn't run off that night by the lake, we wouldn't even be in this mess. Sissy and her goon were waiting to grab the kid, not me. When that failed, they improvised."

"I disagree. I think kidnapping Mony was always the primary objective, at least for the big Indian. Abducting you was simply a means to an end. He wants something from her. This whole ransom thing didn't evolve on the fly. It's too well planned, evident by the elaborate road-block set up to delay Gomez's response team." The attorney winced when he shook his head. "At first, I was convinced Monroe had been behind it. Now, I'm not so sure."

"Why is that?"

"I don't believe any member of the Three Affiliated Tribes community would be cooperating with Monroe Oil. Man, after what you told me about Sissy, Mony's going to have an uphill battle protecting the younger sister."

John furled his eyebrow. "How can she protect what she doesn't have? Shit, I can't believe I was supposed to be on that plane."

"What do you mean?"

He shared with Ferguson what the detective had told him about the plane crash. "I got to tell you, there is no love lost between me and your brother, but what I'm about to say doesn't mean I wish him ill will—everything in this major clusterfuck points to Jason's style of hostile takeover. I mean, two of your company's three owners are missing. What the hell are you going to do?"

Before Ferguson could reply, the orderly returned to collect his patient. "Mr. Ferguson, they're ready for you."

"Thanks, Alex." To John he said, "We'll continue our discussion shortly."

The CT scan ruled out a brain bleed as well as a skull fracture. It was nothing short of a miracle. If the scan had shown any abnormality, or worse, that Ferguson required surgery, it would have been off to Billings. Even so, the lawyer had suffered a severe concussion, requiring rest and close observation for the next forty-eight hours. He and the senator showed up at the detective's debriefing anyway. Matthew instructed the orderly to park his wheelchair next to John. The senator took the chair on the other side of his son. Detective Gomez began by addressing John.

"Mr. Finch, I've spoken with Sheriff Wagner and the North Dakota justice department. You have been officially cleared as a suspect in the murder of Shannon McDonald. Your record will bear no mark of illegal misconduct. The Bureau has seen to it that your former employer will reinstate your position with the law firm without penalty and compensation for work time lost. Your cooperation with this investigation has been invaluable. As soon as we're finished here, you and I will discuss arrangements for your transportation back to Chicago, along with any resources you require."

John blew out a sharp breath. He should have been elated by the news. During his three months of living in hell, going home was all he'd thought about. Now that normalcy was within grasp, he wasn't sure he wanted it.

"We will focus on the kidnapper, Todd Blankenship, aka 'Fox Can't Be Caught.' He's been on the Bureau's radar for the past two years, and—"

John interrupted, "Wait just a goddamn minute. What about Ramona?"

The detective's voice went flat. "The search continues for Ms. Strong. Her tracker indicates they're still on the move. What I was about to point out is that it wasn't happenstance Fox Can't Be Caught sustained a non-life-threatening gunshot wound. He is a decorated Navy Seal veteran. We believed he used himself as a diversion to help his female companions escape with Ms. Strong."

John threw up his hands. "If you know where she is, go get her."

Her jaw tightening, Gomez replied, "We can't risk another failed rescue attempt. The abductors don't know Ms. Strong has a tracker implant, giving us the element of surprise. Our timing must be impeccable."

"Agreed, but you can't let them choose when and where to make a stand."

"We won't, John," Matthew interjected, "but if we can get him to talk, this Blankenship may hold valuable information on how we can achieve a win-win outcome. Detective, tell us more about this fellow."

Gomez appeared grateful for the lifeline. "Todd Blankenship, or Fox Can't Be Caught, is an organizer dedicated to protecting the environment and advocates for the recovery of missing and exploited Indigenous women and children. He'd recently brought various tribes together this past April to successfully protest a white supremacist group holding a jamboree in a small community southwest of Bismarck. The man possesses a wealth of inside knowledge regarding the illicit activities happening in North Dakota."

"Sounds like the sort of guy we'd want on our team," John muttered. "But explain how a guy like this goes from advocating for the protection of exploited Indigenous women to kidnapping?"

"Todd has . . . unconventional methods of operation. Allegations surfaced this past winter of his potential involvement in a rescue and retrieval mission of five Indian women from a man camp near Sidney, Montana. It was a bloody, gruesome mess. Several of the camp's male residents were found scalped. We're not sure if that was before or after they'd been castrated. Seven men died of hypovolemic shock. One died later in the hospital from tetanus poisoning and septicemia. When the community learned what had been done to those women during their captivity and the matter in which it was managed, folks turned a blind eye to the whole affair. The man camp was dismantled, and the investigation fizzled out."

"Vigilante justice," the senator muttered.

"Sounds like the bastards got what they deserved," John said with vehemence.

"The situation remedied—it seems that's how the local folks regarded it as well. Todd may or may not have been involved with the rescue, but it fits his MO. He fell off the radar until resurfacing as the organizer of the protest against the Nazi group, then disappeared until today."

"That doesn't answer the question: why turn to kidnapping?"

"We'll know those answers after we talk to him. He's being treated for a minor gunshot wound, then transferred to the Shelby correctional facility, where he will be detained until we decide what to do with him."

John considered Todd Blankenship's history. Initially,

it seemed at odds with what he'd witnessed of the man. *Or does it?* The big Indian had to be aware of Sissy's mistreatment at the hands of Dwight Mitchell and Harland Richards. John had suffered the misfortune of being present during Mitchell's final justice; Sissy had made a vow that Harland Richards was next. John tried not to picture what sort of "justice" was awaiting that son of a bitch. "Does the Bureau have grounds to hold Blankenship?"

Gomez blinked in surprise. "So far, we have two counts of kidnapping as well as obstructing, then fleeing a crime scene. There's the physical assault on Mr. Ferguson. So, yeah, there's plenty to hold him."

"Have any charges been officially filed?"

The detective seemed perplexed by the question. "Well, no, not officially, yet. What are you getting at, Mr. Finch?"

"I'm considering all the ways in which we can motivate him to talk." Maybe Sissy Moonbeam wasn't the linchpin to Monroe's downfall after all—*but this Blankenship fellow certainly could be.*

Matthew sat in front of a vending machine. "So, Counselor," John asked him, "where do we go from here?"

Ferguson pushed the Diet Pepsi button. "It may sound unorthodox, but I think we need to get this Blankenship fellow on our side."

John smiled. "Have you heard how the detective's interrogation is going?"

Ferguson cracked open his soda can with a hiss. "Not so good. The guy hasn't uttered a word."

John fished for a dollar bill in his pocket. "Do you think we could talk the detective into letting us take a crack at him? I may have something that might sway Blankenship's cooperation. If he has knowledge of illicit activities happening in the man camps, he might have something tangible on Monroe."

Ferguson inserted several quarters into the machine. "Pick your poison."

John pushed for a bottled water, cracked it open, and took a gulp. "More importantly, do you think Ramona will go along with it?"

The attorney lifted an eyebrow. "That will depend on what happens to her or Sissy during their detention. If Blankenship or anyone has harmed Sissy in any way to gain her cooperation, I doubt Mony will go along with any of it. She has zero tolerance for abusive men, especially ones who would harm a kid."

John thought about the slap Blankenship had given Sissy in the cab. "The guy's got a temper." But Sissy had a dark side too. Ramona needed to stop thinking of the girl as some feral kitten in need of a saucer of milk and get with reality. "The one I'm more worried about is the Moonbeam girl. If she's in on the whole thing, and I think she is, I doubt she'll give us the time of day."

Ferguson took a guzzle of his soda and smiled. "John, when are you going to learn to stop underestimating Mony? Can't you see? She's holding the ace card—the one thing Sissy wants."

John thought Ferguson overly confident. "We don't have her."

"We will, soon enough."

"And how, pray tell, do you know this?"

"I've already spoken with Nate. He, the girl, and the two dogs are safe for now."

"Okay. When do we talk to the detective?"

"Already done. I'm heading over to the correctional facility right now. Care to join me?"

John didn't even have to think about it. "Most definitely."

"Good, cuz you're driving."

CHAPTER 16

MASSEY

Because of his head injury, Massey had to relinquish the wheel of his RV to John. He managed to hold comment at the inept handling of the large diesel rig until the driver negotiated the security gates of the prison. "You're lucky it's a Mercedes," he said with a nervous laugh.

His driver had other things on his mind. With a low whistle, John exclaimed, "Wow, what a shithole. I've seen my share of correctional centers—Joliet, Cook—but this . . ."

Just west of Shelby, the privately operated facility was the only prison of its kind in the state. Opened in 1999, it had been built for a capacity of 664 men and assigned as multi-security. The walls had long since exceeded the maximum limit. The joint housed notoriety— a former NFL quarterback who'd been caught breaking into a Montana residence to steal prescription drugs, for one. There was the usual corruption; managed by a for-profit conglomerate, the facility had been the center of controversy over the years. There were allegations of hiring inadequate and untrained staff in an apparent attempt to save money—those savings went toward expenses such as extensive lobbying, bribes for governing officials, and legal costs. Violence among inmates went unchecked, along with the lack of appropriate medical care. A recent case filed against the facility was investigating the premature death of a medical marijuana provider who had died only a few months into his sentence. Mental health care for prisoners was nonexistent.

"I've been here once," Massey said, pointing out a place to park. "Wait until you get inside. You'll want to burn your clothes and shower as soon as you get out."

"I can't wait," John replied.

Todd Blankenship, aka Fox Can't Be Caught, sat in a small detention room, his hands cuffed and chained to the interview table. He was a big man, bigger than Massey had first thought. Hunched over the truck engine, he hadn't really gotten a good look at Blankenship before the other man had knocked him over the head. Entering the room, it was daunting how the man seemed to suck out all the oxygen. John had picked up on the vibe as well. It was him the detainee looked up at as they entered.

"Look at you, standing all upright. I told the feisty woman I didn't kill you. She wouldn't believe me."

As Massey and John took the chairs across the table from the incarcerated man, Massey noticed John's left leg begin to involuntarily shake. He tried to ignore it. "Mony doesn't place much stock in the word of a child abuser. Why would she believe you?"

"Did she tell you that?"

The question surprised Massey. "Are you saying you didn't strike Sissy in the truck cab?"

Avoiding eye contact, Blankenship leaned back, a mild expression of remorse tarnishing his face. "I react badly when people speak disrespectfully."

"That doesn't answer the question," John interjected.

Blankenship looked at him and smirked. "And you! You're one lucky son of a bitch. Did Sissy and I treat you so bad you had to play chicken with a train? I'd have let you go once I had the money."

"Same way you let Mitchell go?"

The Indian scowled. "Mitchell got what he deserved for what he'd done to my Sissy."

"Sissy won't be yours for long."

"She will *always* be my Sissy."

Massey took over the conversation. "Do you know Mony Strong is planning to take both of the Moonbeam girls?"

Blankenship snorted. "I doubt that."

"Do you seriously believe you're the only one playing charades?"

The Indian grimaced. "The feisty woman has no legal standing. It doesn't matter what game she plays."

"A child defined as abandoned does not require permission from the family to adopt."

At that, Blankenship's cool composure faltered. "The state has no jurisdiction over Native American child proceedings. Those girls belong to the tribe. The Indian Child Welfare Act ensures the tribes can and must act as parents for their children in the absence of biological parents. It is required that preference be given to tribal communities when children can no longer live in their homes. AIM has advocated for this self-determination. Their father, my brother in arms, had many friends in his community. Any member of the Three Affiliated Tribes would be honored to raise the girls. They will receive preference. But being a white lawyer, you know all that. Sissy and Lil Sis will be cared for. We have the right to intervene in adoption and foster care."

"Is that what the money was for—to secure these proceedings? Does the tribe have enough resources to properly raise these two girls?"

Blankenship didn't respond.

"Mony will win. Grandmother Moonbeam has already declared her a 'fictive kin,' after Mony agreed to pay for the old woman's medical expenses." Massey removed the document from his shirt pocket and handed it to Todd. "She has a positive relationship with both the girls, and is both willing and more than capable of providing a suitable home."

Blankenship brushed the document aside. "Looks like she's pulling the old 'kill the Indian, save the child' scheme. Leave it to wasicu law to twist the role of the Indian community and meddle in a culture they don't understand."

"Do you really think there's a court of law that would willingly hand those two girls over to a rapist?" John broke in.

The Indian barked out a laugh. "Is that what you think I am?"

"It's what I know."

"And how do you know this?"

"I was there in the room when you raped Mitchell."

"Oh—tell me, what did you see?"

John's face turned fire red. "You know I didn't see anything. It's what I heard."

"Tell me, then, what did you hear?"

John sat quiet. It seemed Massey's partner hadn't divulged all the details about his captivity. Leaning toward Finch, Massey whispered, "Counselor, a word—"

"What in the Sam Hill is wrong with you, throwing a curveball at a time like this?" Massey growled at Finch in an adjacent room. "We were supposed to be on the same team, coercing Fox Can't Be Caught to our side. Remember?"

"Threatening to take the children—that was part of your grand plan? How'd that work out for you?"

Massey had intended to use the information not as a threat so much as a bargaining tool, but John's revelation that Todd may have been involved in sexual violence was a dealbreaker, especially where Mony was concerned. It didn't matter that it had been done to an adversary, or that Mitchell had probably deserved it. Mony would never concede the children's welfare to such an unsavory character. "John, tell me now, did or didn't Blankenship violate Mitchell? And for Christ's sakes, where did you last see him?"

Finch revealed Mitchell's whole story, from the time of his own capture to when he'd been carried away. "I heard the threat, but I didn't actually see anything. They'd placed a sack over my head before they got started on him. Man, if it wasn't rape, it sounded damn convincing."

"Perhaps that was the point: to look or sound convincing."

"What do you mean?"

"I'm thinking about what Detective Gomez said about Blankenship. Castration would seem more his style, not rape. Humiliation would be fair game. Videos and pictures can easily be altered with the right equipment."

"And be just as damaging."

"Exactly." Massey scratched his chin. "Enough of this cloak-and-dagger business. We need to ask direct questions and share what we know to work out an agreement."

"A lawyer playing it honest. That's a new twist."

"I don't see how we can build trust any other way."

When Massey and Finch reentered the room, Blankenship sat with his eyes closed, chanting quietly. The lawyers stood for several minutes, honoring the prayer; then the Indian opened his eyes. "I did not rape Mitchell or kill him—though by now, he'll wish I had. And your feisty woman is in charge of her own safety as long as she cooperates."

"Cooperates with what, exactly?"

"She'll know when the time comes."

"Sounds cryptic. You have no idea of her status or her safety."

Blankenship lifted his cuffed wrists. "You can see I don't have access to the current situation."

Massey changed the subject. "Did you murder Shannon McDonald or Cindy Van Dyke?"

"The redhead and the social worker? No. Sissy deserves to be with her sister and live with her people."

"Do you work for Monroe Oil?"

"That cocksucker? He is my mortal enemy."

Massey and John exchanged a glance. "All right, then," said Massey. "I have a proposal, but first things first." He reached into his pocket to retrieve a packet of cured organic tobacco and began sprinkling the loose leaves onto three pieces of paper. "I need to bring you up to speed on a few things," he said, talking between each cigarette roll. "You're perceptive enough to know we are not your enemy, but we share a common one."

"All wasicu are the enemy."

"Then we're an enemy you'll want to keep closer. You understand the woman you call 'feisty'—her concern for the children's welfare, misguided as it may be, is genuine. Mony Strong will do everything within her power to keep them safe despite your protest, or theirs. It will be up to you to prove the tribe can achieve the goal of providing for them and keeping them safe. Kidnapping her isn't helping your cause."

For a while, Blankenship just stared; then, looking down at Massey's hands, he said, "We're not allowed to smoke inside the prison."

"Then we'll need to go somewhere where we can."

The three men sat at a picnic table in an abandoned

roadside rest area just outside the prison gates. Fox Can't Be Caught lifted his face to the sun, looking like a man who'd just been released from a life sentence to solitary confinement instead of a brief detention. John remained nervous. Massey took the cigarettes he'd rolled from his pocket; Blankenship accepted them and said, "Too bad we don't have time for a good sweat, but we'll make do."

He held the cigarettes up toward the sky and began to chant. Next, he held them low to the earth, then offered them up in the four directions. His manner was centered, his intent sincere. When he'd finished, he lit his cigarette first, then John's, then Massey's. It had been nearly three decades since Massey had smoked an unfiltered cigarette; the tendril of tobacco burned all the way down his throat and seemed to close off his airway. John, on the other hand, blew practiced smoke rings, looking the most relaxed he'd been all day.

Only when everyone had finished their smoke did Blankenship speak. "There is a simple solution to of all this. Lil Sis for your woman, and we can call it even."

"There is nothing simple about this situation," Massey countered. "Not only have you managed to piss off the one person with the authority to give you money or the child, you've demonstrated your dispassion toward violence. Nothing moves forward without Mony's say, and she will never trust you without an extreme show of faith."

"I'm a warrior—of course I am comfortable with violence. I protect my people, whatever it takes."

Massey had no doubt about that. Blankenship held

strong convictions for what he believed in, a quality to be admired. The issue was his deplorable habit of physical violence. Massey was versed in a diplomatic approach, using words to defend and protect. "We need to find common ground for either of us to get what we want."

"You already know what I want, negotiator. What do you want?"

"I believe you can help solve two murders in Williston."

"That's what you lead with? What about your feisty woman?"

"As you pointed out, Mony's well-being is in her own hands."

The response seemed to unsettle Todd. "If I help you, what will you give me in return?"

"We got your ass out of jail—"

Massey threw John a silencing look. To Blankenship, he replied, "You need our help breaking up the human trafficking ring."

The Indian gave a harsh laugh. "Breaking the human trafficking ring is Sissy's mission."

"Sissy?"

"Do you think your feisty woman is the only one concerned about our young girls in the sex trade? My Sissy has sacrificed much to gather information on the ringleaders."

Massey reared his head back. "My God. She's so young."

"And determined. Your enemy, this Monroe—he has a mercenary, a Russki by the name of Kuznetsov, doing his dirty work. He is good at agitating the Nazis and making them do things. Sissy saw the Russki kill the social worker, though no one's sorry about that. Killed the redhead too—that might have been an accident. The sheriff was there, may have even pulled the trigger himself."

John was shocked by the revelation. "Wagner killed Shannon McDonald? That's got to be a lie."

"Sissy does many things, but she does not lie. She'd been working with him, up until the redhead was killed. She didn't like the woman much. Said the redhead was too bossy and should have picked better friends. She might still be alive."

"If breaking up the human trafficking ring isn't your mission," Massey asked, "what is? I mean, why kidnap John, then Mony? Why the ransom money?"

"My mission is simple. I support my people in driving out the white man any way I can. These man camps, drug dealers, murderers, and rapists are killing our communities. The false promise of fast money is turning our young people away from our traditional ways, addicting them to drugs and alcohol. Our way of life has been under attack for centuries through genocide and the theft of our children. It has to stop. A couple of million dollars would go a long way providing for our people."

Shaking his head, Massey ground the remains of his cigarette between his fingers. "You don't understand. Mony would have given you all those things without all this drama."

"No, negotiator. It's you who doesn't understand. Without this drama, you and I wouldn't even be talking."

As a black Suburban SUV carried Blankenship back

to the prison, Massey and John returned to Shelby, where Detective Gomez had moved her base of operations from the hospital to a local hotel. Kip sat at a table in front of a stone fireplace, Gomez next to him, their expressions solemn.

"What's going on, Dad?" asked Massey.

His father looked up from his soda. "We just got an update on the search for Nathan. He and the girl are missing from the crash site. It's been over an hour. The desert temperature is already 100 degrees and climbing. No one knows if they have water. The SAR team is getting desperate. I think one of us needs to go and look for him."

Massey turned to the detective. "Do you have someone you could send?"

"I already asked her that," Kip said. "She needs her team to find Mony. I've decided to fly to the crash site myself and join the search."

"Dad, you turn the AC on as soon as the temperature gets over seventy," Massey countered. "You're in no better shape than I am right now for such an arduous task."

Desperation showed on his father's face. "I—I can't just sit here and do nothing."

Gomez turned to John. "What about you? Since you're so determined to remain a part of all of this, you might as well make yourself useful."

"Me?" It was true, John had declined the detective's offer to return to Chicago, even after the phone conversation with his sister. Lyn had been furious with him—and fearful. But looking at him, Massey could tell the feeling of unfinished business gnawed at him like overactive gastric juices in his stomach. Still, he hesitated. "I mean, I meant it when I said I don't wish your brother ill will, but you know, I'm no tracker. I'm a navigator—on water. I read nautical charts, lake and weather patterns. I have no skill reading signs on dry land. Besides, your brother hates me."

The small group fell into an uncomfortable silence. Time was of the essence, and the level of trepidation weighed heavily around the table. Kip suggested, "Perhaps we can send our own SAR team from Williston, pay the expense."

"And tie up more resources?" the detective countered. "No. We just need one person for Nate to trust so he'll come in from the heat."

Something new suddenly occurred to Massey. "John, you don't have to be a tracker, just part of the team. The tracker I have in mind won't require convincing or a lot of money, just a moderately long leash."

Raising his eyebrows, John asked, "Are you suggesting what I think you're suggesting?"

"To earn trust, we have to give it."

"How in the hell can we be sure Blankenship won't cut and run as soon as they land?"

"Because his niece's life is tethered to Nate. He will find them."

John didn't look convinced, but the only further argument he offered was a shaky exhalation. "I hope to God you're right."

CHAPTER 17

JOHN

John hung on to the oh-shit bar as they traveled up a steep switchback road to the crash site. Passing himself off as Matthew Ferguson was easy compared to explaining what the hell Blankenship and the two custodial guards were doing there. The black suits, white shirts, and ties the latter pair wore made them look more like secret service members than part of an insurance adjuster's team. As for Blankenship, John hadn't even bothered giving him a backstory.

Ranger Daniels from the Hurricane Valley fire district had been assigned to meet the group; he and two other team members drove them directly to the crash site. The scene was anything but quiet. An FAA investigative team was already rummaging through the rubble, while a helicopter from a local news station roved the air above.

Up close and in person, John gave a low whistle as he gazed at what was left of the company jet. The wing and starboard engine lay scattered among the debris, as did most of the right side of the jet. Someone had really wanted to make certain Ferguson was taken out regardless of the collateral damage. "Je-sus *Christ*. It looks like a fuckin' war zone."

"What do you know about war?" Fox Can't Be Caught muttered with disdain.

Depends on the war, John thought, but kept the comment to himself.

Picking up on the tension, Daniels recounted what he knew about the incident. "After one of our sharpshooters neutralized the attackers, the SAR team tended the wounded. It took a while searching the wreckage before we realized anyone was missing."

Todd kicked at a piece of metal debris. "Who's missing?"

Daniels looked to John, confused. "Mr. Ferguson . . . I mean, Nathan Ferguson, of course. Isn't that why you're here?"

"What Mr. Blankenship is saying is, you have everyone accounted for on the flight except for Mr. Ferguson," John broke in. "Is that correct?"

"Well, yes. That, and we think two dogs might be with him."

"Dogs?"

"There are two wrecked dog kennels in the main cabin."

John looked skyward. "What does the media know?"

"We couldn't release much except that a private jet out of Williston, North Dakota, belonging to F&A Oil, had crashed near the Hurricane Cliffs area. Three members of the flight are hospitalized. There was a firefight at the crash site, and the search is continuing for additional survivors."

"Have you released any names?"

"No, not officially. Like I said, the media is assuming it's your brother who's missing."

"Anyone else?"

Daniels furrowed his eyebrow. "Should there be?"

"Mr. Blankenship and I are here to determine if anyone else may have been involved."

"You mean more attackers?"

John didn't answer.

The look of confusion on Daniels's face deepened. "Well, we did find two sets of human footprints alongside dog prints leading toward the outbuildings over there. Our speculation is that whoever made the tracks may have hunkered down there and then taken off sometime after the jet engine exploded. I guess they didn't want to wait and find out who won the skirmish."

"You have a funny notion of winning," Todd spat. "I heard someone died during the rescue."

A repentant look came over Daniels's face. "Regrettably, SAR team leader Della Welch took point and sustained a gunshot wound shattering her femur. Kyle Winters was caught in the crossfire. He will be grievously missed. Your pilot's in pretty rough shape too, in surgery as we speak. The two female passengers are recovering at Dixie Regional with contusions and first- and second-degree burns. Local law enforcement has assigned a guard to all three per a Detective Gomez with Arizona CID, until things can be sorted out."

"Has anyone updated Senator Ferguson on the progress?" John asked.

"Yeah, dispatch notified the senator directly about twenty minutes before your plane landed."

Fox Can't Be Caught wandered off in the direction the officer pointed. John followed two steps behind. The man was difficult to read. One minute he was all Zen-like, humming softly to himself the entire flight. Next, he was instigating an argument with the very team trying to help them.

You didn't have to be a tracker to see the dog and human tracks in the soft soil. The two men followed the foot-prints, which stopped at the edge of a small building. "It looks like you're correct about someone else being in-volved," Daniels told John. "There's a set of smaller foot-prints alongside your brother's, and he has the two dogs with him."

"Does anyone have any thoughts as to where the people who made these footprints may have been hiding?" John asked.

"The theory is they may have held up on top of the building," Daniels informed them. "With Virgin near the base of the mesa, they were probably going for help. We have a helicopter flying over the area. So far, no one's reported anyone walking around with two dogs."

The smell of urine still lingered at the base of the build-ing where the dogs had marked their territory. They fol-lowed the paw and foot tracks around the side of the building away from the crash. Blankenship was examin-ing a large rock propped below a window; John pointed to a smear of dirt on the rock and said, "It looks like they started here. A sweaty palm touched here—then moves in . . . this direction."

Blankenship looked at him with genuine surprise. "The way you are pointing is too steep for my niece's short legs." Todd proceeded to climb where John had pointed. He reached the roof of the small building, looked around, and said, "Humph—The kid must have grown an inch or two since I saw her last."

John climbed the same route and joined Blankenship, kicking at the loose gravel on the flat roof. Removing the canteen from his belt, he took a long drink. *Man, it's hot.* Other than a random puffy cloud, there was no reprieve from the blistering sun beating down on them.

Climbing up onto the roof, Officer Daniels mopped an arm across his forehead and said, "Whoever was here, they couldn't have gone far without water."

John was inclined to agree; the lateness of the day did nothing to diminish the intensity of the heat beating down on them. He shaded his eyes and checked the lay of the land. It was a scenic view. The airstrip where the jet had landed sat atop a wide, flat, elevated land formation with steep sides. The end of the airstrip actually dropped off at the edge of the cliff. If a pilot failed to keep the nose of the plane up, it was over a thousand-foot drop to the valley floor below. He asked Daniels, "Where is the closest town located?"

"Same way we came. Highway 9 follows along the mesa basin and runs through Virgin."

"And north?"

"Nothing. More mountains and a few scattered ranches in the valleys. On the other side of that mountain range west is Toquerville and I-15. Beyond that, you're getting into the Red Cliffs area. East are some hiking trails, then Zion. The mesa overlook is in that direction; you could easily make it on foot to Flying Monkey trailhead from there. It's close and popular with the mountain bikers and ATV enthusiasts."

"Flying Monkey?"

"Yeah, they used to strap chimpanzees into the ejection seats for testing. You know, they wanted to see how a living creature would respond after ejecting. The chimps were easy to get into the cockpit for their first trip, not so much after that. Do you think they went that way?"

John looked to Blankenship for an opinion. He offered no comment.

Daniels said, "I'd half expected to see Mr. Ferguson walking along the road we drove up to the test site. Other than by plane, it's the only access."

Blankenship climbed down off the roof and started walking in the direction of the hiking trail. John recapped his canteen and hurried to catch up. "What did you see?"

Again, Blankenship declined to answer.

Growling, John turned to Daniels. "We know someone is out here and that they're on foot. Worst-case scenario, they're lost and without water. If they're fortunate, they have a phone and can use the GPS to head for the nearest water source."

"That's why I'm surprised we didn't see Mr. Ferguson along the main road. We passed a gas station and convenience store at the bottom of the mesa. From there it's a short walk to Virgin. Probably could have hitched a ride. It's not uncommon for locals to help out a lost hiker who relied on GPS as a guide. A consistent signal gets dicey the closer you are to the mountain range."

"Would you hitch a ride with some stranger after you'd been shot at?" Blankenship asked.

The Indian made a valid point.

"If my brother has witnessed a firefight as you suggest," John told Daniels, "he would assume his life is in danger. It maybe he's trying not to be found."

"What do you suggest?"

It was Blankenship who answered. "You need to have search and rescue back off that TV chopper. It's impeding your search efforts. And get your people on the ground, or we'll be looking for buzzards. How can you tell one hiker from another in the air?"

Daniels looked to John. "Just so I'm clear, we're supposed to follow this guy?"

John softened the tracker's demand. "What could it hurt? It shouldn't be too difficult spotting a person or persons with a couple of dogs wandering off trail."

"You'd be wrong about that, Mr. Ferguson."

He was about to find out just how wrong.

From his years of experience sailing, John had possessed the wherewithal to pick up a bandana along with a wide-brimmed hat before leaving the St. George airport. Whether on land or water, protecting one's skin was paramount in the blistering sun. Given no time to prepare, Blankenship wore the same dark T-shirt, jeans, and combat boots he'd worn back in Montana. He seemed no worse for wear. His custodial guards were a different story. Accustomed to a more *urban* environment, both men resorted to tying their black jackets over their heads for protection and became particularly irritable when having to leave the comfort of the off-road jeep to follow their ward. Todd had insisted on walking. He chastised the entire team for their reckless destruction of clues. "You call yourself a rescue team? If the quarry's on foot, so am I."

They spent an hour on top of the mesa checking out Flying Monkey Trail. In that time, the search team only managed to scare up a jackrabbit and two bikers who claimed they hadn't seen anyone with dogs. Against Todd's advice, the jeeps drove back down the hill and stopped at the gas station and convenience store. The air conditioning was a welcome relief. Avoiding comfort, Fox Can't Be Caught leaned against the jeep and downed a gallon jug of water. John purchased a tube of zinc oxide and joined him. "Why in the hell is Ferguson circumventing these pockets of civilization? Doesn't he know there are people out searching for them?"

"So is his enemy," Blankenship replied. "It would be hard to know who to trust. Besides, how would a white man explain why he's wandering around the desert with an Indian girl?"

John didn't see the relevance. "He's gonna have to trust someone. They'll die out here without water."

"We don't know they're without water. And death would come sooner if the wrong people find them."

Per Blankenship's instructions, they stayed at the base of the mesa and took a gravel road heading toward the river. The sporadic vegetation became more abundant, and John noted several campsites for tents and RVs boondocking along the way. Todd had the caravan stop near a creek. He asked Daniels, "What is this place called?"

"Sheep Bridge Park." The officer pointed south. "Virgin Falls Park is in that direction. If we stay on Sheep Bridge Road, it will take us to the Hurricane Cliffs recreational area. There's a public campground and access to several trailheads. If we stay on Sheep Bridge Road all the way west, we'll eventually cross over Highway 59 and reach the edge of Hurricane. I highly doubt Mr. Ferguson would take this route with Virgin so much closer."

Blankenship stared long and hard in that direction. He examined the ground and shrubs around him, then proceeded ahead.

"Hey," John shouted, "didn't you hear what Daniels just said? Where the hell are you going?"

"I'm following the trail."

Everyone except Blankenship loaded back into the jeep. He kept an even pace with the vehicle as it continued along the gravel road. When he reached the first trailhead, he broke off from the group and began a slow jog.

Daniels looked to John. "Now where in the hell is he going?"

Forced into an explanation, John came up with a quick

lie. "Mr. Blankenship is helping my family retrieve something of value the dogs may be carrying."

Daniels eyed him with suspicion. "So he thinks the dogs are following your brother along that trail?"

"Blankenship is a former Navy Seal and an excellent tracker."

"That may well be, but I can't take the jeeps on that trail. If I had a mountain bike, yes. This trail gets quite challenging as it winds along the side of a canyon and tributary to the Virgin. You have to call him back."

"I can't do that."

"Why not?"

"He doesn't take orders from me."

As the two custodial guards scrambled out of the jeep and followed after Blankenship. Daniels's eyes widened. "What the hell is going on, Mr. Ferguson? If that's really your name."

John looked down the trail where Blankenship was making his escape and decided to come clean. "My name is John Finch. Matthew Ferguson sent me and Blankenship to find his brother."

"Okay, I'll bite. So why does the Indian fellow look like he's a convict on the run?"

"Well, he is. He agreed to participate in the search because he has a vested interest in finding Nathan Ferguson, alive."

"And the two goons chasing him?"

"His guards."

"Well those two aren't going to last a quarter mile outfitted like that."

Choosing to split up his team, Daniels told his two members to stay with the jeeps and grabbed water and gear from the back. "I hope we're not wasting time on some wild goose chase. Every second lost brings our mission closer to failure."

John couldn't argue with that.

Trudging along the dirt trail, he couldn't for the life of him understand the appeal of hiking in a desert. Conquering the open waters of Lake Michigan—now, that was more suited to his sense of adventure. He pined for the sprays of life-giving water even more when comparing them to the grit and dust of sand. He paused to smear the tube of zinc oxide on his grimy lips and ear tips and looked down at his feet. The ground was hot. Damn hot. He regretted not having a fine pair of hiking boots like the members of the SAR team. He'd already developed new blisters on top of old ones.

At least he was better off than the two custodial guards, who'd become very problematic on the hike. Just under a mile, they both began to stumble. Daniels immediately radioed the team left at the jeeps for assistance. "This entire search has been nothing but a disaster. I've got to get these sad sacks out of here before they die of heat exhaustion. Call your man back, Mr. Finch."

John looked ahead at their tracker. Seemingly unaffected by the heat, sun, or limited water, he showed no signs of slowing. Todd glanced back just then; a wisp of a smile breezed across his lips. *Shit.* "We need to stick together," John shouted. "If they are on this trail, they may be injured or are suffering from dehydration. We'll need the SAR team's emergency aid equipment and refortify our water supply. We need to be prepared."

Blankenship hollered, "I am prepared—and fuck you."

Daniels looked to John. "I don't know what the fuck is going on here, but whatever leverage you have over that Indian just went to shit when your two goons collapsed. My advice is to just let him go. Whoever you're looking for, your brother, witnesses, or whatnot, they're not on this trail. And that guy doesn't have enough water to make it all the way to the campgrounds anyway."

John stared at the soon-to-be fugitive. It wasn't Blankenship's inevitable escape he was worried about. If Ferguson and Lilly were indeed along the creek, it fell on Ferguson alone to stop the Indian from just taking the girl and fleeing. If he failed that, everything set into motion to protect the child, not to mention Ramona's safe return, would have been for naught. "I can't do that. Too many lives are hanging in the balance if he gets away."

When Daniels's efforts to talk John out of pursuing Blankenship failed, the man handed him an extra canteen and one of the custodial guards' revolvers. "You'll need a different kind of leverage if you're going to slow that guy down."

John stared at the weapon. *Violence begets violence.* He took the gun and stuck it in his belt behind his back. "Send help as soon as you can."

"I will. Be sure the safety's off before you shoot."

The loose sand gave way to rock, though the jagged,

uneven surface made the walk no less arduous. It seemed they were walking back the same direction they'd driven. The two-man rescue team reached a historic marker and left the cliff rim of the gorge to follow a trail that led along the river. John placed additional pressure on the already aggravated blisters on the outer edges of his feet to keep from falling down the cliff side. Blankenship didn't even break a sweat, maintaining his steady, grueling pace. The hot, thin, dry air made John's every inhalation feel like there was an elephant sitting on his chest. His stamina waning, he reached in his pocket for his inhaler. They had to find their missing people, and soon, if John was going to be of any use to Ferguson. If he couldn't keep up with the pace, Blankenship would leave him for the vultures.

Traversing through a narrow corridor, they came to a dam on the river. A road paralleled the river and canyon wall. John stopped upriver above the dam, where the water was accessible. He stood at the edge, yearning to kick off his shoes and soak his weary, blistered feet. Todd continued up the road—where it led, it was hard to say. "What makes you think they went in that direction?" John asked.

Blankenship laughed. "Do you see my niece here?" The Indian pressed onward.

The sun was low enough in the sky to begin casting shadows at the base of the cliffs. Blankenship hugged closer to the wall of the canyon in the much-needed shade. For the first time since the trek began, he stopped and reached for his canteen. John felt hairs prickle at the back of his neck. Was the reluctant tracker taking a break, or rethinking his decision to follow the river gorge?

For a moment, he thought about the weapon at the small of his back. Instead, he reached for his canteen, took a drink, and said, "Is it possible we somehow passed them along the way?"

Todd wiped away long hair clinging to the side of his face. "They are close. I can feel it."

"Maybe they didn't follow the trail exactly. Daniels said there were multiple connected trails in the recreational area."

"So, you believe they're here."

John didn't know what to believe anymore. "Any animal could have left those paw prints at the dam we passed."

"You saw it."

He leaned his back against the cliff wall, his vision hazy. *What in the fuck am I doing here?* John looked toward Blankenship, his eyes tracing the outline of a stalwart bear standing on a rock formation above him. The bear lifted its chin to the sky and sniffed at the wind. *Seriously?* He shook his head. *What a fool I am.*

Pushing away from the rock wall, his knees suddenly gave way. He leaned against the rock and slowly slid his back until his butt hit the ground. The abrupt thud made him laugh. *Who's the greater fool? The Indian who claims he could smell his quarry in the air, or the white man who believes him?*

"Don't sit," Blankenship told him. "Your muscles will cramp, and then you're done."

Exhausted, John closed his eyes. Images of Lilly and the dogs began floating off of the back of his lids like shadows on a projector screen. She'd been so mad at him when he'd let the dogs go. It felt surreal. He could hear the frantic barks and Lilly's cries reverberating between his ears as he drove the white van away. *Ferguson will do the same if he has to, in order for the two of them to survive, despite the girl's wails of protest.* His human party of two had no more resources for keeping the animals alive than John had on the prairie, if they were even still alive.

He muttered to Blankenship, "What do you care if my muscles cramp? You're either going to abandon me or kill me anyway."

The smell of corn chips mixed with the pungent smell of wet dog assaulted John's subconscious. He heard a young female voice ask, "Is he dead, Uncle?" A wet, slobbery tongue wiped across his lip.

John opened his eyes to the big German shepherd that stood nose to nose in front of his face. Lilly Moonbeam squatted down on her haunches to his right, the other dog next to her.

All heads turned when Nathan Ferguson shouted, "What the hell did you do to my brother?" The dogs and the girl left John's side. He tried to get to his feet and flopped back to the ground. The moment to act was upon him, and all he could do was sit there like a limp, dirty dishrag.

CHAPTER 18

NATE

Nate stood on the rock formation above the big Indian, a large stone in his hand. *Where is Massey, and what in the hell is Finch doing here?* He looked at the man, lying in a heap with his back against the canyon wall—as useful as tits on a boar. It was times like this that Nate truly questioned his brother's logic.

Right after the explosion, he, Lilly, and the two dogs had left the shelter of the building and made a run for it across the airstrip to a cluster of shrubs. It was nothing short of a miracle they hadn't been seen. His initial plan had been to wait for the cover of twilight to make their way off the mesa. That idea had gone to shit as soon as the FAA team arrived. It would only have been a matter of time before they'd reviewed the passenger manifest and found him missing among the wounded. He and Lilly needed to be far away before that search began.

Since they couldn't leave the way they came, he'd decided to make the arduous task of finding a way off the mesa. The road which led up to the flat-top mountain had been in total chaos. A National Guard unit had set up a checkpoint at the main road entrance to keep rubber-neckers away as area rescue teams shuffled hikers, bikers, and ATV drivers off the mountain using local shuttle services. An old Hummer H2 laden with a rack of mountain bikes had offered Nate and his party a lift down the hill; he'd slipped the driver a hundred to say he and the girl were part of their group. The driver had eyed him curiously, then nodded. By the time they'd reached the bottom, there was so much confusion at the checkpoint that when Lilly started crying that she needed a bathroom, the soldier had let them pass without so much as a second glance.

The town of Virgin hadn't been much better. Crowded with locals, tourists, and rescue personnel, the restaurant nearest the highway was jam-packed. It didn't help that Nate had two dogs with him. Nate had placed an order to go and retreated to a park on the other side of the river to regroup. He'd called Mony first but gotten no answer; next he'd called Massey.

Per his brother's instructions, Nate had laid a convoluted path through canyon and desert trails until Massey could arrange a rendezvous point for getting them out of there. They'd spent the better part of the day trying to blend in with other recreational enthusiasts. Unfazed by their peril, Lilly had been content as long as the dogs were with her. Shep and Rainstorm had proved to be excellent companions, providing a much-needed guise for passing their humans off as a family unit. Adding just the right amount of puppy-dog eyes to play on people's emotions,

Nate had found that strangers' generosity was astounding. Throughout the day, the dogs had helped secure a variety of food, mostly carbs, but also some protein (which Lilly fed to them). Their group had also been given ample water, a necessity when hiking in the hostile environment. Nate had led his party of four to a dam located on the river just above the gorge, which Massey had designated as their rendezvous point.

First, though, he had to deal with this clusterfuck.

Lilly left Finch and returned to his side. Flanked by both dogs, she said to the large man towering in front of them, "Uncle, what did you do to Finch?"

Uncle? Massey had never said anything about an uncle. Nate glanced over at Finch. That bastard was supposed to be somewhere in Montana, a ransomed captive of an Indigenous American. *Is this his captor standing in front of me?* If so, something was definitely wrong. It made him wonder what other information his brother had been withholding. Nate looked each man over for obvious signs of bondage or restraint. None could be seen, so it begged the question, who was ward of whom?

"Come here, Niece—he is of no concern to us. Now keep quiet while your elder speaks." To Nate the man said, "Your brother sent me to find you."

Nate tightened his grip on the rock. That was a lie. Even if there was a slight grain of truth to the claim, any sort of contact between Massey, Mony, and the Indian would surely have been volatile. Massey always came for him; always. Nate widened his stance. "Where is Mony, and what have you done to her?"

His adversary didn't even bother feigning ignorance. "She is safe—for now."

A veiled threat.

"Why would Massey send you?"

"I'm a tracker."

He held up his cell. "Massey could have done that through my phone." Shifting his weight to his non-dominant leg, Nate continued, "This is what I think. I think you're here because you think you can trade Finch for the girl. That's not going to happen. I don't give a shit about him, or that you're Lilly's kin. I made a promise to get her to safety. That is exactly what I'm going to do."

The big man stepped forward. "Typical white man, thinking he knows what's best for an Indian. But you are correct. This is no trade. I take what is mine. Come, Niece—hoka hey."

Nate held on to the girl's hand, and the dogs bristled with hostile growls. The Indian spoke in a calm voice: "Sunka iníla yaŋká yo!" His words had no effect. Looking to the child, the Indian's hardened expression relaxed. "Bring the dogs. Your family is waiting."

Lilly was unmoved.

Against his better judgement, Nate got down on a knee and turned the girl to face him. He'd grown quite fond of Lilly in the short time they'd been together. It was easy to see why Mony had become so invested in her; Lilly continuously amazed him with her quiet calm and wisdom. Even after the jet crash, she'd never once complained about the predicament they were in. She followed his every direction and offered useful suggestions when required. Much like Mony, she had an innate survival instinct, something he admired. Not only was she brave, she was extremely bright and resourceful, a pillar of strength, so long as she had her dogs. Looking into her eyes, Nate asked, "Is that what you want, to go with your uncle?"

She averted her eyes, then looked to her uncle. The confusion on her face was telling. "Is Sissy with you?"

"She is with my sister, waiting for you."

"Mama?"

A shimmer of hope flashed in the young girl's eyes. If it was true Sissy was still alive, it would be a gamechangar. However, while it broke Nate's heart to crush the girl's spirit, he suspected this asshole would say anything to gain the child's cooperation. He looked over Lilly's shoulder at her tormentor. "Prove it."

"Don't need to." The big Indian took another step forward and lunged for Lilly.

Defenseless in this position, Nate tried to move the girl away from the assault. She stood like a rock. The dogs growled ferociously as the child confronted her uncle. "You leave miragawigaʔádagi alone." Her command halted his fist.

The Indian narrowed his gaze at Nate and scoffed. "More like maaʔihaaʔidawikáa. You've named him like a pet. Has he turned you against your family too?"

"It is you turning your back, Uncle, and yes, I gave him this name. White Oak has protected me and the dogs more times that I can count against those bad men. If you would just listen to him—"

A loud moan and a stirring movement drew everyone's attention. Finch cast a hazy-eyed look toward Nate and Lilly, then to the Indian. "Congratulations, Blankenship, you found them." The familiarity in his tone prickled the hairs at the nap of Nate's neck.

The Indian chose that moment to make a grab for Lilly, slamming his fist into Nate's face. As Nate fell like a tree, the girl let out a scream, setting the dogs into a snapping, snarling frenzy. Her captor was turning to leave when the unmistakable sound of a firearm hammer being cocked stopped him in his tracks.

Christ, who gave Finch a gun?

Clinging to the flailing child, the Indian pivoted where he stood and smiled at Finch. "Do you know how to shoot that thing?"

Sliding his back up the rock wall, Finch rose awkwardly to his feet. Keeping the gun trained on the Indian, he walked unsteadily over to Nate and extended his hand.

Nate stared long and hard at the proffered assistance. *Does this viper actually think his deceptive gesture will fool me?* But what choice did he have? Lilly's safety was his highest priority, even if that meant fraternizing with his enemy. He begrudgingly accepted.

Standing shoulder to shoulder with his nemesis, Nate felt an overwhelming urge to reach over and strangle the guy. Instead, he spat a wad of blood at the feet of his phony ally. "So what's the plan, Finch?"

His question was ignored. Finch said to the Indian, "I reckon all I have to do is point and shoot."

"Maybe you miss and hit my niece."

The lawyer straightened his spine. "You willing to take that risk?"

Nate noticed the tremor in Finch's outstretched trigger hand. As he contemplated grabbing the gun, Finch clicked off the safety.

"Maybe I pop a cap in your knee to match the bullet hole in your leg. We'll leave you here, wait for the SAR team to collect you, patch you up. Maybe we haul your ass back to Montana, make you take us to where you're holding Ramona."

Nate was stunned. "What the fuck are you talking about?"

Finch waved the gun haphazardly at his target. "Let me give you the Cliff Notes on what we're dealing with here. This is the asshole who kidnapped me during the handoff between me and your brother. He and Sissy tortured me, brutalized Mitchell, and left him for dead. I managed to escape—unfortunately, not in time to warn my rescuers. Blankenship and Sissy laid a trap, knocked your brother unconscious while playing the Good Samaritan, and took Ramona. Matthew was in the hospital when he learned about your jet crash. In the interim, the detective sent her team to retrieve Ramona, only she got Blankenship instead. Because he's the only one who knows where Ramona's being taken, your brother did some behind-the-scenes razzle dazzle and convinced the detective to send me and Blankenship here to find you and the girl first."

Nate had heard enough. Lunging at Finch, he snatched the gun from the man's wavering hand; then, walking straight toward the Indian, he pointed the gun at his forehead. "Did you sabotage the jet?"

Blankenship abruptly released Lilly's arm, letting her fall to the ground. He took a step back. "Why would I hurt my own niece?"

"Because you're a liar and a murderer, you dirty son of a bitch."

Finch staggered over to help Lilly to her feet and pulled her away from danger. "Jesus, Fergie, settle down," he shouted. "The detective and your brother are handling Ramona's rescue. Blankenship and I were sent to get you out of here. He's a former Navy Seal and has experience in the desert. He also has a vested interest in the child's well-being, so will you quit fucking around? Let's all of us get the hell out of Satan's kitchen. I for one have had my fill of this stinking desert."

Nate kept his gun trained on the Indian, staring at him long and hard. "Goddamn it. You're using my wife as bait."

A gentle touch brushed his arm as Lilly rested her hand on his. "Miragawigaʔádagi, please, don't shoot my uncle."

Nate's resolve began to wane as he tried to make sense of it all. *Why would Massey have trusted Blankenship? And in what universe would he think I would ever trust Finch?* There was too much to sort out, and daylight was fading.

"You said the SAR team isn't far behind you, right, Finch?"

"Yeah. We got separated when Todd's two guards collapsed from heatstroke. They had to be carried out, but it won't take long to come back with reinforcements."

"Then we stick with my plan."

"Plan? What plan?"

"The one that gets Lilly and me out of here undetected."

"That's impossible. You've got every emergency personnel member plus the National Guard out looking for you. I wouldn't be surprised if there are a few bounty hunters sprinkled in there as well. You and the girl's footprints are all over the place near the buildings where you hid. People know you're both here. It's only a matter of time before they find you."

"What makes anyone so sure the prints belong to us?"

"Jesus. Who else would they belong to?"

"They could belong to anyone. Maybe another sniper was perched on the roof."

"Fergie, you're not making sense."

"Why do you think Massey gave explicit instructions not to disclose exactly who you were looking for when you went to the crash site?"

Finch shrugged his shoulders. "I don't know. I suppose because he wasn't sure who he could trust. You're all very distrustful."

"Because you didn't want anyone to know my niece was on that flight," Blankenship said quietly.

"What about the flight manifest?" Finch retorted.

"Did you *see* the actual manifest?" Nate asked.

Finch seemed to struggle processing the information, but Blankenship put it together quickly. "Lil Sis isn't on the manifest to keep the mercenaries from discovering her location."

Nate lowered the gun. "Now do you understand the

danger Lilly is in? If these guys can sabotage a private jet and stage an ambush in broad daylight, what makes you think they'll stop there? This is why my brother sent you to find us. You needed to see with your own eyes just how far they're willing to go to get what they want. Even if that means killing a kid."

Nodding, Blankenship asked, "What's your plan for getting out of here?"

Nate held up his cell phone. "People are coming for us."

Finch gawked at the cell phone in surprise. "Does your brother know about this?"

Nate scrolled through the text messages he had going back and forth with Massey. The word *alive* showed on the screen. "Who in the hell do you think is making the arrangements? He's been tracking my phone this whole time. One-word messages were the only information I could risk."

Blankenship broke into a harsh laugh. "Every major exit from the wilderness area will be monitored by the SAR team, the military, and your enemy. How are you planning to get past them?"

"The dam road loops back to Sheep Bridge Road and the campgrounds, where the detective has someone waiting for us."

"I don't believe you."

"Uncle, will you please listen?" Lilly cried out in frustration.

Ignoring her, Blankenship said, "You're in the middle of a desert. How are you supposed to get there?"

Nate felt a twinge in his gut at disclosing their escape

plan. He didn't trust this man any further than he could throw him, and he was taking a leap of faith trusting in Massey's judgement. Finally, he said, "They'll come for me, Lilly, and the dogs on ATVs. They'll smuggle us out of here in a camper."

Blankenship lifted his chin in Finch's direction. "What about me and him?"

"What about you?"

"Are we included?"

"The truth—I don't know. My communications hadn't taken either of you into account."

"Bad odds," Blankenship grunted.

"Yeah well, it's the best odds we've got right now," Finch said. Turning to Nate, he added, "I'm willing to take my chances as long as I don't have to walk very far. I don't think I could take that."

"What about you, Blankenship? Will you agree to getting Lilly to safety?"

Blankenship gave Nate a hard look. "What makes you think she'll be safe in your white man's world?"

"What makes you think I'm hiding her among white people?"

CHAPTER 19

MONY

Mony felt a sharp pinprick under the flesh of her arm, followed by a long, slow, steady burn. The gentle tug at her skin opened her eyes. Standing over her was a woman about her age neatly suturing the laceration in her arm. The woman made another jab.

"Ouch."

"These next two will be deep," warned her medic.

Mony gripped the edge of the seat with her good hand. Sweat dripped down the side of her face as she watched the woman stitch her skin. Being somewhat of an expert herself, she could see from the precision of the woman's handiwork that she had experience. Her needle was a fine fishhook in design, with the tiniest of eyes to thread the catgut. The dexterity in her fingers required no hemostat. Mony laid her head back on the seat, stifling a grown. *Goddamn, that hurts.*

When the woman had finished, she held a thick paper towel under Mony's arm and poured a cloudy tincture over the sutures. Mony hissed at the stinging sensation.

Next, the woman placed the wet cloth over the wound, finally wrapping Mony's arm with strips of cloth torn from an old T-shirt as her patient gritted her teeth.

"Better to hurt now than later because of infection."

"What's in it—the solution?"

"Stinging nettles. It's a good antimicrobial; witch hazel, lavender, and calendula. It's the best I can do right now. As soon as we reach our destination, I'll try to find an oral antibiotic."

As she gathered her supplies and prepared to leave, Mony made a quick grab for her hand. "Thank you."

The woman nodded, and left.

Taking advantage of the solitude, Mony took in her surroundings. The truck sat in a small parking lot made of coarse, rocky gravel and dirt. Two other trucks were parked beside her. Out the front windshield, she noted a trailhead leading up an incline. Beyond that was a brownish-green grassy prairie covered with the same scattering of rock as the parking lot. A line of pine trees rimmed the prairie farther up the slope. The outline of a low mountain range dominated the skyline, marked with a distinct solitary peak. Considering her last location, Mony assumed she was somewhere near Glacier. Given the ethnicity of the woman who'd tended her wound, she was still on reservation land.

With her good arm, Mony grabbed the hand crank and rolled down the window. Despite the heat of the summer day, a cool breeze wafted in, carrying the comforting smell of a campfire burning somewhere nearby. There wasn't much in the way of human activity or voices. She looked down at her arm. Her sleeve had been cut away; her shirt was stained with her own blood. She checked her face and neck in the rearview mirror, examining the nicks and cuts and dried blood from the tiny shards of glass. "You're quite the mess," she told her reflection.

With no one standing guard, she ventured out of the truck. The moment her legs hit the ground, a wave of vertigo engulfed her head and her legs began to tremble. Bile bubbled in her throat. Leaning against the truck, she took several measured breaths before her equilibrium returned. *No wonder my inability to escape was a foregone conclusion.* Hanging on to the truck, she made her way to the tailgate and discovered a path leading into the woods. She followed to what appeared to be a primitive campground. Despite lacking the typical amenities, the grounds felt intimate, private, a place where one would go for peaceful tranquility or introspection—sacred. It was the sort of place her deceased husband, Bob, would have been drawn to. If there were a lake nearby, he'd have considered it heaven. The memory made her smile.

Further in, a clearing held tents in various shapes, styles, and conditions. The tabernacle of this sanctuary was a tent larger than the rest, covered with sheets of black plastic. Thick-cut logs two to three feet in length dotted the parameter of a great firepit. An elder, thin with weathered skin and long salt-and-pepper gray hair, tended the large boulders among the burning flames. As Mony approached, he looked up and said, "Oki! Tsá kinóóhkanistá'paissp?"

Unfamiliar with his greeting, she simply smiled and

nodded. It sounded friendly. The man was preparing for a gathering—a sweat—maybe a vision quest.

Mony looked toward the mountain range. It would be a rigorous hike for anyone trying to reach that peak, a perfect place to be at one with the divine. She pointed and asked, "What is the name of the mountain?"

"Ninaistako. You call it Chief Mountain."

Behind the tents, Mony noticed smaller tendrils of smoke blending with the cloud coming from the large firepit. An aroma of cooked meat with herbs and wild onions made her mouth water. A heated discussion between two women was in process; she walked in the direction of the voices to eavesdrop on the conversation.

"It was foolish to bring the white woman here during this sacred time." It was the woman who'd mended her wound, scolding a younger associate.

Mony recognized the junior as the woman from the cabin. "Stop worrying," she countered. "We'll be gone before sunset."

"She's dangerous."

"She's pathetic and weak."

"If you think that, you're a fool. She's only hungry and dehydrated."

"I told you, stop worrying! You're too on edge. That shitshow at the cabin wasn't our fault—my brother had everything under control until that SWAT team or whoever they were started shooting up the place."

"Yes, and where is my son Fox Can't Be Caught now?"

The younger woman didn't answer.

"Captured. He sacrificed himself—again, for you and my granddaughter's sake."

"If it weren't for her money and that man who watches out for her, she'd be nothing," the younger woman countered.

"I've seen her eyes. She is a mother bear protecting her cub."

"Lilly belongs to me."

"I've seen how poorly you protect your children, daughter."

"Even a mother bear will abandon her young in order to survive. You take Grandma Moonbeam's side over your own kin."

The older woman's voice softened. "I am always on your side, daughter. That doesn't change the truth."

Before they could continue, Mony cleared her throat and stepped into view. "Excuse me, I'm wondering if you have any water. I have a powerful thirst."

The elder woman broke from her conversation. "Of course. I will get you something to drink." As she walked toward a leather knapsack hanging from a tree, the younger woman stood, arms crossed, and glared at Mony.

The elder woman returned with a bottle of water. "Thank you." Mony cracked the cap and proceeded to drink the whole thing.

"Are you hungry?"

She was famished, but she had no idea if her accepting food would cause hardship for their current preparations. Her stomach emitted an audible growl, betraying her hunger. "If you have something to spare, I could eat."

The woman ladled a heaping portion of stew from the cast-iron pot, then handed the bowl and a spoon to Mony. "Be careful, it's very hot."

It was difficult not to plunge the spoon into the steaming middle and shovel the delicious-smelling stew into her mouth. She ventured conversation to give the food time to cool. "Do you know where your son was taken?"

The elder woman looked to her daughter. "After he was shot, they took him to the hospital; then they took him to that hellhole prison in Sidney."

This is good information. "I suspect he'll be in my brother's custody."

"Why would that be?"

"Massey will make a trade, your son for me. If your son hasn't killed John."

"Who's John?"

A young woman walked to the leather bag. It was Sissy. "He's the man I was telling you about, Grandmother." She cracked the cap of the bottled water. "Last we'd seen him; he was playing chicken with a train."

Surprised, Mony said, "Todd mentioned that too. What does that mean?"

"He got loose in the train yard back in Sidney. If he beat the train before crossing the tracks, he's alive."

Mony remembered the ambulance. "So that's why you stopped on the roadside. You needed a new captive."

"We stopped because the truck broke down. I didn't want either one of you."

The younger woman interjected, "What did you do with my Lilly?"

Mony quickly put the pieces together. Three generations—grandmother, daughter, and granddaughter—were standing in front of her, all wanting the same thing. "Lil Sis is somewhere—safe."

The mother lost her patience. "I want my daughter, now."

Mony looked to the grandmother, who'd remained silent. "You can trade me for your son. I trust he knows how to take care of himself, but not your granddaughter. It's far too dangerous to reveal her whereabouts."

"Typical white bitch," Sissy spat. "Always think they know what's best for an Indian." She pulled a buck knife from her belt and pointed it at Mony. "You can tell me where my sister is, or I can send you back to your brother in pieces."

The elderly man tending the fire joined the conversation. "Enough, granddaughter. Your actions bring maká'pato'siiksi to these ceremonial grounds. Continue, and you can no longer stay."

Sissy clenched her fist like a child about to throw a temper tantrum. Mony understood the feeling of helplessness. She hated the idea of sending Nate away with Lil Sis just to protect the child. It put him at equal risk. At this point, no one could know either's whereabouts. "I will not put that child and my husband's life in danger just to satisfy your conscience."

"They are already in danger," the elderly man said.

Mony wiped a hand over her scarred face. "Explain."

"First, your body and spirit need nourishment. Finish

your stew. You need to bathe and put on some clean clothing. After that, we'll talk."

Mony was given a basin of water to wash and fresh clothes. Her torn shirt was replaced with a T-shirt and hoodie; the jeans were hers, damp but clean. She'd been given a pair of boots; the fit was loose, but a thick pair of socks accompanying the ensemble shored up the fit.

As she rejoined the family gathered round the firepit, Grandpa and Grandma Blackrock, their granddaughter Sissy, and her mother, Florence or Night Owl Moonbeam, sat in quiet contemplation. Mony took the log next to Sissy. Across from her, Grandpa Blackrock packed tobacco in a pipe made of catlinite, calumet claystone. Sissy leaned toward Mony and whispered, "First we smoke, then we talk."

Grandfather held up the pipe again, honoring the spirits, then offered a pinch of tobacco in each direction. In his native tongue he spoke invocations to the four directions, skyward, and toward the earth. He took several puffs from the pipe, waving the smoke toward him in a purification ritual, then offered the pipe to the next person. Mony observed each participant's actions. It would be Sissy's role to offer the pipe to her.

With reverence, Sissy handed Mony the pipe. Despite growing up in a smoker's home, Mony herself had never smoked. Nevertheless, she accepted and followed the example demonstrated before her. As the smoke rose from the pipe, a wave of tranquility washed over her, the smell of pure tobacco familiar, comforting. She felt at peace.

A young man with long black hair carrying two

drumsticks approached the firepit and took up a log beside Mony. Sissy introduced him: "This is my cousin, Howls-at-the-Wind. He just came from Sidney. What's the latest, cuz?"

"Sorry I missed the smoke," he said, pulling a pack of cigarettes from his shirt pocket. He lit one up and took a long drag before he spoke. "I saw them load Fox Can't Be Caught onto a plane headed to Utah, I think. The lawyer went with him."

Mony asked, "Which lawyer?"

Howls-at-the-Wind looked at her in surprise. "Didn't know there was more than one."

"Her brother and Finch are both lawyers," Sissy informed him.

"Then it's the guy you and Fox Can't Be Caught had in the truck."

Mony was confused. "Why would John agree to board a plane with his captor, and for what purpose?"

The young man shrugged. "There are a lot of strange alliances happening. What I know is that two white men, Finch and your brother, took Fox Can't Be Caught away from prison. They sat at a park, had a smoke. The next thing I know, our cousin is boarding a plane with the lawyer. Don't know much more than that except there were a bunch of guys dressed in black suits hanging around the plane. Two of them boarded before they left."

Mony turned to Sissy. "Why did you and your uncle kidnap John?"

The young girl's eyes lit with anger. "I told you; we didn't want him at all. He had my sister and was hiding at your farm. Your brother, the one with you when you found me, was there too. It looked like they were making a deal. We signaled Lil Sis to make a run for it. The two men went after her, then split up. Your brother got my sister, we got Finch. If he hadn't escaped in the train yard, you and I wouldn't be having this conversation."

Mony looked back at the cousin. "And you don't know why your uncle and Finch were getting onto the plane together?"

"No, I couldn't get close enough to find out."

None of this made sense. Massey would never let Fox Can't Be Caught out of his sight, let alone put him together with John. And why Utah? "It's time I talk to Massey."

"Why?" Sissy asked. "So he can trace your call?"

"He doesn't have to trace a call. He knows where I am."

"How?"

"Does it matter? What matters is your uncle is on a flight to Utah and we don't know why."

Grandmother Blackrock broke in: "My son is a former Navy Seal and an expert tracker. He knows how to take care of himself in a desert."

"I have no doubt about that. But only Massey can tell us if Lil Sis is okay."

The women in the group argued amongst themselves, and the young man continued his smoke. Eventually, the elder man interrupted, "Enough of this chattering. Make your call, find out what's going on."

Mony reached for her back pocket. "Fox Can't Be Caught smashed my cell phone."

The cousin took the last drag from his cigarette. "You

don't need a phone. There are other ways of getting word to your brother."

CHAPTER 20

MASSEY

Massey noticed his dad wiping at the corner of his eye as Nate deplaned at the Babb public airport. He held no judgement. The aerial shots of what was left of the company jet had been distressing. Despite their communications, he, too, had been uncertain if he'd ever see his little brother alive again.

Without hesitation, Kip went to his son, engulfing him in his massive arms. Nate offered no resistance. Neither spoke, but a message had been conveyed. Following his dad, Massey pulled his kid brother in for a shoulder hug. "Good to see the three of you didn't kill each other in the desert."

Nate snorted a laugh. "You should have seen us coming back on the plane."

"And your stowaway?"

"She's where she needs to be."

"How is Blankenship taking it?"

Todd walked up to him, answering the question. "I still

think she would be safer with her people, but I understand the risk of bringing her back to Montana."

Approaching on wobbly legs, John said, "That's one hell of a team-building experience you sent me on."

Massey extended his hand. He'd had misgivings sending John to find Nate, but once again the man had proved himself worthy of his family's trust. He could see the verdict was still out for Nate, but was confident his brother would eventually come around. "Thanks for helping to find my brother and bring him home."

Finch accepted his proffered hand. "You have Blankenship to thank for finding him. The homecoming was your planning."

"He wasn't hard to follow," Todd grunted. "Left enough signs a blind person could follow."

Nate winked. "I told him—the clues were meant for you, brother. You have many useful talents; tracking isn't one of them."

Massey was unoffended. "That's why I sent the best." He turned to Todd. "Are you ready to take us to Mony?"

"Why not get her yourself?" Blankenship asked, his voice rising in a challenge. "It wouldn't be the first time the feds trespassed on sovereign Indian lands."

The man did have a right to be irritated there. "That's not how we operate. Besides, I'm sure you have Mony hidden so deep within the reservation, even with her tracker, we probably wouldn't find her for a couple of weeks. We don't have that kind of time to waste."

"Always in a hurry, the white man."

"I can't argue with that. But the Feds' presence is far

more reaching than a hostage retrieval. If we know Mony and Sissy's general location, so does our enemy. You've seen for yourself the lengths Monroe will go to—attacking a wealthy, powerful, white oil family in broad daylight. How long do you think it will be before they come after an impoverished Indigenous community?"

"I know my niece; she won't accept your help."

"Then you need to convince her. This is no longer exclusively our family's fight. He'll dispatch Sissy and her sister, along with anyone else on the Rez in both North Dakota and Montana, if he thinks they're an obstacle."

Blankenship released a heavy breath. "You're not going to like her plan."

"What's there to like?" said Kip. "Both our families' lives have been invaded by this parasite. We need to eradicate it from the North Dakota plains once and for all, before it can do any more damage."

"White people don't care about Indian affairs, nor do they get tangled up in matters that endanger their wealth."

Nate rolled his eyes in exasperation. "Jesus, Todd, we've been over this. Mony's already fully vested in the welfare of the Moonbeam girls, plus whatever baggage comes with her involvement. My guess is, if her mouth hasn't been taped shut, she's probably won over Sissy and her captors already."

Kip concurred. "I don't give a shit what's financially at stake. Wealth is fleeting. A business can be rebuilt. My family's lives, however, can't be replaced. If I need to work with the entire Blackfoot nation and Three Affiliated Tribes to protect them, then that's what I'll do."

Finch, who'd been standing quiet on the periphery, lent his voice to the Fergusons' appeal. "From where I'm standing, neither one of you will achieve your goal without my help. No one knows Monroe's weakness better than me. Combine my inside knowledge of Monroe Oil, your niece's inside knowledge of his illicit business ventures on the Bakken, and F&A Oil's resources, and you have incredible power to achieve both your goals."

Blankenship was stubborn. "You know nothing of my goals. Why should I believe the word of any white man?"

John laid out the cold hard truth. "Don't believe my words. Believe your eyes and the actions of the people who are trying to help you."

At that, Nate turned to the lawyer. "By helping us, Finch, you'll not only lose your most lucrative client, you'll probably ruin your entire legal career. So I have to ask: what's in it for you?"

John placed his hands over his heart. "Fergmeister, I'm touched. And to think all this time I was under the impression you didn't care."

A devious smile bloomed across Nate's face. "Watch it, Finch. You haven't earned that level of sarcasm—yet."

Massey couldn't help but laugh. "He has in my book. What say for now we let Nate and Todd check in on the girls at the Rez, while Dad, John, and I figure out our next move taking down Monroe?"

From the air, Massey watched the RV heading north on Highway 89 as the plane carried him, John, and Kip back to Shelby. His dad was still uncomfortable with the arrangement—Blankenship could highjack the RV and take Nate across the Canadian border within the hour. He had to remind his dad as well as himself they'd reached an understanding with the man. It was imperative they demonstrate trust. Blankenship had finally revealed the mission entrusted to him. His people had just as much to lose if their agreement turned sour.

Detective Gomez escorted the three men to her temporary base of operations in the hotel conference room. A young woman wearing her hair in double braids and eagle feathers for earrings got up from her laptop next to a makeshift terminal. She extended her hand. "Gentlemen, I'm Keri Morningstar, identification analyst for the FBI. Please, take a seat."

Casting images on a projector screen, the detective began, "This is Viktor Ivanov, the sole surviving assailant of the F&A company jet. He's an underling for a known syndicate leader whom we'll call Anton Kuznetsov."

Massey examined the image of Kuznetsov. "That's the guy Blankenship was telling us about."

"The Bureau developed an interest in him following the assassination of a political consultant for a Texas senator."

"I remember that," Kip said. "The senator had been investigating the oil industry's methods of buying and selling mineral rights leases."

"Correct, Mr. Ferguson. We suspected Anton performed the hit himself. We were about to arrest him when we learned of his connections."

"Connections." Kip curled his lip in contempt. "The

guy's a murderer and you let him loose, because of. . . connections?"

"His crimes go way deeper," Morningstar said. "He's linked to a Ukraine-born Russian mob boss financing the Russian separatist group that seized the Crimean Peninsula. We began monitoring him when he popped up on US soil. He's passing himself off as a private investigator under the alias Anton Kuznetsov. He's been working on behalf of high-profile clients in the oil industry, his case load allegedly involving insurance claims. His job is to ensure his clients get paid."

"Basically, he's a fixer," Massey said. "Is Monroe on his client list?"

"At the very top."

Kip became incensed. "For Christ's sakes, are you saying the Russian mafia tried to kill my son?"

"From what we've determined, it appears Kuznetsov is currently working on his own behalf. He's trying to establish his own crime network here in Canada and the US and is using his clients to finance his efforts."

John snorted. "So this guy's bilking Monroe Oil using his mercenary skills to take out F&A, then funnels the company's liquid assets to finance his own affairs. Can I use your computer a moment, Ms. Morningstar?"

She slid the laptop across the table to John, who began typing. An image of the Nasdaq index appeared on the screen. "These initials here represent Monroe stock. It appears he's selling preferred shares, probably to a shell company. I'm guessing he's trying to obtain financing and still maintain controlling stock in his company. Christ,

Thomas is so focused on buying F&A Oil, he's placing his entire corporation at risk."

Massey asked, "Is there a way to find out who's buying up the stocks?"

Morningstar took back the laptop and tapped rapidly on the keyboard. "This is not my area of expertise, but from what I can see, so far not a lot of the shares have moved."

"Why would that be?"

"I'm not sure," she said. "Perhaps with a bit more time and Mr. Finch's help, we can figure it out."

"While you're doing that, I think Dad and I need to re-visit the interview between Sheriff Wagner and Richards. Richards alluded to a Russki giving orders at the Nazi camp. Blankenship claimed that this guy murdered Shannon McDonald and Cindy Van Dyke-Mitchell, and that the sheriff was a witness."

Kip broke in. "What I want to know is, who has the most to lose on the dismantled human trafficking ring, and who is working for who?"

"That may be difficult to differentiate," replied Gomez. "Up to his disappearance, Dwight Mitchell was the local liaison for Monroe regarding the illicit trade on the Bakken."

Massey looked to John at the mention of Mitchell's name. They hadn't shared his fate with anyone. For the moment, he wanted to keep it that way.

Kip said, "Monroe's not only being conned out of his money, he may be getting set up as the fall guy for a double homicide."

A plan was kindling in Massey's brain. "John, you ready to get back to your old job?"

"With Monroe? When hell freezes over. Jason has probably already hired his hitman to take me out."

"I was thinking more of your old law firm. Gabriella has already cleared a path for you."

"I doubt they'll just invite me back to the table. Ethan Rice has taken over representation for Monroe Oil."

"Come on John, think. You're an old pro at this. We need someone on the inside to follow what's going on."

Morningstar spoke up. "I might have a way in for you. Tiffany Monroe-Rice filed a petition for divorce papers two days ago with a judge in New Orleans."

John was shocked. "Not Chicago or Houston?"

"No. She established residency three months ago when she purchased an art gallery along the Plantation River Road. She'd had a long-term lease at the Nottoway Resort prior to her residency. My hunch is she'd been planning her divorce for a while. She may have filed in New Orleans to gain the element of surprise."

"Took long enough," John muttered. "Have those papers been served?"

"Not that I'm aware. But I've learned she's attending a corporate board meeting for Monroe Oil scheduled at your law firm in Chicago, day after tomorrow."

"There you go, John," said Massey, "Naturally, you would be there to represent Ms. Monroe's interests."

John visibly squirmed. "I don't like the idea of using Tia as a pawn or betraying her trust. If I burn that bridge, there's no going back."

"I have no intention of using Ms. Monroe or burning bridges. She is exactly the sort of ally we need in removing Monroe Oil from the Bakken once and for all."

"What about Kuznetsov?" asked Kip.

"One step at a time, Dad. John will lock down Ms. Monroe's holdings in the oil business while you and I get back to Williston. We need to get to the bottom of Sheriff Wagner's involvement in all this. According to Shawn and Nate, he's been lying to us for a while now. We need to know the details. Detective, you may want to put a security detail on Finch while he's in Chicago."

"Matthew, I don't have the personnel for all this. They're all tied up monitoring the inlets to the Blackfoot reservation."

"We can take our focus off Mony and Nate for the moment. As long as they stay on the Rez, they'll be safe. Blankenship will see to it."

"Can you trust him?" asked the detective.

"He's after the same thing we are; he just has a different approach. Let Nate and Mony find out what sort of strategy Sissy has up her sleeve for taking down Monroe and barter a way to dovetail into that plan. The young girl may have valuable information involving the mercenary. If that's the case, she could be the key in helping the FBI to neutralize his crime syndicate."

CHAPTER 21

NATE

Nate turned off Chief Mountain Highway and followed a dirt road heading west. Twilight was approaching. As the sun made its descent behind the mountains, Blankenship instructed him to take another left on a road that seemingly led nowhere. Though it was doable, Nate was becoming increasingly concerned the journey would eventually become impassable for Massey's RV and he'd be stuck with no means of rescue. When they crossed a cattle guard onto a more primitive access road, he asked Blankenship, "Where in the hell are you taking me?"

"To your woman, like you asked."

"And how far am I going to get with this albatross before we have to hoof it?"

"Not far. There is a signboard for the tribal campground up ahead. It's three miles beyond that. Your rig won't make the climb up the hill to the parking spot, but I'll show you where to park. We walk into the camping area from there."

Nate studied the approaching mountain range. "Are we in Glacier or on the Rez?"

"Chief Mountain is, and will always be, part of tribal lands."

He found the sign as Blankenship had said and shifted the RV into a lower gear. Driving at a snail's pace, he was so focused on weaving and dodging through the rocky grassland that he was surprised when Blankenship declared they'd arrived. The line of trees between prairie and foothills didn't look like much of a campground.

The two men got out and walked up the hill, where a couple of four-wheel-drive vehicles sat parked in a level area. Nate smelled the campfire before seeing it, and could hear chanting blend with the rhythmic thrumming of drums.

"What's going on?"

"Come with me and you'll see."

He entered a clearing where a roaring fire lit up the surrounding trees, casting a shadow against the approaching dusk. Off to the right, next to a large teepee-style tent, eight men of various ages beat on a drum made from a hollow tree trunk. Nate was less interested in the festivities and more intent on the circle of people. Finally, after several moments of searching, he found what he was looking for.

Sitting on a log on the far end of the firepit, Mony gazed contemplatively into the flame as if seeking the answer to a burning question. Nate was about to approach when Blankenship held out an arm. "Go around, that way." Nate looked at him, puzzled, but complied with the request.

Mony hadn't seen him approach but felt his proximity. As she looked up, her eyes widened as if she'd seen a ghost, then welled with tears. Nate knelt beside her. It was hard for him not to cry too.

"You're all right. Thank God, you're all right. Why didn't you call me? You should have called—"

"I tried, babe, I tried. It's why Lilly and I weren't with the plane when things went to shit. I couldn't get a signal. I climbed on top of a building. I—"

"You are never leaving me again, you hear?" She kissed him fervently on his dry, parched mouth. Nate didn't care who was watching or what ceremony he was interrupting. Consumed by her love, he pulled Mony to her feet. He kissed her back, squeezing her in his arms. She whimpered.

"What's the matter?"

She wept openly. "Don't you ever leave me again."

As Nate pulled her away from him, holding her at arm's length, she winced against his grip. "Mony, are you hurt? What did they do to you?"

Avoiding his gaze, she gingerly removed the hand holding her arm. "No one hurt me. Not here. It's a long story."

He pulled her close, taking care to avoid her injury. "I guess we both have some catching up to do."

Two shadows passed along the grandeur of the landscape, using the moonlight and Nate's cell phone to light the way. Hand in hand, they headed back to the RV. Despite Mony being a captive, no one among the host of people seemed concerned her husband had taken her away from the campfire.

The air was crisp and cool. A light breeze filled the night sky. The sound of wind harmonized with the distant chanting and drumming as if they were in concert with one another. Along the walk, Mony talked about the two young members of the Blackfoot tribe who'd recently completed a sweat and had been sent off into the mountains for a vision quest. The blue light emitting from Nate's phone reflected in her eyes as she spoke passionately. "It would have been enlightening, being a part of such an extraordinary experience. Of course, I wasn't invited, and it would have been rude to ask."

Nate leaned over and kissed her forehead. "It's in your nature to explore. It's one of the many things I love about you. But haven't we both had enough adventures for one day?"

Mony halted in front of the house door to the RV. The glow of the partial moon reflected off the shiny exterior, illuminating her dark eyes. Nate watched the side of her mouth curve into a knowing smile. "I think we're good for one more adventure today."

She opened the door and reached in for the Coleman lantern. Navigating the narrow galley space, she retrieved two bottles from the stocked refrigerator. He took the water from her outstretched hand, his fingers purposely winding over hers, holding her in place. "Before we get started," he said, "maybe I should go outside, drop the stabilizing jacks and extend the slider."

"Not tonight," she purred. "The bed in the back is all we'll need."

Nate brushed the back of his fingers down the side of her cheek. After all she'd been through—*they'd* been through—she still found him desirable. "I love you, Mony Ferguson."

Mony gave an airy laugh. It was music to his ears.

Taking the beverage from her hand, he set it on the counter along with his own, then helped her out of a borrowed sweatshirt, exposing a soft tissue T-shirt and the wound on her arm. The site was clean, but the sutures looked red and angry. He gently touched her skin. "How did that happen?"

Mony brushed his fingers away. "Flying glass when my so-called rescue team started shooting up the cabin where Todd and Sissy stashed me."

"Will that hurt?"

"Not if you don't touch it."

Stealthy and playful, she moved with the self-assurance of a feline, leading him to the back of the RV. Mony finished undressing herself, a striptease for his benefit, an application of control for hers. He could have helped her, but he understood his lover's method of seduction. She needed to be in charge, and he knew why. They both had to acknowledge the trauma of her past. It would always be part of their life together; that didn't mean it had to rule it. She offered a wicked smile, sending signals of desire straight to his groin. Mony helped him out of his dirty shirt, brushing the sandy grit from the crevice of his arms. "Massey had the water tanks filled before we hit the road. It won't be very warm, but it will give you a chance to clean up. Let me help you."

Taking a disposable washcloth, she began sponging the grime off his face. The shock of the cold did nothing to squelch the desire burning inside him. Mony left a trail of kisses as she washed her way to his torso. When she reached his hips, his heat turned into an inferno. She slid the cloth easily between the apex of his thighs and cupped his scrotum in her hands, washing with gentle strokes. His head fell back when she flickered her tongue over the crown of his penis, firmly gripping his shaft before taking him in her mouth. His knees weakened, and he gripped the edge of the counter. "My God, Mony, I love your mouth."

She began kneading his inner thighs, sucking rhythmically, pulling him deeper into her mouth. She moaned softly. He felt the swell of his desire grow with intensity. "Mony—stop—I'm—going to come."

She didn't stop. His body flushed with longing. It was difficult not to grip her head and take over the pace, but he knew in order for Mony to give her love freely, he had to relinquish control. In all other matters, theirs was an equal power exchange. In lovemaking, Mony was dominant.

The bed in the back of the RV was snug for Nate's height, but if Massey and his wife could fit, so could he and Mony. Using his shoulder for a pillow, she fell asleep quickly after their little sexcapade. It was as natural as breathing, having her tucked under his arm.

He wished the rest of her night could have been as peaceful. Having shared a bed, Nate was aware that his wife was susceptible to fitful dreams—they both were, for different reasons. But her restlessness that night had a different edge, and he worried it might be due to a developing infection in her wound. He planned to speak to Blankenship about it in the morning.

It came all too soon.

The early morning air was crisp and clean as it had been the night before. The moon was still out, but Nate could see the glow of yellow, pink, and red on the eastern horizon. *Red sky in the morning, sailor take warning.* It didn't bode well for getting the RV out of the wilderness. Driving down the ramshackle road was difficult enough dry. A rainstorm would make it impassable.

Nate put his thoughts of the pending weather aside. The prospect of rain and a new day had the birds singing in joyful anticipation, lifting his mood. Crossing the parking lot, he noticed the trucks from the night before were gone save one. Several red-tailed chipmunks scurried around the wheel wells, looking for scraps of food. The sight reminded him he hadn't eaten since yesterday. Hunger hadn't troubled him up until that moment. A waft of something savory in the air changed that.

Despite the absence of people, there was an invisible thrum of energy around the encampment. The large campfire had died down overnight, though if a few logs were to be thrown onto the red-hot embers, it would easily become a roaring fire again. Nate hadn't noticed it the night before, but there were six modern tents set up on the backside of the firepit. Behind the teepee-style tent, tendrils of smoke curled upward, the source of the delicious aroma. He also hadn't noticed the dome-shaped lodge in closer proximity to the firepit. Nate wasn't as familiar with Indigenous practices as Mony, but it appeared preparations had been underway for some type of ceremony.

The dome-shaped lodge was covered in black plastic. The flap lifted. Fox Can't Be Caught emerged from the sweat lodge, wearing a towel wrapped around his hips. He was a muscular man, with numerous scars on his chest. Tall and stalwart, he walked toward the firepit and sat on a blanket next to a log. Crossing his legs in tailor fashion, he closed his eyes and began humming. Despite the public setting, Nate felt like an intruder on what appeared to be a private moment.

His eyes closed, Blankenship called out, "Come—sit." Nate approached, taking a seat on a log next to the blanket. There was an awkward silence between them when Blankenship said, "You should try it some time."

"Try what?"

"A sweat."

"You mean like a sauna?"

"There's more to a sweat than sweating."

Nate thought about that. "Is this part of a ceremony?"

"Yes. Chief Mountain is sacred to my people. Our

young come here to learn the old ways and the rituals of the Sun Dance. It will soon be upon us. Some elders were here last night teaching the young boys the songs for a sweat and how to drum in preparation. Two of our young warriors are on the mountain right now for their vision quest. They will be leaving for the Army soon. Your woman helped prepare the ceremonial meal. My mother said she did very well."

The comment made him feel unusually . . . proud. "I'm not surprised. Mony has great respect for the earth and for Native culture. It's what makes it so difficult for her being the head of an oil company. The industry goes against every fiber of her being."

"Then why does your mountain devil keep it?"

"Mountain devil?"

"It is the name my niece gave her. She fights like a wolverine."

For a brief moment, an image of Hugh Jackman popped into Nate's head. Shaking it from his thoughts, he considered Blankenship's query. He'd asked a valid question, one Nate often asked himself. Mony had a mind for business and knew how to be successful, but did she have the stamina for such an environmentally unfriendly business? "Why? Because she is a mountain devil. The land she owns is as sacred to her as that piece of rock that juts out of that mountain range yonder. It's more than a business, more than dirt, marsh, and prairie. It's memories, family, traditions, connections. It's her legacy to her children. Generational wealth given to her by her dad. She will never sell, unless there were another company out there willing to care for the environment instead of raping it. I'm not going to hold my breath on that."

"Has she considered giving it back to the people?"

"The Three Affiliated Tribes? She hasn't said it, but I'd be surprised if she hasn't thought of it. Though my dad wouldn't be keen on the idea—besides, given the chance, what's to stop the Indians from drilling the land to support their own people? This bust won't last forever, and the wealth of the world still runs on oil. It won't be long before the demand to open US reserves jumpstarts drilling on the Bakken again." Nate shook his head. "Rich men don't care who they have to use or abuse to acquire it. The world's a mess."

Blankenship opened his eyes. "There is nothing wrong with Turtle Island. Á'pistotooki will protect her and the people."

"Your people, perhaps."

"All people. If we don't kill each other first."

"I wish I had your faith."

"You can." Mony strolled into the clearing, carrying a basket laden with animal proteins and cornbread mix. Her eyes had dark circles, and her hair was a tousled mess from a fitful sleep. She set the basket at her feet and took a spot on the log next to Nate. Wrapping her arm around his middle, she leaned her head on his shoulder. "We could use a little divine intervention right about now."

Nate draped his arm over the back of her neck and tucked her into the crook of his arm. "God has nothing to do with it. As long as the world's wealth is controlled by a few, there'll always be injustice. Everyone thinks their cause is the right one, using God as vindication for their atrocities."

"Maybe it's time to change that."

"God doesn't take sides, Mony."

"You are wrong," Blankenship said. "Á'pistotooki is always on our side."

Mony left to join in the food preparations while Nate and Todd rekindled the fire in the large pit. When finished, Todd produced a handcrafted long-stem pipe made of red stone. He lit it and took several long drags, waving the tendrils of smoke toward him before offering it to Nate. "It is good for your mind and spirit. It will bring you clarity."

Nate gave a nervous laugh. "I doubt my pulmonologist would agree." As he'd anticipated, the first drag set his lungs on fire, and he coughed violently. Todd voiced no judgment as he handed back the pipe. Eventually, Nate got the hang of it and both men sat in contemplative silence, enjoying the fresh morning air and the peace that came with sharing a common act.

As the smoke filled his senses, he said to Todd, "I understand why Sissy wanted to bring Lilly to this place. It feels like an eternity since I've felt the nurturing effects of nature. Too much death since the last time my family took their annual hunting trip into Montana. Buddy, then Shannon. Someone's tried to murder me—twice."

"You romanticize my niece's motives. She is here under protest. It is a dangerous world for Indigenous women, being out there alone. She came because I brought her mother here, because they had nowhere else to go. They need to heal in heart and spirit. They need the protection and guidance of the people. Sissy does not want to accept this. She is too angry, too fixated on revenge."

"She sounds a lot like Mony, always striking out on her own, unprotected. But I understand wanting revenge against those who have hurt you or someone you love."

"That is why you and the mountain devil are here. A bitter spirit gives your enemy a great advantage in destroying you."

"Maybe Mony and I should just stay here and let the world go on without us."

"That would be irresponsible. This is a place of reflection and healing, not hiding. You and I are much alike, soohksiisiimsstaan."

"What does that mean?"

"It's our word for meadowlark. The Sioux tribes have a great affinity for meadowlarks. They see them as a symbol of friendship and loyalty. They take great care never to kill them. To the Niitsitapi, or Blackfoot, as you call us, meadowlarks are a symbol of peace, and their presence is a sign a camp or village will be safe from attack. That is why you are here. Many men have interfered with our journey, you and me. But á'pistotooki, the one who made us, has a greater purpose for us, the mountain devil, and my niece. We have too much to do before we sspomóo. We need to be quiet, listen, and accept guidance."

"And what has 'the one who made us' revealed in your quest?"

Blankenship closed his eyes. "The spirit told me to

trust the strange alliance with the mountain devil and a meadowlark."

"I need you to be more specific."

"You and your woman need to confront the enemy in a place of your choosing."

"Our land? We need to lure Monroe back to Williston? How do we do that?"

"Your woman has already arranged it. She plans to cheat your enemy at his own dirty game."

CHAPTER 22

MASSEY

In a raspy smoker's voice, the dispatcher escorting Massey and Kip to Sheriff Wagner's office said, "He's out on a call and said he'd be back shortly. That was forty-five minutes ago. I wouldn't go placing any bets on when he actually shows."

"Does he know we're waiting for him?" Kip asked.

"No," Sophie said with indignation. "Attorney Ferguson told me not to tell him. I know how to follow directions." She lifted her chin and closed the door behind her in a huff.

The two men took a seat in the molded plastic chairs. Massey asked his dad, "Do you think Wagner suspects anything?"

"Possibly, but I doubt it. Besides, let's not jump to any conclusions. I want to hear what Scott has to say before passing a guilty verdict. We're still missing a motive."

"If rumor is true, blackmail. It's Shannon's MO—"

"Son, our dear Shannon had dirt on everyone without exception. The woman had the ears of a bat and eyes like a hawk. She could sniff out a secret like a bloodhound. It doesn't necessarily mean she used the trait against a friend."

"Do you think Richards was telling the truth when he said he'd seen Wagner at Shannon's apartment?"

"No, his timeline is off. If Scott was there, Gunsel got the news secondhand."

"Why would he make an accusation that verifies he was also at her apartment?"

"He never said he was, only that he saw Wagner. I think he's trying to work it within the confines of his alibi, validating himself as an accessory to murder, not the trigger man."

"Hmm. . . casting doubt."

"Exactly. Without his skinhead posse and with Mitchell still missing, Richards can blame whoever he wants with no one around to step forward and challenge it. He can plead to the lesser charges, asserting he did the dirty deed under duress."

"That may be true, but it won't exonerate him of murder."

"Not in the eyes of the law, perhaps, but in his warped perception of things it might."

Sheriff Wagner came barreling into his office ten minutes later. The man looked frazzled, his face as ruddy as if he'd been running a marathon in the heat of the day. Muttering incoherently to himself, it took a beat before he looked up and realize he wasn't alone. "Jesus Christ, how'd you get in here?"

"A little jumpy there, aren't you, Scott?" Kip replied.

Wagner walked behind his desk and sat rigidly in his chair, visibly pulling himself together. Massey could already sense the lies about to spew out of their former ally's mouth. "Can whatever this is wait, Kip? I'm dealing with a lot of bullshit today."

"I imagine so. Trying to wrap up a double homicide while you're up to your eyeballs in it can generate a lot of shit."

"What the hell is that supposed to mean?"

"It means you're too close to this case, and you're losing objectivity."

"There's nothing wrong with my objectivity. Has Shawn been complaining again?"

"It's been a week since I've seen Shawn, and he has every right to demand his sister's killer be brought to justice."

"I'm not saying he doesn't have a right. I'm saying he's been on a bender since Shannon's funeral and he's being irrational. I caught him just the other night with a shotgun in his chassis, driving drunk out to that old abandoned farmstead north of Tioga, where those Nazi rats are camped out. If I hadn't intercepted him, he'd have ended up crashing into the ditch or been beaten to death after accusing them of murder."

"You think so?" Massey interjected. "My guess is they'd have probably thrown Richards under the bus and sent Shawn after him to finish their dirty work."

It appeared that thought hadn't occurred to the sheriff. "Humph. Richards won't be released from the hospital for a couple more days. Shawn could easily—" He broke off and pressed a button on his office intercom. "Sophie, I want you to alert our team guarding Richards to be on the watch for Shawn McDonald."

"Our Shawn?"

"Yes, Shawn. If he steps one toe on the hospital campus, I want him to be arrested, immediately."

"Arrested? On what grounds?"

"On the grounds he's a dumbass and he's going to get himself shot. Better yet, put a tail on him. I want to know his location at all times. Gomez's team is still mulling around in town, don't want anyone getting trigger happy."

"Okay, but—"

"Just do it, Sophie." Despite the air-conditioning, the sheriff pulled a bandana from his shirt pocket and mopped his glistening forehead.

When the sheriff cut the mic, Massey cut to the chase. "We found the Moonbeam girl."

The sheriff gave him a puzzled look. "Which one?"

"Sissy."

"Are you sure?"

"Why would I lie about that?"

"I didn't say you weren't telling the truth. I asked, are you sure?"

"Are you saying I can't distinguish one Indian girl from another?"

"Finch couldn't."

"Jesus, I've met the girl—in person. She claims she saw you and Richards at Shannon's apartment the morning she was killed."

"Unlikely. What time did I arrive?"

"Somewhere between five and five-thirty."

"Did she actually see me arrive?"

"She didn't say—"

"Well, there you go. She's lying."

"She saw you leave. She didn't see you arrive, because you'd entered from inside the bar through the interior stairwell," Kip said flatly.

The existence of the interior stairwell from the kitchen to the upstairs apartment wasn't common knowledge. Only members of the McDonald family and close friends like the Fergusons, Buddy Altman, Virgil, Vernon, and the sheriff were aware of it, mostly in the event of an emergency or fire. In Nate's case, it had been a means of stealing a quickie during one of Shannon's shift breaks. "According to the fingerprints lifted by Detective Gomez's team, you'd traveled those stairs quite frequently prior to Shannon's death."

"That doesn't mean anything."

"It points to you spending a lot of time going up and down those stairs, Scott. Perhaps having an affair with Shannon."

Wagner scoffed. "Where in the hell did you come up with such a crazy idea?"

Massey changed up his line of questioning. "Tell me about your scuba diving training this past winter."

Prior to their blowout, Shannon had informed Nate she was flying to Cozumel for a destination wedding. "You told my dad you had planned on taking your wife Wendy to Mexico, but it fell through when she developed a severe case of the stomach flu at the last minute. As I recall, you'd used the time off to recertify your underwater rescue and scuba diving license. Except you didn't. You used that time to shack up with Shannon in Cozumel."

"That's ridiculous," Wagner retorted. "I'm a married man."

"All the more reason to keep the rendezvous a secret."

"It's a flimsy theory, Massey. Besides, there's no proof."

"Oh, there is plenty of that," Massey countered. "Not only are your fingerprints all over the banister, but there's Shannon's confession. You see, she got pretty wasted one night and spilled her guts to her brother about the trip. She even asked him for advice on choosing between you and Nate. With my brother MIA in Vegas, your odds were improving."

"That's not evidence, it's conjecture."

Massey wanted to punch him. "You were the one who placed the crystal decanter in the trash."

"Watch it, Massey, you're teetering on slander. Where's your proof?"

Massey pulled out his cell phone and paged through his uploaded photos. He handed it to Wagner. "Is that proof enough?"

Wagner tapped on the photo, enlarging it and studied it carefully. He handed the phone back to Massey. "I'm likely picking the decanter out of the garbage, not putting it in."

"I thought you might say that." Massey pulled up a seventeen-second video depicting Wagner coming down the back stairs off Shannon's deck, carrying the decanter and a paper bag in his hand. He dropped the decanter into the garbage, then placed the paper bag over the top and walked back up the stairs.

Wagner sat silent.

Kip lost his composure. "For the love of God, Scott. This is serious. Gomez's team found your blood on the interior wall of the stairwell."

Wagner sat stone-faced for a long moment before breathing a sigh of resignation. Abruptly, he unpinned his badge from his uniform shirt and tossed it on his desk. He then reached into his bottom drawer and pulled out a half-empty bottle of bourbon along with three tumblers. Pouring three fingers into each, he raised his glass in a mock toast and tossed it back, then shuddered. "Drinking's just not the same since Shannon's been gone."

"Are you going to tell us what really happened?"

Wagner sighed. "Things have been rocky between me and Wendy for quite a while now. The trip to Mexico was our last-ditch effort to rekindle some sort of spark in our marriage. When Wendy got sick, it felt like an omen. Shannon had already covered the expenses in Cozumel so it wouldn't show up on my credit card bill. I paid her back, of course."

"I already know that," Massey interjected. "Shawn found Shannon's bank statement. Tell us what we don't know—like why your blood's in the stairwell, and why you threw away the decanter?"

Wagner sat motionless, looking like a man lost in a dream. "Shannon was the best part of my day. Sometimes we'd just sit and talk; most mornings we made love. She was always up for it. The morning Mony found her in the lake, I'd gone up to see her. I knew right away something was off. When I unlocked the door, the space felt cold, dark, and empty. You remember how Shannon could always light up a room. I looked around—saw the rumpled bedsheets, the empty bottle of whiskey—two tumblers. She'd told me she was inviting Finch for dinner. Said she was doing it for Cindy and that it didn't concern me. I'd tried talking her out of it. Told her no good would come from hooking up with a sleazy lawyer from Chicago. She told me to mind my own business—she knew what she was doing. It was a lie."

"The smell of hard sex lingering in the air sickened me. I threw one of the Waterford crystal tumblers I'd given her for Christmas against the wall. I must have cut my hand when I swept the shards into a paper bag. I threw it out with the decanter because, well, I was pissed. I wanted to hurt her. The decanter had been handed down from her great-grandmother. I didn't know it was a murder weapon until afterward."

"Is that why you didn't meet up for coffee that morning?" Kip asked. "Because you already knew Shannon was missing?"

"I didn't say she was missing, I said she wasn't in her apartment. I drove around town a bit, checked her usual stops—came to the office. It wasn't long after that Mony radioed she'd seen something floating in the lake."

As Massey listened to Wagner's account, his annoyance grew. It reeked of contradictions. "Can anyone corroborate your story?"

"Probably not. My wife can't tell you what time I left

our home because our bedrooms are on opposite sides of the house. She's usually still sleeping when I leave. Sophie can verify what time I arrived at the office."

In exasperation, Kip burst out, "Jesus Christ, Scott, you were having an affair with a woman you just admitted you wanted to hurt, and you have almost three hours unaccounted for. Plus, you're videotaped tampering with evidence at a crime scene. What the hell were you thinking?"

Wagner rubbed a hand over his face. "If only she'd have listened to me, she'd still be alive."

Kip stood from his chair and leaned over Wagner's desk. "You have to step down from this investigation, Scott, and let the feds handle it."

Wagner hung his head. "I still can't believe she's gone."

"Detective Gomez is on her way here, right now, with a warrant for your arrest."

"Kip, I—I loved her."

"You need to stop talking, Scott, and get your shit together. Call your lawyer, now, before the detective arrives."

"I swear to you, Kip, I didn't kill her."

"Maybe, maybe not," Massey interjected. "Either way, you're not telling the whole truth. Dad's right, Sheriff. You need to lawyer up—now."

CHAPTER 23

JOHN

John set his satchel and coffee on his desk and plopped down in his chair, exhausted. Walking into his office at the law firm of Temple, Rice, and Goldman, he felt like an alien touching down on another planet. The obvious stares and whispers that followed him down the hallway were unnerving. An air of impending doom seemed to drift throughout the office suite. Taking a sip of coffee, he surveyed the familiar space. Everything seemed in its proper place, so why did it feel like someone had rifled through his entire office? Searching for what, he couldn't say.

An electronic notepad and a couple of brown bags in his hand, Franklin entered the office and greeted him in the usual manner. "Good morning, boss. I stopped at Freshii and grabbed a couple of green juice cleanses, two Buddha satay bowls, and that spicy lemongrass soup you like. Plus, I got a dozen energii bites. I'm guessing we're working straight through the morning while I bring you up to speed. By the way, has anyone told you that you look thinner? Oh, welcome back."

It was nice to know some things hadn't changed.

They spent the morning reviewing John's case load, which had been distributed to other junior associates in his absence. Because most of his time had been spent in preparation for Monroe's attempt to take over F&A Oil prior to his departure, there wasn't much unfinished business left on his plate. Franklin took a bite of the protein chew. "You already know the outcome of the Altman land acquisition debacle. But did you know it's been a losing streak for Ethan Rice ever since?"

"How so?"

"Well for one, he lost that restaurateur mogul's divorce case."

"Are you kidding me? That case was practically a freebie. Not only was his client's asshole husband caught embezzling from her company, but he'd gotten his side piece knocked up. She should be having the kid by now."

"Remember how you never got involved with the client until . . . after the case was over?"

". . . he didn't."

"Several times, apparently."

John shook his head. "Idiot."

"It might also please you to know Ethan's wife Tiffany found out about the affair. She kicked him out of the house in true jilted lover's fashion. Left his clothes and personal effects on the front yard with a sign, 'Free for the taking.' I guess this ain't her mama's broken heart. Anyway, she's your two o'clock this afternoon."

"Well, shit." That had fallen apart much quicker than he'd anticipated. John had always been on good terms with Tiffany Monroe-Rice, but representing her in a divorce case would not only place him in an awkward position, but do the same for the entire firm. "Aren't Randall and Ethan meeting with the Monroes here later today?"

Franklin gave him a sly look. "As a matter of fact, they are. She wants to serve him the papers at the meeting."

"Do Fran and Goldman know all this?"

"Nope—just me, now you."

John got up from his chair and stood in front of his west-view window. The sky was mostly sunny, giving the city a glossy new glow. "Holy Christ. This entire building is about to become ground zero for the Monroe meltdown."

"That meltdown would be to our advantage, wouldn't it?"

"That depends on Tia. She revels in a good drama. If she goes too far off the rails, she may make a hasty decision and really fuck things up. I need her to keep a level head and an open mind. Attorney Ferguson has suggested arranging a meeting between her and Ramona Strong."

Franklin reared his head back. "What on earth for?"

John had experienced the same reaction. The oil heiresses were about as opposite as two women could be. Matthew had assured John he had a solid motive for the proposal. That wasn't the half of it. "At this point, the less you know, the less potential there is for an unwanted visitor showing up on your doorstep in the middle of the night. If you thought things were violent before, let me tell you about my abduction, then you can decide how much you really want to know."

Fashionably late, Tiffany Monroe-Rice was dressed to the nines in a blush pink bodycon dress, a simple Tahitian pearl necklace with matching teardrop earrings and bracelet, and a pair of white slingback strap Louboutin. She looked every bit an oil heiress. Her appearance was in direct contrast to Ramona Strong, whose wealth superseded Tia's twelvefold. She air-kissed John on the cheek. "You poor, poor dear. Didn't those terrible people feed you? Why, it's uncivilized. There's nothing left of you."

Since his return to Chicago, John had avoided a mirror, especially after his trainwreck reunion with his sister and her wife. They'd bawled unabashed for twenty minutes, offering him food, protein drinks, and carbs. He waved off the comment. "You know I'm a creature of strict habit. A few weeks back in the dojo and I'll be as good as new. But enough about me. Please, Tia, have a seat. Tell me what I can do for you today."

He took the visitor's chair next to Tia and let her rant and rage about Ethan's whole affair. Thirty minutes into the exposition, John was glad they had this moment in private, rather than in the boardroom in front of her soon-to-be ex. Clutching a floral print handkerchief, she dabbed at the corner of her eyes, careful not to smear her liner. "I shouldn't be so upset. I've known about Ethan's infidelity for a long while. But my dignity can no longer abide his brazen contempt. It isn't as if he'd found someone better. I mean, honestly, look at me. I have the perfect pedigree, wealth, family, education, and etiquette." She gestured at herself from top to bottom. "What could possibly be a step up from this?"

John patted her slender shoulder. "He's a fool, Tia, blinded by his own inflated ego."

She breathed a resolute sigh. "This just seems a good time to end the relationship, you know? The prenup will protect what is mine, and I'm perfectly willing to let him keep what is his." She gave a devilish laugh. "If it hasn't been stolen off the lawn already. All I want from you is to make certain he doesn't come after what is mine. We have no pets or children to complicate the matter. I believe this will be good for me. I've been wanting to become more involved in the oil business."

John rolled his eyes inwardly. "As your lawyer, I would advise you that now is not a good time to become involved in the oil business."

She stiffened her chin. "And why not? Daddy says the business is expanding. I'm sure there would be plenty for me to do."

If only. "Wouldn't you rather establish your own business brand? Oil is a dirty, corrupt, undignified, cutthroat affair."

Tia placed a hand on his knee. "You don't think I'm capable of dealing with a few unruly men? Remember where I came from. I've been around cowboys all my life."

John rephrased his comment. "What I'm saying is, the oil business just isn't a good investment at this time—it's headed toward a bust, and things will only get worse. I'd even advised your father against expanding before my unsubstantiated detainment. Besides, I have it on good authority that F&A Oil has no intention of selling the business cheap. Even if it were cheap, your father simply doesn't have enough liquid assets. He would go bankrupt in his pursuit." John mimicked Tia's seductive gesture. "Now, financing a salon, spa, or resort? That would be a great investment. Far less volatile and much more suited to your creative aptitude."

"But I want the oil business," she pouted prettily. "Before my irresponsible brother ruins it."

John hid his surprise at the remark—it seemed his debutante knew more about the situation than she was letting on. He weighed his next words carefully. "Tia, do you trust me?"

She blinked at him with doe eyes. "John, I'm hurt by the insinuation. Of course I trust you, I'm here, aren't I? You've never steered me wrong and have always looked out for my best interest." Her eyes began to well again.

He searched for sincerity behind the waterworks. "Then please, trust me when I say that you won't have a business to get involved in by year's end."

Tia's eyes suddenly narrowed, her expression hardening. "Do you have proof to substantiate such an audacious claim?"

"Yes, Tia, I do. Unfortunately, I'm not at liberty to share it."

She frowned. "Then it is you who lacks trust. Does this have something to do with that dreadful investigation headed by that inept sheriff?"

"No, the FBI is running the show now. I can put you in contact with the lead detective on the case—we're on a first-name basis—but before I do that, you need to promise you won't share any of the information with your father."

"My God, are you asking me to betray my family?"

"Tia, do you know how your father supplements his oil wells in North Dakota?"

"John, you're scaring me. What in heaven's name is wrong with Daddy's business?"

He fingered the Tibetan pearl dangling from her ear and whispered, "Sweetheart. Are you prepared to sacrifice your lifestyle for someone who has already betrayed you?" John reached in his shirt pocket for a clean handkerchief and handed it to her. "Best you get all your tears out now, then use my private washroom to freshen your makeup. When you've finished, I'm going to need your answer."

Thomas Monroe sat on the opposite side of the table, flanked by his son Jason and son-in-law Ethan. Randall Rice sat next to his son. Fran Temple joined John and Franklin on their side, with Quincy Goldman assuming the head of the table. The tension in the room was palpable.

John began the meeting. "Franklin is distributing an updated summary of Ramona Altman's business holdings in the oil company, along with the property she owns in North Dakota and the frack sand quarry in Minnesota. Despite the oil industry heading for a bust, not only has the company increased its profit, but the value of her properties has increased exponentially. She's diversified a great deal of her investments in the entertainment industry in response to her partner returning to the music business, which is also showing a significant profit. If you're serious about buying out her oil business and property holdings, you're going to have to come up with a purchase agreement she can't walk away from."

John cued Franklin, who distributed a single-page document. "This is her asking price."

All eyes studied the information intently—all except Ethan's. "Why sell now? What's wrong with the business?"

Fran Temple answered, "Ethan, read the information in front of you. There is no indication she's selling, nor is there anything wrong with the business."

"Broadly speaking," John broke in, "two of the three owners are showing a growing disinterest in running the oil business. Senator Ferguson is ready to retire. You've expressed an interest in purchasing the business. They're giving you first opportunity."

"Generous," Jason sneered. "She couldn't have come to that conclusion a little sooner?"

"It is what it is, Jason. Perhaps she and Mr. Ferguson are tired of having their lives threatened. She's already lost two close friends in connection with the oil business."

"We had nothing to do with that," Thomas snapped. "That incompetent investigative team and their slanderous accusations will earn them a billion-dollar lawsuit if they don't back off."

"I'm not saying you did anything, sir, just relaying what I know."

"The cops seem damn convinced we did."

"Hell, Dad," Jason cut across him, "let it go. This is what we've been working toward. Don't give that bitch a chance to change her mind."

Fran Temple's face lit with fury. "I've warned you for the last time, Mr. Monroe. I will not tolerate your derogatory language. If you can't keep a civil tongue, our firm will no longer manage your account. Is that understood?"

Randall Rice's face flared equally red. "Says who? After all, we should be creating an environment for all our clients to speak freely, without judgment."

Fran stood her ground. "We are professionals, Randall. I will not idly stand by and let a foul-mouthed sexist mar the integrity of this firm. Either Mr. Monroe speaks in a respectable manner or he leaves this building, immediately."

In a tone of derision, Monroe Senior said, "Let's all just take it down a notch. My son can keep a civil tongue in his mouth, can't you, Jason?"

Fran challenged, "I want to hear that from him."

Randall, Thomas, and Ethan collectively glowered in Jason's direction, bullying him into submission. His tone contemptuous, he grumbled, "I'll be civil."

Fran gave him a scathing glare. "We shall see."

John brought the meeting back on point. "As you can see, Ms. Altman has stipulated in a purchase agreement that all members with a claim or holding in Monroe Oil must be in unanimous agreement before proceeding with any further transaction."

Ethan spoke out of turn: "That's no problem. We're all in agreement."

Jason concurred. "Yes, everyone is in agreement."

"I'm afraid you're incorrect," Fran interjected. "Ms. Tiffany Monroe-Rice isn't here to validate that statement."

Ethan retorted, "I speak on my wife's behalf. She'll see the investment opportunity once it's explained to her."

"Your word has no weight in this matter, Ethan," John told him.

"Don't be an ass. My wife and I are always on the same page."

"Is that so?" John handed Ethan his divorce papers. "You mean this page?"

Ethan snatched the document and began reading, his eyes widening with horror. "What the hell is the meaning of this?"

"Isn't it apparent? Your wife is choosing to speak on her own behalf."

Monroe Senior reached for the papers. "Let me see that." He scanned them briefly, then tossed them back at John. "What sort of sick joke are you playing here, Finch?"

There was a soft knock at the conference room door. Fran's secretary announced, "Please excuse the interruption. Ms. Monroe is ready to join the meeting."

Per John's advice, Tia immediately rejected the F&A purchase proposal, sending the other side of the table into a tailspin. Monroe Senior approached the matter with all the subtlety of a neon sign hanging in a tavern window.

His daughter deflected each approach with the ease of a horse swishing its tail at a pesky fly. "I just can't right now, Daddy. I'm in the middle of a divorce. I need to take care of myself."

Jason flung a few insults at his sister in a last-ditch effort to break her, but both sides of the table forced him into an austere silence. Talks deteriorated after that, Tia's resolve not far behind. When it appeared she'd reached her limit, John suggested tabling the matter for a later date.

Like two sparring boxers, each team retreated to their respective corners. Franklin escorted Tia to Fran's private washroom, while Fran walked with John back to his office. The moment they were behind closed doors, she snapped, "Are you willfully trying to destroy this company?"

John had always retained the utmost respect for Fran, not least because she'd often sided with him in past disputes. Since his incarceration, however, he no longer held her favor, nor did he regard her with the same esteem. Fran had never kept it secret that the reputation and integrity of her law firm had always been her highest priority. The Monroe-Rice fiasco that had just played out in the boardroom would surely be its demise. John knew she would stop at nothing, go down swinging if she had to, to protect her company. First, though, she had to get her own partners to regard their company with the same tenacity.

"I'm not the one you need to be concerned about," he told her.

Fran gave him a scathing look. "Oh, but I am, John. I

only allowed you to keep the Monroe account because you assured me you could handle it."

"I can handle the Monroe account. It's the dissolution of Ethan and Tiffany's marriage that you should be focusing on. Ethan's made a real mess of his nuptial bed, and now he'll have to sleep in it—soiled sheets and all. If Randall sides with Ethan, which I fully anticipate, they will likely drag the matter out in court. You and I both know they will lose, badly. You've seen the prenup. It's rock solid. That's what will split your law firm straight down the middle, leaving Goldman the tiebreaker. We both know he has neither the stomach nor the heart to shoulder that burden. Thomas and Jason are coming to grips with their own business failings. Things will return to the status quo in a day or two."

"A day or two? Don't be arrogant, John. It doesn't become you."

"It's not arrogance, it's fact. The business became muddied when Ethan lost the probate challenge and decided to publicly humiliate his wife. Once he's out of the picture, daughter, father, and brother will come to their own terms regarding the business. Thomas never liked him anyway, and Tiffany has a right to extricate herself from a loveless marriage."

"I'm not saying she doesn't have the right or just cause," Fran retorted. "I'm saying, why did you take the case knowing full well the strife it would cause in this office?"

"Simple: because she asked me to."

"Now you are being obtuse. There is nothing simple about this matter."

"With all due respect, I disagree. I've known the family for more than twenty years. I know all of their dirty little secrets. There is only one thing that drives them—money. I have devised a strategy for Ms. Monroe to exit her adulterous marriage and satisfy her brother and father's goal of acquiring the F&A business, if they have the money to do so."

"Ms. Monroe made it clear that she has no intention of consenting to the purchase of Ms. Altman's business or property holdings."

"That is true. As long as she holds a claim in Monroe Oil, she will not invest in expansion. But what if she relinquishes that claim?"

"John, why would she give away her inheritance?"

"Who said anything about giving it away?"

Fran lifted her hand. "I don't want to hear any more of your plan, but I will say this. Make no mistake, Mr. Finch, I'm holding you responsible for any negative publicity brought to this company. We've already been forced to rebrand ourselves because of your incarceration in North Dakota. It doesn't matter that the FBI have cleared you of any wrongdoing—the public still considers you culpable, me included. You were given your job back only because to do otherwise would have resulted in a lawsuit that wasn't worth the investment." She held up her pointer finger. "You are one slip-up away from termination."

"I'll accept responsibility for my actions, but let me make this clear to you. I will not be the scapegoat for Randall, Ethan, or the Monroes' actions as they impact this law firm. The onus belongs to each individual alone, exclusively."

Fran pursed her lips. "Where's your decanter? I'm in serious need of a drink."

CHAPTER 24

NATE

Nate reached for Mony's hand under the mahogany table. She gave it a reassuring squeeze. He hated the pre-meeting façade—the greasy handshakes, schmoozing, cocktails, and hors d'oeuvres. Mony, by contrast worked the room like a lioness in sheep's clothing, stalking her prey, smiling, laughing, stroking egos. She'd even melted the icy female lawyer's exterior by discussing how best to reduce her Yorkipoo's risk for Legg-Calve-Perthes disease, whatever the hell that was. She had smitten the sailors by talking about her experience on Lake Michigan, and enthralled the portly lawyer with her aviation tales. Even Monroe Senior wasn't immune to her wit and charm. Monroe Junior, however, remained aloof.

The tall, silver-haired man, complete with a spray tan, capped teeth, and a face full of Botox, took charge, introducing his team in a smooth baritone voice. His condescending grin set Nate's nerves on edge. Explaining Finch's absence in a sentence, the F&A team feigned indifference to the matter. If given a choice, Nate would have almost preferred his rival over the viper staring back at him. At least he knew that enemy and his wife's persuasive power over him.

To the slimy lawyer's left sat the taut-faced woman and the perspiring, porcine man; to the right, Monroes Senior and Junior and another person who looked familiar, his name elluding him. Behind them sat a line of paralegals, each with dark circles under their eyes and riding a caffeine buzz. Nate chuckled to himself. Massey's assistant Jesse was preparing to leave for Dickenson to catch his daughter's Bantam softball tournament. Jealous, Nate wished he were going too.

The opposing lawyer continued, "Thank you for agreeing to meet with us on such short notice and in such sumptuous accommodations. Ingenious to have a conference room in an airport terminal." He eyed the bar. "I don't think even O'Hare has a conference room as—should I say—well stocked as this."

Massey launched the first volley of the morning. "We completed the build on this wing in 2009 to accommodate the increased business clientele flying in and out of Sloulin International." He pointed to Monroe Junior. "Some members of your team, including John Finch, have already enjoyed our hospitality in this very room."

Nate suppressed a laugh. He remembered that meeting—Monroe Junior had pissed himself.

Massey continued, "I've been informed by the company's attorney, Mr. Finch, that you have a purchase proposal for F&A Oil Company."

Rice gave a smirk and waggled his finger at Massey.

"Straight to business. I like that. My team will distribute copies for everyone's viewing." The paralegals sprang from their seats as if their asses were on fire, laying thick spiral-bound books in front of everyone at the table.

Kip didn't bother to crack the binder. "You could have saved yourself a long trip and faxed or emailed this."

"Yes," said Randall with an easy smile, "we could have. But we like to do business the old-fashioned way. It's the personal touch that drives America, don't you think?"

The F&A Oil team prudently perused the document. It was for show—Finch had already shared the details. Kip launched the second volley, nitpicking a couple of clerical errors and discrepancies, sending the paralegal team into a frenzy. Tuning out of the conversation, Nate mindlessly flipped through the pages as he focused his attention on the other side of the table. Monroe Junior was as disengaged from the meeting as him, looking down at his phone—he could have been playing a video game for all anyone knew. His actions did not go unnoticed—Monroe Senior shot his son a stern look, and Junior shoved the phone in his pants pocket.

Nate felt Mony's body lean toward Massey. She was pointing to something on one of the pages. Massey flipped to the same page and jotted a few notes. "Is this correct? You plan to use your own oil company as collateral to make the purchase?"

"Yes, we have already secured preapproval for the dollar amount listed on page five. The market value on Monroe Oil is considerable. We would like—"

Mony interrupted, "Let me get this straight—the bank

gets your company when the oil business goes bust, and we get—what? Looks to me like you're counting on a quick sale because for some reason you think the pending bust will undervalue our assets."

"Ms. Strong, let me explain—"

Mony crossed her arms. "As a shareholder, you're thinking you can recoup your money by promoting the sale of pieces of our business and land parcels when the bust is over. Not on my watch. Absolutely no loans. This is a cash purchase only, or no deal."

Sweat began to bead around Randall's lips. "Ms. Strong, no major business has the liquid assets necessary to cover this type of purchase. We need—"

"We do. If we don't have the cash, we don't make the purchase. Even if our company were public, which it isn't, you couldn't afford two shares with this paltry offer." Mony slapped the book closed. "Mr. Finch had assured us there would be a legitimate offer at this table. If this is the best you've got, it's an utter waste of our time."

Nate noticed the female lawyer's lips crack into a millisecond's smirk. He struggled to suppress his own. My, how his woman could push just the right buttons to infuriate a man. "And another thing," Mony added. "Where is Ms. Monroe-Rice? The stipulation was that all members of the Monroe family were to be in agreement on this purchase."

Monroe Junior was snorting from the nostrils like a bull ready to charge, Monroe Senior not far behind. He made excuses, trash-talking Finch and his incompetence. The man whose name Nate couldn't remember tried to join in the fray, but Old Man Monroe shut him down with a dirty look. As much as Nate hated letting Mony step into the line of fire, he loved watching her shred her opponent. He let her go a few minutes before it was time for him to post up.

As the Monroe team scrambled for footing, Nate said, "Hold on, Mony. You don't want to run the oil business, and neither do I. Maybe we should, you know, sell some shares and transition out of the whole thing."

Mony shot him an incredulous look. It made him shiver. "Are you out of your mind? We're taking all the risk. Add together our mutual fund assets and cash, subtract liabilities, and divide by the number of shares outstanding. This is a hostile takeover."

Kip stoked the argument. "Will you two just calm down? If that's how you really feel, maybe this is something we should consider. I can't run this business by myself forever."

The phrase *calm down* was a major trigger in just about any argument. Mony unleashed hell as they argued among themselves, pretending to be oblivious to their audience. Maintaining a degree of seriousness in this make-believe fight was difficult; before long, Nate had to tap out, letting his other three actors continue to sling insults. Fifteen minutes passed before Mony made her dramatic exit, storming out of the room.

Composing himself, Nate's brother feigned embarrassment and smoothed his tie. "How long did your team say they planned to be in town, Attorney Rice?"

The two lawyers worked out the timeline and logistics

for reviewing the offer. As the rest of the Monroe team filtered out of the room, Nate overheard Randall remark, "You got a real spitfire on your hands with that one."

Monroe Senior added, "My daughter has better business etiquette than that woman."

Randall concurred. "I've seen it time and again—women don't really have the emotional fortitude for business talks."

Nate couldn't help but thinking that, had Mony heard the remarks, she would have buried Monroe Oil's business on the spot. Leaning over to Monroe Senior, he asked, "Is that why you left your daughter at home?"

CHAPTER 25

MASSEY

Massey entered his office reception area expecting to find Mony. He found Sheriff Wagner waiting instead. Striding in behind Massey, Kip saw his old friend and asked, "What are you doing here, Scott?" When last they'd spoken, Detective Gomez had placed the sheriff on administrative leave after his interrogation. She'd held him in a safe house, pending further investigation of his involvement in murder.

The sheriff pulled his cell phone from his pocket and handed it to Massey. "I want you to take a closer look at this video."

It was the video forwarded by Sissy. Nate and Kip looked on over his shoulder as they watched the video start to finish. "What are we supposed to be seeing, Scott?"

"Look again."

"I have this video too. I suggest we go in my office and sync it with the flatscreen for a better look."

It was a low-resolution file, making the foreground blurry, but Massey was able to make out the images in

the back of the parking lot. He recognized the man—
Anton Kuznetsov, with his hand covering Cindy Van
Dyke's mouth.

"Jesus," he hissed, "no wonder we missed it. And you
didn't know about that at all?"

"That's what I want to talk about," said the sheriff. "He
arrived in Williston shortly after Buddy Altman's funeral.
Pulled up a bar stool next to me at the Blarney Stone one
night, started pummeling me with questions about the
crime rate in the area. As you can imagine, there was a
lot to tell."

"Did he ever ask about Mony or our family?"

"He asked about all the oil companies in the county.
Which ones were legit and corrupt, which ones had a good
reputation for taking care of the workers, the environment, no illicit side activities, that sort of thing. Of course,
your company floated to the top as being squeaky clean,
despite Candy Man—ah, I mean Cayden Peckersch's efforts to smear you in the papers. He told me he had an
understanding of the demands on law enforcement, especially in remote areas where conglomerates were clamor-
ing for the same resources. He knew how the jobs often
drew *undesirables* to a community."

"Did you hire him?"

"More like he was hiring me. He certainly had credible
references, plus considerable experience in the oil industry in both Russia and Ukraine. He understood what I was
up against."

"So how did the two of you become . . . *associates*?"

"He just randomly showed up when first responders

found Sissy Moonbeam half beaten to death behind the Lake Zahl bar. Shannon was on that call. She didn't like his involvement. Said he had a bad vibe. Anyway, he accompanied me to Harland Richards's trailer after we figured out she was one of his girls. I'm telling you, he started busting heads."

"Why?"

"Said he had no tolerance for human trafficking. Claimed his baby sister had been taken in a trafficking scam back in Russia. Harland told him there was no human trafficking, they were all working girls making money for themselves."

"He bought that bullshit?"

"The girls all corroborated his story."

"Of course they did. Either they were too afraid to tell the truth or they'd been threatened. Besides, what minor is going to admit to prostitution in front of a cop?"

"Anton said the business seemed legit and told me to let it go—said I had bigger fish to fry. Most of the girls were runaways anyway and had nowhere else to go. Up until Mitchell got involved, that is."

"Who teamed up with Mitchell?"

"Richards was the go-between. Why, I'm not sure. His operation had been sliding under the radar for the most part until kids in social services' custody started disappearing."

"Why did Richards and Mitchell take the girls in Cindy's care?"

"Outside pressure. The oil boom was clearly going bust. Potential clients were leaving the Bakken hand over fist.

Their business was plummeting. Someone was trying to muscle in and control the prostitution market before it moved on to the next location."

"Someone like Monroe?"

"You'll have to ask Mitchell that question, if you can find him. As long as I wasn't finding half-beaten kids lying in street gutters or our high school students strung out on drugs, I stayed out of it."

"Jesus."

"Better than the alternative. Violent crime against the citizens of Williston dropped considerably after Anton came on the scene."

"Was that all this Kuznetsov helped you with?"

"No. We raided several man camps, busting up drug sales, meth labs, gun runners, you name it. Sometimes we'd go together when the location was remote, but most of the time I led the raid with my deputies under Anton's direction."

"And you never asked yourself why he was doing this or how he knew so much about the illicit business happening on the Bakken?"

"I figured he was working for a private agency. Man, it was too good to be true. We worked well together. You might say we even became friends."

"Christ, Scott, he was vetting you," Kip exclaimed.

Massey asked, "Did he ever mention Monroe or being on his payroll?"

"Not directly, but I overheard a conversation when we were busting up a meth lab over in Big Meadow Township. It was the same night Finch fuck—went to Shannon's apartment. Anton took a call in the middle of the raid. He mentioned Monroe's name and chewed his ass—royally. I overheard him say, 'You don't send a bunch of wannabe skinheads to dispatch an important hit.' At first I thought he was talking about the local chapter, until he mentioned the location—Arizona."

"And you didn't arrest him then?"

"On what charges? For knowing something about someone?"

Kip was livid. "You had some deep Donnie Brasco shit going on, didn't you? You knew he sent those goddamn Nazis to kill my son and you didn't say anything?"

"Who was I going to tell? None of you were around, and things went to shit so fast. Mony reported Shannon's body in the lake that morning, and by nightfall, you, Mony, and Poppy had flown to Lake Havasu City. You know the rest of the story."

"Let's back up to the video," said Massey. "You knew Kuznetsov had taken Cindy, didn't you?"

The sheriff nodded.

"And you know who killed her."

Wagner hung his head. "Richards is being framed for Cindy's murder, but Anton pulled the trigger."

"You know this? How?"

"I was there."

"And Shannon?"

The sheriff's face contorted into a pained expression. "I killed her."

As Massey and Kip stood there in shock, Nate became furious. "Did you actually pull the trigger?"

"I may as well have."

Nate grabbed the sheriff by the shirt collar. "You're not making sense."

Wagner began to sob. "She just couldn't stay out of it. I told her Cindy was already a dead woman long before that stupid video."

"What do you mean?"

"They fucked up. She and Mitchell fucked up."

"Fucked up what, for Christ's sake?"

Wagner was no longer talking to the room. "Neither of them should have trusted Monroe. Anton warned them do not draw attention. Said they were expanding the business too quickly. That was about the time the Moonbeam girl decided to go rogue."

"Are you saying Sissy tried to take over the operation?"

"I begged Shannon not to tag along with me out there. I told her, stay out of it. I said she was going to get herself killed. She wouldn't listen. She thought I would protect her. Me, the Williams County sheriff. How wrong she was."

"She was there when Kuznetsov kidnapped and murdered Cindy."

The sheriff didn't respond.

"He took Cindy; you drove Shannon out to the Altman farm, where they were both murdered."

The sheriff gave an uncontrollable wail. "I told you: I killed her."

As Wagner used Massey's private bathroom to pull himself together, Massey told Nate and his dad, "He's going to need to tell the whole story over again to the detective."

"If he doesn't kill himself first," replied Nate.

"That would be too convenient."

Kip reared his head. "For who, Monroe?"

"No, the mercenary. I think he was dragging his feet dispatching Mony and Nate on purpose so that Monroe would become impatient."

"Do you think this Kuznetsov is setting Monroe up to take the fall?"

"Remember what Gomez's analyst said. I think he's tired of working for dipshits like Monroe and is making a power play to control all the illicit activity on the Bakken." Massey looked toward the bathroom door. "We need to get Scott to the safe house as soon as possible and call the detective."

"I'll take him," said Kip.

"I think one of the detective's team should take him."

Kip persisted, "I said I'll take him. No matter what he's done, he isn't a killer, and he's still a friend in trouble."

"Be careful, Dad. Kuznetsov has been five steps ahead of us thanks to his alliance with Wagner. Without his safety net, the mercenary will likely tie up loose ends before he leaves the Bakken."

"If you're right, we need to get Richards out of Williston too. He's a sitting duck in that hospital bed. Being a witness, he'll be next on the hit list."

"And what about Mony?" Nate put in. "Why isn't she here like she said she'd be?"

"Knowing Mony, she got tired of waiting and went back to the house. You should give her a call, Nate, and tell her to come back to the office. We can offer you both the greatest protection here until we get this mess sorted out."

CHAPTER 26

MONY

Mony sat in the front seat of the black SUV, staring out the windshield, the purchase proposal draft in her lap. Kuznetsov had used no force in her abduction, simply uttered veiled threats to gain her cooperation. Wagner and his deputies would not be coming to her rescue. "The Williams County sheriff has essentially neutered himself," he said in a smug tone. "If you don't want any harm to come to your family, you'll follow my instructions." She knew when to heed a warning.

Her abductor chose to abandon his vehicle at the intersection of US Highway 85 and State Highway 50, where a helicopter sat on standby, and they headed west. It was easy to see he wasn't quite sure of the flight path. They hadn't traveled far, just barely across the Montana border, when the expanse of Medicine Lake came into view. Mony was familiar with the area. At 3,100 acres, the refuge was part of a unique plains ecosystem that offered many different recreational opportunities. For the Ferguson and Altman clan, it was hunting. Despite the vast acreage of the lake, no motorized boats were allowed, and the two-thousand-acre Sandhills Wilderness area was completely roadless, allowing only walk-in hunting. It wasn't where they were headed.

There wasn't much time to take in her surroundings before Mony was ushered inside the trailer, but the bolded letters painted on the oil silo made her location clear. The burner stack a few feet away spewed a foul methane smell, much like the stench from the owners of the property. She was somewhat surprised to see Thomas and Jason Monroe there, along with Ethan Rice, already waiting. Jason promptly walked up to Mony and gave her an open-handed slap across the face, the force turning her head. "Goddamn, I've been waiting a long time for this."

Calmly, the mercenary said to him, "You may want to wait until the contract's signed before you do that."

Monroe Senior agreed. "He's right, son. Best not damage the goods too much until our work here is done. After that, I don't give a shit what you do to her."

Jason whirled to face his father. "I'll do as I damn well please, in the order I choose." Before anyone could stop him, he kicked Mony low in her pelvis. She doubled over, falling to her knees. Blood seeped from the laceration across her cheekbone and trickled into her mouth. Kuznetsov stepped around Jason and offered her a hand up off the floor.

Mony looked up at him with cold eyes. "Seems rather chivalrous when you plan to kill me anyway."

Monroe Senior's expression soured. "Who said anything about killing?"

Mony hesitated before reaching for the proffered hand. When she and the mercenary were eye level with one another, she spat in his face. "Murderer."

"Do you see the shit I've been putting up with from this cunt?" Jason sneered. "Go ahead, give her a good smack."

The mercenary ignored the insult. Pulling a handkerchief from his trousers pocket, he wiped the saliva and blood from his face, then cleaned the blood oozing from Mony's laceration. Smiling, he said to her, "There will be plenty of time to humble you. For now, we'd best finish business."

"Goddamn you, Kuznetsov," Jason snapped. "Stop undermining my authority. You're paid to take orders from me, not the other way around. Remember that."

The mercenary was unaffected by the remark. "You're paying me because you're a coward."

Monroe Senior raised his hands. "Enough bickering. Let's just finish the contract."

Ethan Rice grabbed the papers from Mony's hands as the mercenary sat her down in the office chair. Leaning over her, Ethan laid the purchase proposal on the desk and slapped down a pen. "Sign it."

Unimpressed by the posturing, Mony glanced around the room. "My signature alone means nothing on this document. Unlike Monroe Oil, F&A makes its decisions unanimously."

Jason came up to her and backhanded her across the head. "Stop stalling and sign it."

Mony stared down at the piece of paper. "There's no way my partners will agree to this."

He hit her again. "Not your worry. Sign it."

As Monroe Senior and the mealy-mouthed lawyer chastised Jason for his brutality, the mercenary just stood back and watched. Ears still ringing from the blow, Mony tried to fathom in what universe a document signed under duress would stand up in a court. *Does it matter?* Apparently, her nemesis believed it. Her delay tactics played out, Mony complied.

Rice picked up the document with shaky hands and studied it. When he seemed satisfied, he said to the Monroes, "Everything's in order. Now, where's my cut?"

Jason gave Kuznetsov a subtle nod. The mercenary walked up behind Rice—before Mony could cry out, he'd given the man a quick turn to the neck. The lawyer fell to the floor in a heap.

Monroe Senior gasped in horror. "Did you have to kill him?"

The mercenary grabbed Mony by the arm and wrenched her out of her seat. "He was a weak link. My work here is complete."

"No, it isn't." Jason pulled a gun from his jacket. "You're not taking her anywhere."

Blood draining from his face, Monroe Senior turned to his son. "Jason, what are you doing?"

The son turned on his father. "Shut up, old man. I'm just getting started." He pointed the gun at Kuznetsov. "Give her the handkerchief."

The mercenary smiled and pressed the blood-soaked cloth into Mony's hand. "Give it to me," Jason told her.

With his gun trained on the mercenary, Jason began wiping the handle and trigger with the bloody cloth. The mercenary laughed. "Seriously? Who did she murder?"

Jason responded by shooting a slug into Ethan Rice's corpse.

Mony fully expected to be the target of the next bullet, but when the shot rang out, the smoking gun was in the mercenary's hand, pointed at Monroe Senior. Stunned, the old man looked down at the mortal wound to his chest. "You dirty son of a—"

Monroe Senior took two staggering steps forward before face-planting on the floor.

Jason looked down at his father, his expression unreadable. Pulling a second gun from his jacket, he left the one smeared with Mony's blood next to his father's corpse. He pointed his gun at the mercenary. "Now what do we do with her?"

Mony knew she was as good as dead if she boarded the chopper. The obvious plan was to dispatch her on reservation land. It would take weeks to find her body, if they found her at all, and tribal law enforcement had no jurisdiction over non-Indian affairs. She glanced at the two men on either side of her, each pointing a gun at the other. *No trust among thieves*, she thought bitterly. Kuznetsov was clearly the superior killer, but skill could be thwarted by overconfidence and an unpredictable opponent. She focused on how she could divide and conquer. Perhaps if she could form an alliance with the pilot, it would even her odds.

That hope became reality.

A shock of disbelief marred the two men's faces as they fell backward, a single bullet hole in each forehead. Still in their hands, Mony fell with them, then scrambled to get away from the ooze of death.

Blankenship deplaned and lent a hand to pull her to her feet. She looked down at the corpses, a primal anger consuming her, and kicked at the bodies as if the bullet to their brains wasn't enough. Todd lifted her off her feet, holding her tight in his grip. She squirmed, a source of protection and intimidation. "Put me down," she demanded.

The big Indian obliged. "They can no longer hurt you, Mountain Devil. Your revenge is complete. Now it is time for you to keep my people safe."

"I will keep my promise," Mony said with vehemence. "But what are we going to do about this mess?"

"Don't you worry, Mountain Devil, I have a plan for that."

Mony sat still as the ER physician pulled the last stitch through her cheek. "I've tried to keep the sutures small to minimize scarring. You'll need to keep it free of infection, so I'm prescribing an antibiotic."

Standing on the other side, Detective Gomez pulled back the curtain. "Ms. Strong, please accompany me to the conference room. It's time to share your story."

Epilogue

In 2005, an obscure oil and gas company made one of the first proposals to lease land from the Fort Berthold Indian Reservation for drilling. Supported by the Bureau of Indian Affairs, or the BIA, the proposal called for ten thousand tribal acres to be leased at a 16 percent royalty and a $35-per-acre bonus. It sounded like a lot of money, especially to an impoverished people who had lost most of their ancestral lands in the name of progress. But as the oil industry boomed on the Bakken, the Indigenous people saw little by way of wealth, and bore witness to the irreversible damage hydraulic fracturing (fracking) made on the environment, polluting their drinking water and further decimating their way of life.

Flipping was a common industry practice whereby companies sold off leases for profit to whomever they chose, without tribal consent. This left landowners confused as to who would pay royalties owed, if they were paid at all. It didn't take long to understand that once again, the people were on the losing end of the agreement. Learning from the Three Affiliated Tribes' experience, the Turtle Mountain Band of Chippewa Indians hoped to fare better.

In an effort to preserve the environment, a draft by No Fracking Way Turtle Mountain Tribe unanimously voted to ban fracking as a means to exploit oil reserves in November 2011. In December of the same year, the tribal council amended this resolution to direct the BIA to cancel oil and gas bidding on forty-five thousand acres of tribal land, which was scheduled to begin on December 14, 2011. The cancellation went into effect on December 9, 2011. Companies that held existing leases within tribal land and had not yet started drilling were left in the lurch. Without the preferred and most economical means of drilling, companies found themselves in a financial predicament despite the boom, holding leases they could neither sell nor utilize. For one small Houston-based oil company in particular, the impact of the Tribes' decision was great—their empire, which had been built at the expense of the people, began to crumble.

Mony leaned back in the saddle, adjusting her feet in the stirrups as her mustang descended into the rocky gorge behind Gloria. The sensation made her feel anxious and out of control. Gloria called back to her, "Resist pulling on the reins. The horse's nose will go wherever you pull, taking the stability out from under the both of you. Trust your horse. She knows what she's doing." Taking a deep breath, Mony did as instructed.

From the safety of the gorge floor, she looked back and watched the two young riders make the same descent with the ease and confidence of a couple of pros, Slow Joe bringing up the rear. She called to Sissy and Lil Sis, "Remember, we can't stay long—we have a concert to attend this evening."

When news of Mony's abduction had reached Slow Joe via Rez wire, he'd immediately led Lilly, Gloria, and the two dogs into hiding. Following the Bill Williams River on horseback, they had cut through the very gorge Mony had just entered and held up in an area of the Swansea Wilderness, a spectacle rarely seen by humans. Lil Sis had not only learned how to survive; she had thrived in the desert environment, and was eager to share her newly honed skills with her sister.

It had been a pleasant surprise when the girls' mother had allowed them to stay at the ranch the remainder of the summer, though what their future held after that was uncertain. It shouldn't have come as that great a shock. Fox Can't Be Caught was indeed a man of his word. There seemed no limits to what the man could accomplish, including a multilayer homicide cover-up.

Found bound, gagged, and blindfolded in the helicopter which had transported her to Monroe Oil Well Number Three, there weren't many facts Mony could substantiate when questioned by Detective Gomez. Thanks to Todd's planning, he was able to provide plausible denial as to any involvement he may or may not have had in events that took place prior to the office trailer's destruction. Mony could honestly say that it had been the mercenary who had brought her to the location, and that she'd heard gunshots prior to the explosion. She remained nondescript about the pilot, and let it be assumed the mercenary had flown her himself.

As the fire and rescue team had retrieved his remains from the trailer ashes, Mony could account for the mercenary. She had to feign ignorance about the others, and did her best to appear shocked when she was informed of the names. Her reaction turned sincere, however, when Dwight Mitchell's body was counted among the corpses. She didn't know why Fox Can't Be Caught had added Mitchell to his list of victims. Perhaps it was to protect Sissy. If that had been indeed his motive, it had inadvertently become Dwight's one and only act of redemption in a lifetime of cruelty and tyranny.

Mony also shared the mercenary's remarks regarding Scott Wagner with the detective. Sheriff Wagner's demise was indeed tragic. A member of Detective Gomez's team had entered the safe house and found him at the kitchen table with a self-inflicted gunshot to the head; a Waterford crystal tumbler and decanter filled with Irish whiskey stood in front of him. Kip Ferguson disputes that the incident was a suicide. The investigation is ongoing.

The surviving heir of the Monroe Oil Company, Tiffany Monroe-Rice, lost all interest in becoming active in the oil industry. A month after the deaths of her family members, she and her attorney, John Finch, met with members of the Turtle Mountain Band of Chippewa Indians to discuss the sale of leases held by the company on off-reservation trust land, in eastern Montana and western North Dakota. Thirty thousand acres were purchased for a fair market price via funds made available to the tribe through an anonymous benefactor. Tiffany sold Oil Well Number Three and what was left of Monroe Oil to rival company F&A Oil. She and John are currently sailing in the Florida Keys.

The investment in Monroe Oil has suspended the horizontal drilling planned for Oil Well Number One, per the decision of F&A Oil's newly appointed board members Kat, Dane, and Mindy Strong and Matthew Ferguson. Fracking wasn't used when Well One was established, thereby leaving groundwater and aquifers unsullied. There isn't much the company can do to reverse damages caused by Monroe Oil Well Number Three, a mere fifteen miles away. The new members, however, can change the future. Reducing methane emissions from oil and gas operations has become one of the new board's high priorities, and they've made a point to partner with environmental specialists, including area Indigenous communities.

Mony poked her head out from behind a side curtain, watching eager fans returning to their seats. The intermission did nothing to diminish the energy emanating toward the stage, especially after Tim's dynamic drum solo. The concert was one big party, a celebration of Mile

High Club's newly finished renovation project and the band's official return from retirement. Scanning the auditorium, Mony was glad to see a strong security presence. Though the imminent danger was past, Mony was grateful Trevor had finally conceded to her warnings; it had taken little convincing, especially after Gem had been approached by an unknown assailant leaving her office last spring. A brown belt in Krav Maga, she'd easily fought off the attack, but the event had legitimized Mony's excessive security lectures into a sharp reality.

An outburst of laughter drew Mony's attention to the green room down the hall. The sound was music to her ears—Nate's bandmates and her family were finally getting along, especially Gem.

Nate had taken it upon himself to personally inform Gem of her brother's demise. Prior to Mony's abduction, a hospital security camera had revealed a man the same height and build as the mercenary, dressed as a nurse, entering the hospital through the main entrance only to leave twenty minutes later. The footage coincided with the guard assigned to Richards leaving his post, allegedly to use the bathroom. A code blue had been announced over the PA system just as the nurse imposter exited the hospital. The official cause of Harland's death: poisoning by lethal injection.

The whole ordeal between Gem, Mindy, and Kat had long since been forgiven, and the three women had spent the earlier part of that day exploring the details of the renovation. Despite all the coercing, begging, and pleading required, even Kip and Poppy seemed to be enjoying the spectacle, and all the ostentatious display of flamboy-ant behavior which accompanies fans at a rock concert.

A pair of strong, familiar hands rested on her shoulders, and the voice of her lover whispered in her ear. "Trevor has asked me to do a solo before the rest of the band re-turns to the stage. I'm feeling a little nervous. Will you stay right here until I've finished?"

Mony pivoted in his arms. "You, nervous? That seems unlikely, but I'll stay here and listen from the stage."

Nate pressed his lips to her forehead. "Thank you."

He made his way toward the piano, which had been moved center stage, his path illuminated through the smoky haze in the dimly lit beam of the PAR lights; those seated toward the front of the auditorium became imme-diately aware that Mile High City's favorite member had walked onto the stage. Despite the fan hysteria, an ethe-real hush fell over the crowd. A single spotlight focused on the man and his instrument as he began to sing.

Sung in vibrato, it was an unconventional love ballad, the dynamic eliciting a sense of urgency and longing. It was a song written from experience, the lyrics poetic in tone. The question Nate expressed in his lyrics was the same question he'd asked Mony as they stood on the tarmac before their separation. They'd talked about trust, fear, and vulnerability. Mony felt the tightening in her chest as he beseeched the heavens to make his dream a reality. Filled with passion, Nate built to a crescendo, in a key which would elicit the natural passaggio, the transi-tion area between his vocal registers. She heard the crack as he passed from chest to head voice, yet it had been incorporated so seamlessly into the music, it seemed as natural as if it hadn't occurred at all.

Gem whispered into Mony's ear, "Isn't it beautiful? I told him when he was composing the song to leave it in."

Tears welled in Mony's eyes as she nodded in silence. In that moment, she vowed to spend the rest of her life empowering Nate to find value in himself, so that he would never have to ask that question of her ever again.

When the song was finished, the flood and spotlights resumed their brilliance as Nate rose to a standing ovation. Several minutes passed before the crowd settled in for what was to be a brilliant second half. He expressed a sincere thanks to the audience for their years of steadfast loyalty and support, the chant *M-H-C* building in volume as he spoke. Then, he said something that blindsided everyone.

"Several times throughout the years, I've been asked the question: what is the inspiration behind my music? Is there a special someone to whom my songs are dedicated? The answer to the question is, yes, there is—and tonight, I would like to introduce that person." Nate turned to face the side stage. "Gem, will you escort our guest onto the stage?"

Gem Richards linked Mony's arm in hers. "Ready?"

Mony felt the blood rush to her head, her knees going spongy. She looked at Gem, half terrified, half in shock. Gem told her, "He knew you wouldn't go if we told you ahead of time. It's okay to smile."

As the two women walked arm in arm onto the stage, Mony recalled only twice before when she'd been in front of a crowd to lecture—and those crowds had been a quarter the size of the present audience. Murmurs and whispering scuttled through the auditorium as Gem handed her off to Nate. He bound his arms around her waist; it was difficult for Mony to know whether she was standing on her own power or being held up in his powerful arms. He pressed his lips to the crown of her head, then said to the audience, "I'd like to introduce my wife, Mony Ferguson."

The response from the crowd was overwhelming. The whoops, whistles, cheering, and clapping were deafening, and unexpected. It had always been Mony's perception that Nate's acknowledgement of being a married man would somehow diminish his popularity. It appeared the opposite. True fans wanted one thing of their favorite musician. His earlier work was filled with two main themes—one of regret, loss, and anguish; the other of rebellion, recklessness, and a carefree lifestyle. Coming full circle, Nate had finally found happiness, and his fans were elated.

"My music career began on a cold winter's day, long ago at a farm in North Dakota. I sat waiting for my best friend to finish her piano lesson so we could go outside and play. My friend was being especially obstinate that day. From the kitchen, I heard her say to her teacher, 'I always play better when Nate sits next to me on the piano bench.' That wasn't true, of course. We had never sat side by side at the piano, but I welcomed the invitation. Reluctantly, the piano instructor conceded. From that day forward, we never missed a lesson. When the weather was especially cold and stormy, we would sit together and play Handel-Halvorsen's Passacaglia, the 'Impossible Duet.' It's more often performed as a cello and violin duet, but we played it on the piano. I wonder; would you do me the honor of playing it for this wonderful audience tonight, Mony?"

The uproar from the crowd was unimaginable. Mony found herself in a vacuum of sound, barely hearing Nate when he leaned over and murmured, "Just pretend they're not there. That's what I do."

Mony and Nate slipped into a familiar pattern, he to her right, she to his left. Though a duet by title, on the piano, this arrangement could be performed by a solo pianist. For Mony and Nate, it became something of a challenge, matching wit and skill, deviating from the sheet music and incorporating all the nuances of the string duet into a creation of their own.

When they'd finished, Nate leaned his forehead to hers, a bedazzling smile brimming across his lips. Lost in a world of their own, they sat side by side, finding peace in the presence of an unconditional love—a bond tested by fire, made unbreakable, unyielding in power and might.

ACKNOWLEDGMENTS

A note to aspiring writers: Becoming an indie author doesn't mean the work is finished with the last written page. It requires a team dedicated to the successful publication of your work. With humility and gratitude, I would like to acknowledge my team:

Wise Ink Creative Publishing project manager Amy Quale, editor Abbie Phelps, cover designer Jay Monroe, Donya Claxton at D.J. Claxton Photography, cover models Kevin R. Davis and Miranda Lynn, and virtual assistant Cori Ramos.

I want to thank author Kimberlee Ann Bastian for her inspiration and being my sounding board.

Finally, I want to thank my husband Doug for his continued emotional support and encouragement. Without your understanding and patience, there would be no Bakken series.

Julien Bradley never aspired to become an indie author, but she does love telling a good story. She used time between jobs to hone her documentation skill and do some free-writing—the exercise resulted in 1,100 pages! Encouraged by her daughter, Kimberlee, she pitched the story idea to Wise Ink Creative Publishing; the "draft," after professional editing, became the first installment in the Bakken series.

With more than thirty-five years in the health care industry, Julien writes stories that reflect a culmination of real human experiences to create organic women's fiction/romance. Her books give an honest look into the lives of ordinary people, elevate the underrepresented voice of women over fifty, and breathe new life into the unexpected depth of the "normal" day-to-day.

Born and raised in Minnesota, Julien lives with her husband atop the bluffs overlooking the beautiful Hiawatha River valley. She is a member of Midwest Fiction Writers and Romance Writers of America. *Beyond the Bust* is the third in the Bakken series.